PLACID HOLLOW

A Walter Hudson Mystery

CHARLES AYER

outskirtspress
DENVER, COLORADO

Placid Hollow
A Walter Hudson Mystery
All Rights Reserved.
Copyright © 2016 Charles Ayer
v2.0

Cover Photo © 2016 thinkstockphotos.com. All rights reserved - used with permission.

Outskirts Press, Inc.
http://www.outskirtspress.com

ISBN: 978-1-4787-6497-7

Library of Congress Control Number: 2015921416

Outskirts Press and the "OP" logo are trademarks belonging to Outskirts Press, Inc.

PRINTED IN THE UNITED STATES OF AMERICA

DEDICATION

This book is dedicated to my Brother:

ROBERT WELTON AYER
1966-2009

The Sweetest Soul I Ever Knew

ACKNOWLEDGMENTS

I would like to thank my sisters, Susan Ayer and Rebecca Lenahan; my brother, John Ayer, and my sister-in-law Janice Ayer for generously providing their guidance and feedback. I don't know what I would have done without them.

I'd also like to thank the entire team at Outskirts Press, many of whose names I will never know. They turned my ugly duckling of a manuscript into a thing of beauty that I can always be proud of.

1

F EDERAL DISTRICT COURT JUDGE T. FRANKLIN "TEDDY" BRAXTON had been called many things during his long, controversial life, but "dead" had never been one of them, at least not until 1:18 AM on Saturday, May 9, in the Presidential Suite of the recently opened Empire-Excelsior Hotel in New York City.

"He's dead," said the tired-looking house doctor, glancing at his watch and putting his stethoscope away in a worn leather bag as the EMTs looked on, wearing vaguely guilty expressions of relief, knowing their services would no longer be required.

"Shit," said Officer Eduardo Sanchez, his broad, dark visage betraying fatigue while the young, scantily- clad blonde sitting next to him on the large sofa that rested in the middle of the spacious room looked on disconsolately, like a stripper who'd shown up at the wrong party. An unopened bottle of Veuve Clicquot champagne, a card hanging around its neck on a small chain proclaiming it to be "Compliments of the House!" sat in a bucket of melting ice on a table in front of the sofa, a lone sentinel standing its guard in the midst of a lost battle.

The crime scene photographers clicked away, taking the hundreds of photos from all conceivable angles and distances that Sanchez and the other NYPD investigators would be staring at for as long as it took them to solve the crime. And solve it they would, because the man who would lead this investigation, Detective Lieutenant Walter Hudson, solved his cases and stamped them "Closed." No exceptions allowed.

But Sanchez knew that he couldn't rely on photos alone. In his experience, direct observation at the crime scene often told him things that a photograph could not. He also knew that Lieutenant Hudson's first questions of him would be about what he had observed personally: not just what he had seen, but what he had heard; what he had smelled; the off-hand comments; the transient expressions on people's faces. These were the things that solved crimes, taught the lieutenant, who, though only in his mid-thirties, was an old-fashioned cop who believed that cops solved crimes, not computers.

They were in the living room of what must have been the largest suite in the hotel, guessed Sanchez as he gazed around at the spacious, high ceilinged room. It was painted a pale green, and the furniture looked, at least to Sanchez's eye, expensive, though what did he know? His experiences with hotels were limited to Comfort Inns on the Jersey Shore. Diaphanous drapes covered floor to ceiling windows that looked down thirty-five floors onto the brightly lit streets of midtown Manhattan and west over to the Hudson River. Down a carpeted hallway were two bedrooms, each with its own bathroom.

The woman, whose name according to her driver's license was Caroline Schuyler, and who had described herself as a "colleague" of the Judge, had been found standing in the middle of the room holding a handgun when the police arrived.

"I'd like to put some clothes on," she said to Sanchez.

"Sure, ma'am," said Sanchez, "but don't lock that door, you hear me?" Not standard procedure, Sanchez knew, but there was nothing he could do about it. There was no female police officer on the scene, and he wasn't about to expose any of the other officers to harassment charges. Besides, he'd already swabbed her hands for gunpowder residue, printed her, and examined the small overnight bag that sat at her feet.

Everybody tried not to look, and everybody failed, as she stood up, but she either didn't notice or didn't mind. She was wearing nothing but a G-string and a sheer bra that hid nothing, but she took her time as she walked down the hallway to the bedroom off to the right. He heard a bathroom door close.

"Can we leave now, sir?" said one of the EMTs, whose nameplate said, "Manning."

"What, now that the show's over? Sure, as soon as you all give me your names," said Sanchez, although he knew most of them from previous cases. They did and hurried out.

He bent down and picked up one of Teddy Braxton's well-manicured hands, his left, which was adorned only by a simple, yellow gold wedding band. Judging from the way it had sunk into the flesh of the ring finger, it hadn't been removed in many years. He noticed, too, that wrapped around the man's left wrist was a simple, slim, gold wristwatch with the words "Patek Philippe" printed on its face. Sanchez didn't know much about watches, but he knew that the watch cost more than he made in a year. The hand was limp and, though cooling, still warm. The crime scene pathologist would give him an accurate time of death, but Sanchez knew from experience that it was less than an hour ago.

The man lay on his back. He had removed his suit jacket and his necktie, both of which had been carefully folded and draped over the back of a chair, so the three bullet holes in the front of his starched white shirt were clearly visible. They were in a tight grouping just below the man's sternum, where his heart would be. Whoever had fired that pistol had a steady hand and knew what he, or she, was doing. There was very little blood around the wounds, which led Sanchez to believe that the man had died almost instantly.

The doctor had known enough to leave the body alone, so he lay as he had fallen, flat on his back, arms oddly folded over his stomach, a placid expression on his face as if he'd merely lain down for a nap. A small smudge of what Sanchez guessed might be a pale shade of lipstick brightened his left cheek like a faint blush. Sanchez bent down closer and thought he detected a faint floral aroma. His thick, dark hair was still in place, as if he'd just run a comb through it. There were no signs of struggle at all, and Sanchez was left with the strong impression that the man had been taken completely by surprise.

The young woman emerged from the bathroom a few minutes later carrying her overnight bag, looking demure in a gray, knee-length wool skirt and a lilac-colored cashmere sweater. Her hair was combed and tied back. The makeup she'd been wearing was gone, and her shoes were simple flats.

"May I leave now, Officer?" she said.

"No, you can't," said Sanchez.

"What? Why not?"

"Ma'am," said Sanchez, "perhaps you don't understand your situation. You were found holding a gun in the same room where a man was lying dead on the floor with three bullets in his chest. You are, ma'am, our prime suspect at this moment, and you are not going anywhere."

"I understand my situation perfectly well," said Caroline. "I am an attorney licensed to practice in this state, and I'm an expert in criminal procedure."

"Then you know," said Sanchez, "that we have probable cause to charge you with the murder of Judge Braxton, and we can't just let you walk out of here."

"Officer, as I have already explained to you, I was in the bathroom showering and changing with both the bedroom and bathroom doors closed when the murder took place. I saw nothing and heard nothing. I called in the emergency, for God's sake."

"I know that ma'am, but...."

"I walked into the living room and discovered the body on the floor. He was clearly dead when I got to him. No breathing, no sound, no movement. I had no idea what had gone on, and for all I knew the murderer might have been still lurking in the suite. I saw the gun and picked it up. What would you have done, Officer?"

"I understand all that, ma'am, but still....."

"'But still' what? You've already swabbed my hands for gunpowder residue, which you know will come back negative, printed me, and pawed through my belongings. You have my name and address. What more do you want?"

The problem, thought Sanchez, was that he tended to believe her. The gun, a vintage Colt .45 with a large silencer attached, looked almost as heavy as the young woman. He doubted whether she would have succeeded in injuring anyone but herself, even at point blank range, if she had tried to fire it. But he also knew that if he just let her go it would probably cost him his badge, not to mention the brand new detective's shield that was waiting for him at the end of the month.

"Tell it to the judge at the bail hearing," he said. He turned to the only other cop still in the room, a tired looking kid named Peters, and said, "Cuff her, and let's get out of here." He looked at his watch. It was 1:51 AM. He still had a long night ahead of him.

It suddenly got longer as a tall, silver-haired man in a blue pinstriped Brioni suit, silk tattersall shirt, and burgundy tie marched into the room followed by a helpless looking hotel security officer. He ignored Sanchez and walked straight up to Caroline.

"Dear Caroline, are you all right?" he said.

"Oh, Arthur, thank God!" said Caroline. "Yes, I'm all right, but you got here just in time. I was about to be hauled off to the hoosegow." She nodded in the direction of Sanchez.

The man turned toward Sanchez and raised himself to his full height, which was a good three inches taller than the six-foot cop. Sanchez was a powerful man, and he had grown up hard on the streets of Spanish Harlem, so he was not intimidated by the man physically. But the suit, and the bespoke Italian leather shoes that were probably worth more than his car, made Sanchez suspect that this was not going to go well.

"Officer Sanchez," said the man, staring at Sanchez's nameplate, "what on Earth is going on here?"

"Perhaps you ought to identify yourself," said Sanchez, trying to gain back at least some of the initiative.

"I am Arthur Hurley," said the man, sounding a little put out that he hadn't been recognized immediately, "of the law firm of Hurley, Hanlon and Dawes. I am also the personal attorney of Ms. Schuyler's father, Mr. Carlton Schuyler; and as of this moment Ms. Caroline Schuyler is also my client."

This is not a good development, thought Sanchez. Even he had heard of Carlton Schuyler, the hedge fund billionaire who was a golfing chum of the president, and who had played polo with the Prince of Wales in his younger days. Ten years ago he'd bought a thirty-five million dollar mansion in Greenwich, Connecticut, overlooking Long Island Sound only to tear it down to the ground and build another one on the same space. He liked the view, he'd been heard to say. His legendary wine cellar was rumored to be worth ten million dollars, even though he was a teetotaler. He wanted to make sure his guests were comfortable, he'd said.

"Then you need to know, sir," said Sanchez, "that your client was found standing over the body of a dead man holding what is presumably the murder weapon in her hand."

"I am aware of the circumstances, Officer, and I am also aware of the fact that my client has given you a perfectly sound explanation, as well as allowing herself to be subjected to your customary humiliations. She and her family are prominent members of this community, with strong roots and a spotless reputation for integrity. She will, of course, cooperate fully with your investigation. Here is my card. You may contact her through my office at any time. Now, come along, Caroline." He put his well-manicured hand behind her back and gently guided her toward the door. Sanchez blocked his way.

"With all due respect, sir," he said, "I don't particularly give a shit who you are. The circumstances dictate that I take Ms. Schuyler into custody and bring her before a judge for an arraignment and a bail hearing. You are welcome to come along."

The doctor from the Medical Examiner's office gave the "all clear" sign, and they left the room just ahead of the stretcher bearing the body of Judge T. Franklin Braxton, a man who in his lifetime had not been accustomed to bringing up the rear.

The arraignment hearing took approximately five minutes before a tired looking magistrate. Caroline Schuyler was released on her own recognizance. Neither she nor Arthur Hurley acknowledged Eduardo Sanchez as they left.

Sanchez's boss, Lieutenant Hudson, liked to say that every day was a good day to be a cop, but he'd never said anything about the nights, thought Sanchez. He rose from his chair tiredly and left the courthouse.

2

"**S**HE'S LYING, LIEUTENANT," said Officer Sanchez, looking exhausted as he sat in Detective Lieutenant Walter Hudson's cramped cubicle in the Detectives' Squad Room of the Midtown South Precinct House. The ancient analogue clock hanging over the door said it was eight o'clock on Saturday morning, and his body ached for sleep. "I don't know exactly what she's lying about, but sure as shit, she's lying."

Hudson was tired, too, but his job had nothing to do with it. Well, almost nothing, he thought. He had walked out the front door of his family's modest home in Fresh Meadows, Queens in the dark after receiving a phone call from Sanchez, but he'd already been awake for hours.

He and his wife, Sarah, had welcomed their third child, their first son, into the world just two months ago, but they were already wondering what they had gotten themselves into. The first two, now ages four and seven, had been a joy from their first days: making all the requisite gurgling, happy baby noises, eating well, napping at all the right times, and sleeping through the night within a few short weeks. So when Sarah quite unexpectedly found out that they would be having a third they had thought, why not? We're pretty good at this, and it'll be fun to have a baby in the house one more time.

But from the moment young Daniel Walter Hudson had entered the world they knew that he had been cast in a different mold. Walter remembered holding Daniel for the first time and realizing that, unlike his daughters, he couldn't make the child comfortable in his arms. He'd given him to Sarah thinking that he was hungry, but after nursing for only a few short minutes he'd stopped and begun to squall. He never seemed to sleep for more than twenty minutes at a time, and both Walter and Sarah were at their wits' end.

Their pediatrician had told them that it was colic and he would outgrow it. When? That, it seemed, was anyone's guess.

Walter's mother, who lived just over the Nassau County line in Port Washington, had done nothing to make things any easier.

"Oh, he's a chip off the old block, that one," she would announce gleefully to anyone within hearing range. "Little Walt was just like this one. Crying all the time, never sleeping. And the child never stopped throwing up! I used to say to the doctor, 'I don't know what's keeping the child alive! He throws up more than I feed him!'"

"Mom, mom," Walter had said, as he felt the walls of their small house close in around him. "Please, I know you're trying to help, but it's just upsetting Sarah." But he knew it was to no avail.

"I'm just trying to warn the both of you," she would say. "You're in for a long siege, let me tell you, so you'd better get used to it."

Walter's father had been a placid man, dying as he had lived, with a contented smile on his face. Walter, knowing that he was not his father, prayed for guidance.

"What makes you say that, Eduardo?" said Walter, snapping himself back to the present and shifting his large frame in his seat. His thick black hair was carefully combed and he was freshly shaved, but his face sagged with fatigue.

"Well, first, Lieutenant," said Sanchez, "the young woman displayed no emotions whatsoever, not at the murder scene and not at the arraignment. You know what it's like. People who are telling the truth aren't afraid to let their emotions show. Liars have to control their emotions and stick to the script."

"That's true," said Walter, thinking back on his own countless interrogations. "What else?"

"She just kept repeating the same lines over and over again, like she was afraid that she might slip up and reveal something if she said anything else. But I guess it's more than that."

"What do you mean?"

"Just lots of little things, Lieutenant. She wasn't checked into the hotel, and she said she was planning to go back to her apartment at the end of the evening. So why was she carrying an overnight bag with a change of clothes and a toilet bag?"

"What did she say?"

"She said that she was pretty sure that the Judge would ask her to have a drink with him and a couple of the other attendees afterwards, and she wanted to be able to change out of the formal dress that she was wearing if he did."

"Sounds at least plausible," said Walter.

"Perhaps," said Eduardo. "But then why was there only one bottle of champagne, and no snacks? But how the hell should I know? The last formal event Angelina and I went to was our wedding, and we served Asti Spumante and mixed nuts."

"So tell me again, Eduardo," said Walter. "When you examined her overnight bag, what exactly was in it?"

"Like I told you, Lieutenant, there was the long black gown she said she'd worn to the dinner, the clothes she eventually changed into, a toilet bag, and some other, you know, underwear."

"Was the underwear carefully folded or just thrown in there?"

"How the hell am I supposed to know? I've never folded women's underwear, but I guess it looked like it had just been thrown in there, on top of the gown."

"Was it fancy stuff, like the stuff she was wearing when you found her there?" said Walter.

"Lieutenant," said Eduardo, starting to squirm, "what I know about women's underwear could fit on the back of a postage stamp. But I guess it was more, like, regular. It was white and I think it was cotton; nothing, you know, silky or anything."

"Sarah tells me that there's a reason that the fancy stuff is called 'lingerie' and not 'underwear,'" said Walter.

"What's that?" said Eduardo, wanting badly to get off the subject.

"She says you can't call it underwear because women don't buy it to wear under anything. They wear it to be seen in it."

"And so you're thinking…"

"That she was there to have sex with the Judge. I think they were having an affair."

"And that makes her a prime suspect in the Judge's murder, no matter what she says," said Eduardo.

"It sure as hell does," said Walter. "Now, tell me another thing."

"What's that?" said Eduardo, relieved to be moving on to another topic.

"You got a pretty good look at her body, right?"

"Geez, Lieutenant."

"Eduardo, Angelina's not here."

"Oh, I've already gotten the third degree from her, don't worry. She called me at seven this morning after she heard the news reports on TV about 'policemen bursting into the hotel room and discovering a nearly naked woman holding a gun over the corpse.'"

Angelina Sanchez was barely five feet tall and weighed a hundred pounds dripping wet. They were a happy couple, and Eduardo loved her deeply, but the big cop was petrified of his tiny wife.

"What did she look like?"

"You know, like a female, I guess."

"Look, Eduardo, I know this makes you uncomfortable, but this is important. You said she's about five-two and weighs maybe 110, and you said it was hard to believe that she would have been able to handle a silenced .45."

"Okay, but look, I just got finished swearing on all that's holy to my wife that

I only glanced and I really didn't see anything. She said it was like a venial sin, whatever that is, if I looked. You gotta promise me this doesn't get back to her."

"Eduardo, as a good Catholic you're supposed to know what a venial sin is," said Walter, not able to help himself.

"I am? That's why we have priests, right?"

"And wives, apparently."

"Damn right," said Eduardo, with feeling.

"Seriously, Eduardo, she has to understand that you were just doing your job."

"Oh, no she doesn't."

Walter tried not to laugh at the man's predicament while he waited for him to continue.

Eduardo paused briefly, then said, "Okay. I mean, she was built, Lieutenant. Not an ounce of fat on her. Great muscle tone in her legs and arms and a flat, hard stomach. She looked like she worked out, a lot. And her ass, Lieutenant, holy....."

"Let's not get carried away, Eduardo, or Angelina's ears are going to start burning."

"Sorry...."

"But the point is, you still don't think she could have shot the gun?"

"Lieutenant, I'm six feet tall and weigh 185...."

"Two-ten."

"Yeah, yeah, but the first time I shot a .45 I was still 185. I missed the target by five feet at a range of twenty feet and my shoulder hurt for two days afterwards."

"But you eventually learned how to handle it."

"Yes, I did," said Sanchez, "with a lot of practice."

"And in your professional assessment, Officer Sanchez, based on your own experience and on your physical observation of the suspect, could she have managed, with practice, a .45 caliber pistol with a silencer attached?"

"Lieutenant," said Eduardo after a long pause, "when you put it that way, I wouldn't bet my life she couldn't."

———————

EDUARDO LEFT FOR HOME, and Walter was getting ready to do the same when his phone rang. He assumed that it was Sarah wondering when he'd be getting home, but he was wrong.

"Levi! Hello!" he said, pleasantly surprised to hear the voice of Leviticus Welles on the other end of the line. Just a few months earlier Levi, then a sales representative for the now bankrupt TransAt Corporation, had helped Walter solve the most important case of his career. He was now employed in the Intelligence Division of the NYPD and rapidly gaining an outstanding reputation there. "How are you? How's Julie?" Levi had met Julie Remy, now his wife, while working on the same case.

"I'm fine," said Levi, "and so is Julie. How are Sarah and the new baby?"

"Let's just say we're all a little bit tired right now," said Walter. "We're waiting till the little guy stops crying before we get him baptized, but at this point we may be attending his high school graduation first. But don't worry, you'll be invited."

"Thanks," said Levi, "it'll be great to see you all."

"But I bet you're not calling me on my work number on a Saturday morning just to chitchat."

"I'm afraid not," said Levi. "I just wanted to make sure that you had what might be some pertinent information regarding the Braxton murder. You may be way ahead of me, and if you are I apologize for wasting your time."

"If I'm way ahead of you, Levi," said Walter, "it'll be a first. So what have you got?"

"It's regarding the young woman who was at the scene of the crime."

"Caroline Schuyler?"

"Yes. Caroline Schuyler."

"What about her?"

"Her name rang a bell when I heard it on the news this morning," said Levi, "so I decided to do a little research."

"And did you find anything?"

"Well, yes I did," said Levi. "It turns out that she was on the U.S. Winter Olympic Team at the Games in Sochi."

"She was an Olympic athlete?" said Walter, picking up a pencil and starting to write. "What was her sport?"

"She was a biathlete. She competed in all the events in the Women's Biathlon."

"You've got to help me here, Levi. I'm a Mets and Jets fan. I don't follow the Olympics. What's a Biathlon?"

"It's a combination of cross country skiing and shooting."

"You mean, shooting as in a gun?"

"Yes, with a rifle. You ski from station to station, and then earn points for shooting accuracy. Your total score is a combination of your elapsed time around the course and your shooting score."

"Sounds tough," said Walter, furiously scribbling on his pad.

"It is," said Levi. "You have to be strong and in terrific physical condition."

"And I bet you have to be a hell of a good shot."

"That's why I called."

"Thanks, Levi. Stay in touch, okay?"

"Sure will."

Walter had no sooner hung up the phone than it rang again. He groaned inwardly as he glanced at the Caller ID screen.

"Good morning, Captain," he said. It wasn't that Walter disliked Captain Eugene Amato, his boss. He just wasn't Walter's kind of cop. In a way, he envied Amato for possessing the political skills that had gotten him to the rank of Captain before he'd turned forty, the same skills that he knew he lacked. But it seemed to Walter that Amato wasn't as much interested in being a cop as he was in navigating the treacherous bureaucracy that led to the Commissioner's office, and Walter would rather go back to walking a beat than be that kind of cop.

"So I see you landed yourself another hot one, Lieutenant," said Amato.

"We'll have to see," said Walter. "I'm hoping we can wrap this one up pretty quickly."

"What, you think you're just gonna hang a 'guilty' sign around Caroline Schuyler's neck and walk away?"

"I wasn't saying that, Captain."

"You know who her old man is, right?"

"Yes, sir, I do. But I think we have some preliminary evidence......"

"Lieutenant, Lieutenant, I didn't call you up to discuss the minutiae of your investigation."

"No, sir, of course not."

"I'm calling you up to warn you," said Amato, either ignoring the jibe or oblivious to it, "that you're going to be getting a lot of help on this one."

"What do you mean?"

"I've already received personal calls from the commissioner and - are you ready? - the mayor's office."

Crap, thought Walter. "Is it because of Carlton Schuyler, Captain?"

"No, that would be too easy."

"So, what then?"

"It seems that both the commissioner and the mayor have some kind of connection to Judge Braxton and his family, and they both want his murder solved like, yesterday. And you're right, they also know Carlton Schuyler, who donated heavily to the mayor's election campaign; so you better be damned sure of your case before you go accusing his daughter of murder."

"Thanks for the heads up, Captain."

"Always glad to help, Lieutenant."

3

WALTER WAS TEMPTED TO GO STRAIGHT HOME, but he knew that he couldn't leave the city before making a visit to the Empire-Excelsior Hotel. The hotel was on the site of the old, recently demolished Hotel Pennsylvania, across the street from Penn Station and Madison Square Garden. It was a beautiful, warm morning, so he decided to walk from the Midtown South precinct house. He hoped that a brisk walk in the fresh air might revive him.

The brand new hotel sparkled in the sunshine as Walter crossed over 7th Avenue, but he was jarred by the absence of the magnificent old edifice of the Hotel Pennsylvania, like the first time he had seen his grandfather with his new dentures. All he'd been able to see were the teeth.

As he walked through the large rotating doors at the entrance he spotted a sign that said: "Now Appearing in the Glenn Miller Room - Wynton Marsalis! Call PE6-5000 for Reservations!" At least some things never changed, Walter mused.

The lobby itself was clearly meant to impress, and it succeeded. He felt rich carpet beneath his feet, and everything looked and smelled new and expensive. What it lacked were the crowds of people he'd expected. The check-in and check-out counters were relatively quiet, and what looked to be a bar/lounge area was practically empty. He wondered how many guests had hurriedly checked out when they heard that a murder had taken place the night before. But Walter was dazzled nevertheless. People like him didn't stay in places like the Empire-Excelsior. Walter was not an envious man, but he couldn't help thinking how tickled Sarah would be to check in to a place like this. Maybe someday....

But any fascination he'd felt evaporated as he walked through the office door marked "Stanley Kraszcinski - Chief of Security." The office was windowless, but a large lithograph of the Brooklyn Bridge under construction graced the wall and it was spacious, well lit, and expensively furnished. It smelled like new paint and air freshener. And right now it also smelled like failure.

Stan was perhaps 45 years old, guessed Walter, about ten years older than he was, but right now he looked 60. Stan had recently left the NYPD, where he'd been a detective captain, to take this job at the Empire-Excelsior, a job, he had crowed, that paid more than double his NYPD salary and had more regular hours. And stock options, he'd said. "Can you believe it? Stock options!" If Walter had known what stock options were he probably would have been more impressed.

But now Kraszcinski's graying red hair was unkempt, his clothes were wrinkled, and he looked up at Walter with bloodshot eyes.

"Do you think you can get me my old job back, Walter?" he said, attempting a smile but failing.

"C'mon, Stan, you don't really want to go back to that coffee, do you?" said Walter. Despite the age and rank difference, he and Kraszcinski had always been friendly and had shared a mutual respect. Unlike Captain Amato, Kraszcinski had always been a cop's cop, and Walter hated to see him so miserable.

"I'll drink it by the gallon and be grateful for it," said Kraszcinski. "I may be out of this job before lunch."

"What do you mean?"

"I mean the Regional VP is showing up here any minute, and the scuttlebutt is the first thing he's gonna do is can my sorry ass."

"For what, for God's sake?" said Walter. "It was just bad luck that you had this happen on the first night that the hotel was open. I'm sure you've got a great staff put together and a great system set up, and once they see that you'll be fine."

"That's the problem," said Kraszcinski, looking even more miserable.

"What's the problem?"

"I fucked up, Walter."

"Aw, c'mon, Stan, I just don't believe that," said Walter, his heart beginning to sink not just at the predicament of an old colleague, but for what this might mean to his investigation.

"Well, start believing it, Walter, and you might as well hear it from me, because you're not gonna like me too much anymore once you find out what a mess I've left you with."

"Why don't you tell me about it, Stan," said Walter, settling himself into a chair opposite Kraszcinski's desk. It was leather and it was comfortable, but right now that was all wasted on him.

"Walter, I've had since the first of the year to set up this operation, and I busted my butt. I put together policies, procedures, and training manuals, and I scheduled dozens of training sessions for all the employees. Front desk people, back office people, kitchen staff, maids, you name it. I've been working night and day, seven days a week non-stop ever since I started this job. My wife's ready to divorce me. But after all that, the second we opened the doors yesterday at noontime, it all fell apart."

"How could that happen? It sounds like you did all the right things."

"First of all," said Stanley, "you have no idea how, uh, fluid a hotel staff is. I mean for chrissake, Walter, three quarters of them are illegal aliens and the rest have criminal backgrounds. They're always on the run from something. I told them as directly as I could without getting myself in trouble that I wasn't going to look real hard at that stuff, as long as they were good at their jobs. And they were, Walter. With only a couple of exceptions they were good, smart, hardworking people, people just looking for a chance. But then a rumor would come drifting into the hotel that Immigration agents were going to be showing up, or the police were coming to do background checks, and they'd just about trample each other heading for the doors."

"So all that training was wasted."

"Half the people we had on staff when the doors opened yesterday were hired in the past week and a half. There was no way I could get them all trained."

"I'm sorry, Stan."

"But my biggest mistake, the one thing that I completely underestimated, was the impact of the crowds. It's one thing to teach them how to follow a process in a training class, but when there are a thousand people in the lobby, all screaming for attention at the same time, the training just falls apart. I should've known that and made sure Human Resources doubled up on the staff for the first couple of days."

"Which they probably couldn't have done anyway," said Walter.

"Ah, you're probably right," said Stan, throwing up his hands. "But somebody's gonna have to walk the plank for this, and that somebody's gonna be me, I fucking guarantee you. Margie's gonna kill me. I walked away from a great job, my pension, everything."

"I hope you're wrong."

"We'll see," said Stan, "but when a big shot like that gets murdered on your watch, nothing good can happen."

"So what are you telling me here, Stan? What am I up against?"

"I've been here all night, Walter, interviewing as many employees as I could before they ran out the door on me. I talked to at least a half dozen front desk staff who admitted to me that when people came up to them asking for a spare key card for their rooms they didn't even bother to try to verify who they were. And the ones who didn't admit it were lying to me. They were handing them out like candy at Halloween."

"Shit."

"No, it gets worse. I had three chambermaids, *just on the floor where the murder took place,* admit to me that they let strangers into rooms when they came up to them and said they couldn't find their keys but really needed to get into their rooms. It's amazing what a twenty dollar tip will get you. And the tech guys just got finished telling me that half the surveillance cameras were never turned on and the other half were never aimed accurately. They're either pointed at the ceiling or each other. Worthless."

"Jesus," said Walter.

"I'm sorry, Walter."

Before Walter had a chance to reply there was a knock on the office door.

"Come in," said Stanley.

"I'm sorry to interrupt, Mr. Kraszcinski," said a scared looking young woman whose name tag said, 'Terri Dunkel - Training Associate,' with a little yellow smiley face on the bottom, "but there's a Mr. Lucas Trask here to see you. He says it's urgent."

"Here it comes," said Stanley, turning ashen.

"Who's Lucas Trask?" said Walter.

"He's the Senior VP of Security for the entire hotel chain."

"You're a good man, Stan, don't forget that," said Walter, not knowing what else to say.

"Walter, I hate to beg, but at this point I've got no choice. I've heard that you have the commissioner's ear these days. Could you put in a good word for me? I'll do anything to get back onto the force."

"I'll do what I can, Stan, I promise," said Walter as he stood to leave.

"Thanks, Walter, you're a real friend."

But Walter wasn't thinking of friendship as he left the hotel. He was thinking that any chance that he had of ever solving the murder of Judge T. Franklin Braxton may have just evaporated as quickly as poor Stanley Kraszcinski's new job.

4

WALTER WAS IN NO MOOD to be driving up to the small village of Placid Hollow in Westchester County on a Sunday morning in an unmarked car he'd borrowed from the motor pool. It had been another long night with little Daniel, and Sarah had been tired and surly when he'd left. He had initially thought that he would be able to interview Judge T. Franklin Braxton's immediate family at their residence in one of the most expensive residential buildings in Manhattan, on Park Avenue; but when he'd called, a butler had informed him that the family was spending the weekend at their "cottage" in Placid Hollow, as was their custom. He pronounced "weekend" with the accent on "end."

In any event, it was early on a Sunday morning, the traffic was light, and the drive went quickly. At least he hadn't had to go to Mass.

IF THIS IS A COTTAGE then I'm the Sheikh of Araby, thought Walter as he pulled up to the massive Victorian mansion set on a high knoll that he was sure gave its residents a commanding view of the Hudson River. It was a three-story, gabled structure that Walter guessed must have had seven or eight bedrooms and an equal number of bathrooms.

Placid Hollow itself was a bustling suburban village, its roads chock full of late model Mercedes Benzes, BMWs, and more than the occasional Bentley, a far cry from the quiet Dutch farming village that had been founded by a friend of Peter Stuyvesant in the 17th century.

The village was small and concentrated, though, and less than a half mile out of town the road narrowed and the countryside turned leafy and quiet. The "cottage" sat about fifty yards from the road on what Walter estimated to be twenty acres of fallow but well-tended rolling farmland. A large barn sat behind the house. Two chestnut horses grazed lazily. A small sign at the entrance that looked like it had been freshly painted announced it to be "The deGroot Family Farm." Judge Braxton had apparently married well.

As he pulled up to the house two middle-aged men came out to greet him, both dressed in dark suits. He got out of the car and started to button his blazer, but then thought better of it. The off the rack 50 Long was snug on his lean but large frame, and he didn't want his service revolver and shoulder holster to be too obvious.

"Lieutenant Hudson, I presume?" said the first man. He had a full head of dark, slicked back hair and was clean-shaven. Walter didn't have to be told that he was the one in charge.

"That is correct," said Walter.

"Welcome to deGroot Farm, Lieutenant," he said. "I only regret that your visit was precipitated by such a tragic occurrence. My name is Albert, and I am the family butler here at the Farm."

"Pleased to meet you, Albert, although I, too, regret the circumstances."

Albert gestured at the other man and said, "Richard is Mrs. Braxton's personal chauffeur. If you don't mind, he will park your car for you."

"Thank you very much," said Walter, handing the keys to Richard, who eyed the five year old Ford with a mixture of distaste and suspicion as Albert led Walter into the house.

⟞⟝⟞⟝

THE EXTERIOR OF THE HOUSE was impressive, but the interior was breathtaking, each room looking like the ones Walter saw when he occasionally perused one of Sarah's "House Beautiful" magazines. The furniture looked handcrafted, and all the art looked, at least to Walter's untrained eye, original and expensive. He felt like he'd get yelled at if he touched anything, like when his parents used to take him to the Museum of Natural History, or his grandparents' house.

Albert led him into what Walter guessed would have been called a drawing room, or perhaps a sunroom. It was large and well-lit, with floor-to-ceiling bow windows with window seats on the inside and flower boxes on the outside gracing the exterior walls; and it indeed commanded a breathtaking view of the Hudson River. He thought he heard a robin chirping outside, but it may have been his imagination.

The four occupants of the room looked at him expectantly: A striking silver-haired woman, probably in her sixties; a younger man, probably mid-thirties, with lank, sandy-colored hair and an unfortunately weak chin that made him look like an incomplete copy of the older woman, who was clearly his mother; a pretty, shy looking blond-haired woman of approximately the same age, who Walter guessed to be the man's wife; and a dark-haired woman, thirtyish, whose features were too strong for her to be called beautiful, but who exuded a confidence and authority that she had obviously inherited from the Honorable Judge Braxton, whose portrait dominated one wall of the room and whom the young woman strongly resembled.

The older woman rose and offered Walter her hand. He couldn't help but notice the youthful, alluring figure that belied the silver hair.

"Good morning, Lieutenant Hudson," she said in a clear voice and patrician accent. "I am Barbara Braxton, the late Judge's wife or, I guess I must say now, his widow. My friends call me Bunny."

"It's a pleasure to meet you," said Walter, taking that to mean that it would be 'Mrs. Braxton' to him, "although I deeply regret the circumstances. Thank you for agreeing to see me at such a painful time for all of you."

"Think nothing of it," said Barbara Braxton with a dismissive wave of her hand. "We all have our duties. In the interests of justice for my late husband you have to do yours, and it is our duty to help you to the greatest extent possible." She looked at the others in the room and they all nodded, perhaps a little halfheartedly.

"Please allow me to introduce everyone," said Barbara, to which Walter nodded.

"This is my son, Theodore Franklin Braxton, Jr.," she said, motioning to the sandy-haired young man with the weak chin, "and sitting beside him is his lovely wife, Alicia Chadwick Braxton. Young Ted is a partner at Braxton & Pierce, the law firm my husband founded. Alicia is also an attorney, having clerked for the Judge as well as being employed at the U.S. Department of Justice for three years, but she is currently working full-time managing their increasingly complex household."

"Do you have children?" said Walter to the couple.

"No, but it is in our plans," said Alicia, as "Young Ted" nodded beside her.

"And where do you live, if you don't mind my asking?" said Walter.

"When we're in the city," said Alicia, "we stay at the townhouse on Park Avenue."

"It's very spacious and the Judge and I enjoy the company," said Mrs. Braxton.

"And we also own a home here in Placid Hollow," said Alicia, "which we are currently in the process of renovating, so we stay here at the Cottage quite a bit these days."

"And this is our daughter, Virginia Elise Braxton," said Mrs. Braxton, nodding toward the other woman. "We call her 'Ginny.'"

"And I call myself 'Virginia,'" said the woman, reaching out to shake Walter's hand. Her small hand disappeared in Walter's enormous paw, but her grip was firm and dry. Barbara Braxton's expression remained impassive, but Walter thought he saw a quick flicker of annoyance in her eyes.

"And are you also an attorney?" asked Walter.

"Thank you so much for assuming that, but no," said Virginia, looking at Walter with knowing, hazel eyes like she was appraising livestock at a state fair. "I'm a money manager."

Okay, thought Walter, a live wire. "And where do you work?" he said, trying not to react to the jab.

"I initially worked for Goldman, Sachs," she said, "but two years ago I moved to Avista Asset Management. It's a boutique firm that manages the assets of only a small number of very high net worth clients. I doubt you've heard of us."

"So do I," said Walter, looking right at her and smiling. She smiled back, and Walter got the sense that Virginia Braxton liked men who pushed back.

"And to answer your next question, I own a loft in Tribeca, where I live by myself." Walter took down the address.

"Lieutenant Hudson," said Barbara, "I'm afraid we're being terribly rude. Please, take a seat, and may we get you something to eat or drink?"

"I'd love a cup of coffee, ma'am, if you wouldn't mind," said Walter. He was famished, but that would have to wait. Walter looked around at the delicate looking furniture and was suddenly self-conscious of his large frame.

Noticing his discomfiture, Virginia patted the cushion next to her on the small sofa where she was sitting. "Come sit here, Lieutenant. The furniture is sturdier than it looks, just like me, and I promise not to bite, at least not right away." The others looked mortified, but Walter smiled and took the seat.

Coffee appeared momentarily and they were all served. Walter asked for his black and Virginia said, "I didn't think you were a milk and sugar kind of guy."

"Well, then," said Barbara, her eyes shooting daggers at Virginia, "I'm sure the lieutenant didn't come here to engage in witty repartee, and I'm also sure that he's a very busy man. So, Lieutenant, why don't you ask us your questions."

"Thank you, Mrs. Braxton," said Walter, "and, once again, thank you all for your patience and hospitality at this difficult time. But I do have some questions, and I hope you won't find them too painful or personal."

"We will do our best, Lieutenant," said Barbara.

"First, I believe you know that a young woman named Caroline Schuyler was in your husband's hotel room when the police arrived, under fairly awkward circumstances."

"What do you mean, awkward circumstances?" said Barbara. "You mean, that she was holding a gun?"

"No, Mother," said Virginia, looking mischievous, "he means that she was standing there in her unmentionables, holding a gun."

"Good God," said Young Ted, almost under his breath, staring at his sister.

Walter winced inwardly. How did this stuff get out? Every newspaper in New York was already carrying lurid descriptions of the crime scene, which the Braxton family had obviously already seen.

"Do any of you know Ms. Schuyler?" said Walter.

"We all know Caroline Schuyler," said Barbara, staring at Virginia, who for once backed down. "She is not only a fine clerk for the Judge, she is a dear family friend, as is the entire Schuyler family."

"So you weren't surprised to learn that she was with the Judge at the time of his death?" said Walter.

"Not at all," said Barbara. "The Judge considered her to be one of the finest clerks he had ever employed, and he had taken a great interest in furthering her career. He had expressly invited her to attend the Bar Association meeting with him. There were to be many of the most influential members of the New York legal community in attendance and Teddy, the Judge, thought it advantageous for her to meet some of them."

Walter thought he felt Virginia shift beside him, but she remained silent.

"I'm sure that by now you are aware of her alibi," said Walter.

"Yes, we are," said Barbara, "and we take her at her word. All of us."

"Perhaps we should take a step back," said Walter. "Can you tell me why the Judge was at the Empire-Excelsior Hotel on Friday night?"

"He was there," said Barbara, "to receive an award from the New York State Bar Association, a Lifetime Achievement Award I believe they called it, and to give a speech. The Judge is, was, a fine speaker, and he was in constant demand throughout the Northeast, and even nationally."

"Did any of you attend?" said Walter, looking at Young Ted.

"None of us attended," said Young Ted. "I was invited, of course, and I intended to go, but some last minute work kept me at the office until quite late."

"And the rest of you?" said Walter, turning to Alicia. "Ms. Braxton, you are an attorney and you've previously worked for the Judge. I'm surprised that you didn't attend, given that it was to honor him."

"I would have loved to attend," she said, "but I had a long standing dinner engagement and it would have been awkward for me to cancel."

"And you, Virginia?" said Walter, turning to the young woman sitting beside him, who met his eyes with a frank stare. Somehow, Walter got the uneasy feeling that she had had her eyes on him all along.

"I was hosting a group of investors from Asia," she said, "who didn't seem to appreciate the concept of Friday night, and I went straight home from there, although I'm not sure I would have attended in any event. The idea of spending the evening with that many lawyers in one room kind of gave me the creeps, even more than having dinner with a bunch of leering, middle-aged Asian men." Her large eyes glinted with humor, and her lips curled in a smile that made him feel like she was sharing a private joke with him.

"It is our long time custom to gather here for dinner on Friday evenings," said Barbara, giving Virginia another hard stare, "although with our busy schedules that doesn't always work out. Nonetheless, I had travelled up here on Friday afternoon."

"Did you drive yourself up?" said Walter.

"Surely not," said Barbara, giving him an amused smile. "Richard drove me up, of course. The Judge was scheduled to arrive yesterday afternoon. He had a brief breakfast meeting scheduled at the hotel with some senior Bar Association members from out of town, which was why he had booked a room there for the night. Of course, I had to travel back to the city yesterday to do all the necessary things, but we all decided to meet here yesterday evening nevertheless. It is a place of solace and comfort for us all." Again he felt Virginia beside him, seemingly barely containing herself, like a thoroughbred racehorse waiting for the gate to open.

"Couldn't Judge Braxton have just stayed at your Park Avenue home?" said Walter.

"Of course, he could have," said Barbara, "but his colleagues were staying at the hotel, and it was just more convenient for him to stay there."

"It seems the Judge was a very popular man," said Walter.

"He was not just popular, Lieutenant," said Barbara. "He was beloved."

"But he must have had some enemies, right?" said Walter. "I mean, anyone who had been in the legal profession for as long as the Judge was must have angered people along the way."

"Lieutenant," said Young Ted, " as Mother just told you, my father was a well-loved man, both in his personal and his professional life. I doubt any of us can think of a single person who would have wanted him dead. We have no reason to believe that this was anything other than a random act of violence. This is New York City we're talking about. As you must know, these things occur there every day."

"We have not discounted that possibility, Mr. Braxton," said Walter, "but there are also reasons to believe that the crime may have been committed by someone the Judge knew."

"And what reasons might they be?" said Young Ted. "By the way, please call me Franklin, which is the name I go by in my professional life to avoid confusion with my father."

"As if that would ever happen, " said Virginia, but so softly Walter doubted anyone but he had heard it.

"The hotel has outstanding security," said Walter, lying, "especially when someone as prominent as the Judge is staying there. Their security personnel noticed nothing unusual."

"It's a big hotel, Lieutenant," said Young Ted, "and Friday was its grand opening. I can only imagine how many flaws there still are in their security procedures."

"Not to my knowledge," said Walter, lying again, not wanting the conversation to go in that direction, preferring to get the family members a little off balance. "The thing that sticks out in my mind is the fact that it appears that there was no forced entry. The doors automatically lock when they're closed, and both the doors and the frames are very sturdy. It's quite possible that Judge Braxton knew whoever killed him and let him, or her, into the room voluntarily."

"Has it occurred to you," said Virginia, "that the killer was already in the room when my father and Ms. Schuyler entered?"

"Yes, it has," said Walter, "and that's why we have not discounted the random act of violence--that perhaps your father interrupted a robbery in progress; though it's odd that Ms. Schuyler didn't mention hearing any sounds of a struggle. But, your father was a very well known man and reputed to be extremely wealthy. He would be a prime target for such a thing and I do not discount it."

"So why don't you just assume that was the case unless you find specific evidence otherwise?" said Young Ted, whose voice tended to rise in pitch to a nasal whine when he became argumentative. Walter found himself unable to think of the man as anything other than the patronymic "Young Ted," not only because he knew it was what his family called him, but because it seemed to fit him far better than "Franklin."

"Because in my experience," said Walter, "and in the experience of the NYPD in general, murders like this are personal; they are committed by someone known to the victim, quite often by a family member."

"Dear Lord," said Barbara, sounding genuinely upset, "you can't possibly suspect any of us? We are an extraordinarily close-knit family, and we've already been completely forthcoming as to our whereabouts on Friday night."

"Lieutenant Hudson," said Young Ted, "we are all trying to comprehend a tragedy that struck our family less than two days ago. We are exhausted and we haven't had the chance even to begin the grieving process. We agreed to meet with you because we want to find out as badly as you do what precisely happened to a dear man we all loved. But this conversation is becoming very upsetting, and perhaps we need to be left alone now. We will all make ourselves completely available as your investigation progresses."

"I agree," said Walter. "I am truly sorry for your terrible loss, and you have my sincerest condolences. Thank you for providing me your whereabouts on the night of the murder. We will, of course, follow up to confirm your alibis, but we will try to do that as unobtrusively as possible."

"'Alibi' is an awfully distasteful word, don't you think?" said Alicia.

"Well, murder is a distasteful business, Ms. Braxton, but I do understand your feelings, and I do not wish to intrude on you any further. However, I would like to speak to your mother in private before I leave," said Walter, turning to Young Ted.

"For God's sake," he said, "I thought I made myself clear. I think we have all had enough for one day. Especially Mother."

"Thank you for your concern, Ted," said Barbara, "but I don't mind. More than anything, I want your father's killer found. I will be more than willing to talk to you, Lieutenant."

The others headed for the door: Young Ted, looking none too pleased, followed by his wife, and Virginia, who surprised Walter by giving him a soft pat on his shoulder, her hip brushing his arm as she rose from the sofa.

The door closed behind them, and Barbara took a seat on a sofa adjacent to the one Walter was seated on.

"Now, Lieutenant, I'll be curious to know what you wish to discuss with me that you think is not suitable for my adult children to hear."

"Mrs. Braxton, I really hesitate to bring up this subject at such a sensitive time, but is it possible that your husband was having an affair with Ms. Schuyler?"

"Lieutenant," said Bunny, staring at him frankly with large blue eyes, leaving Walter overcome with how beautiful the woman still was, "I completely understand that it is your professional duty to ask difficult questions, and please rest assured that I take no offense. But to answer your question directly: No, I do not believe that my husband was having an affair with Caroline Schuyler."

"It's just that, you know, the situation appeared to be suggestive of that type of thing, what with the lingerie and all."

"Lieutenant Hudson, it has been my experience that men, no matter what their age, and no matter what their marital status, know pathetically little about women in general, and what they wear under their outer clothing and what motivates them to wear it in particular. Caroline was always completely at ease with my husband, and I have absolutely no problem believing that she would have been quite comfortable going up to his suite to change. I believe that is all there is to the matter."

"That is completely consistent with what Ms. Schuyler herself has told us."

"Well, then, there you have it."

"Again, I hate to ask a personal question," said Walter, "but would you describe your marriage with your husband as a happy one?"

"It was more than happy, Lieutenant," said Barbara. "We were made for one another. I fell in love with Teddy the first time I ever saw him, and I believe it was the same for him; and we never stopped loving each other, not for one day."

"Then you were a very lucky woman, and he was a very lucky man."

"Very lucky, indeed," said Barbara. "Now, I must admit that I am tiring. Is there anything else that you would like to ask of me?"

"No, Mrs. Braxton, I think that will be enough for today. Thank you so much for your patience."

"You're welcome," said Barbara as Albert, as if by some telepathy, appeared at the door. "Please excuse me if I do not accompany you out, but as I said, I am quite tired."

Walter rose and shook her hand. "I completely understand, ma'am. Again, please accept my condolences for your loss." She remained seated as he left the room with Albert.

He was surprised to see Virginia in the hallway as he left, standing by a small table and examining what looked to be a stack of mail.

"Oh, hello again, Lieutenant," she said, looking up. She was petite, but by no means fragile looking. Her strong features were striking in the late morning light.

"Hello, Ms. Braxton."

"Please, call me Virginia," she said, staring at him with those disconcertingly penetrating eyes.

"Yes, well, it was a pleasure to meet you, although I'm sorry it was under such sad circumstances," he said.

"You sound like a funeral director, Lieutenant. Please, it's all right. It was nice to meet you. I imagine we'll be seeing each other again."

"I'm sure we will," stammered Walter. Somehow she had made it seem like they were making a date. "Well, I'll see you later," he said as he stumbled out the door behind Albert. Richard was waiting outside, and he handed him the keys to his car with a disapproving expression on his face.

As he drove back to the city Walter reviewed the conversation in his mind. He'd deliberately held a lot back from them, wanting more than anything to get initial impressions of all of them and hear their alibis from their own mouths, but all in all it seemed to have gone well. He hadn't come away with any firm suspicions; but it also confirmed why, as emotionally difficult as it usually was for all involved, it was critical to have these interviews as soon as possible, before questions could be anticipated and answers coordinated and rehearsed. Because that is what Walter couldn't help feeling that he had just witnessed: a performance, but a performance that was just a little under-rehearsed. And Walter's finely tuned ear had definitely detected some wrong notes. He had a lot to think about.

But mostly, he thought about Virginia Braxton.

5

"ARE WE GOOD?" said Sarah Hudson, settling herself into her husband on the sofa in their small living room. Walter had never thought of the house as small, but the visit to the Braxton's "cottage" had altered his perceptions.

"Good as gold," said Walter, liking the warmth of her beside him.

It was the refrain of their marriage, countlessly repeated over the years. Walter and Sarah had met in high school and had been inseparable ever since. Their marriage was the unshakable foundation of their lives and the envy of many; but even the best of marriages has its difficulties. For Sarah and Walter it was mostly the financial strain of living on a cop's pay and coping with his irregular hours while they tried to raise a family.

But now it was a little mite named Daniel, whom they had both already come to love more than their own lives, but who was exhausting both of them and stretching their patience, especially with each other, to the limit.

When Walter finally got home that evening he'd found their two little girls, Beth and Robin, quietly playing in the living room and clearly trying to remain inconspicuous. He'd gone into the kitchen and found Sarah holding the crying Daniel in her arms, weeping, while a pot of water boiled on the stove and a boxful of uncooked pasta lay scattered over the linoleum floor.

He'd tried to take the baby from her, but she had pushed him away and cried harder, so he had cleaned up the pasta, opened up a fresh box, and heated some store bought marinara sauce. Sarah would ordinarily not even hear of store bought sauce in her home, but desperate times called for desperate measures, and since Daniel's arrival they had all gotten used to dinners from jars and the freezer without complaining.

Sarah had retreated to the bedroom with the baby while Walter and the girls ate in silence. He had tried to talk to them and cheer them up, but they weren't having it, and he couldn't blame them. He'd cleaned up the worst of the mess in the kitchen and got them bathed and into bed. They usually fought bedtime, but tonight they had withdrawn to their room gratefully.

He went back into his and Sarah's bedroom where he found Sarah still awake, her eyes tired and swollen. Little Daniel, at least for a few precious moments, slept quietly beside her. He sent her out to the kitchen to get some supper while he stayed with the baby and changed out of his work clothes. Then he snuck back out to the kitchen to clean up after Sarah and send her off to take a quick shower. And now, with Daniel still miraculously asleep for what Walter was convinced was a record amount of time, they finally had some peace and privacy.

"I'm so sorry," said Sarah. Her normally abundant, well-groomed dark hair hung lifelessly down to her shoulders, and her large brown eyes, which usually held a hint of mischief and, when Walter was particularly fortunate, a sultriness that he found irresistible, were dull and hinted only of exhaustion.

"There's nothing to be sorry about, honey," said Walter.

"Are you kidding?" said Sarah. "The house is a wreck, I haven't cooked a decent meal in weeks, I've become nothing more than a shrew who even my own kids are terrified of, and we haven't had sex in months, like anybody would want me. I look like a hag."

"It's all temporary," said Walter, kissing the top of her head. "The kids and I love you, and we'll all somehow manage to survive on store-bought food for a while. And you're still the most beautiful woman I've ever laid eyes on."

"Liar. I think this is the longest we've gone without making love since we were married," she said. "That's not right."

"You know, Sarah, my mother always wanted me to be a priest."

"Yeah," said Sarah, laughing for the first time in weeks, "especially after the first time you brought me home."

"Mom loves you, you know that," said Walter. "She just has a funny way of showing it sometimes."

"You can say that again," said Sarah.

"So, anyway, this is a good opportunity for me once and for all to understand just how bad a decision that would have been. I mean, I would have taken one look at you after I was ordained and gotten myself defrocked in world record time."

"Your mother would have shot me dead first."

"Don't worry about it, OK?"

"It's just not right, that's all. And I miss it, too, you know."

"Well, c'mon, who wouldn't?" said Walter.

"Dope," said Sarah, punching him in the shoulder.

"I think this is the longest Daniel has slept," said Walter. "Maybe he's finally getting over his colic." As if on cue, they heard him begin to fuss.

"Jinx," said Sarah.

"Look, you get into bed and get some sleep. I'm not tired yet, and the little guy and I need a little quality time together anyway."

"Thanks. I haven't even asked you about work. How's it going?"

"It's a weird case, I'll tell you that. The Braxtons try to come off as the perfect family, but I get the impression that they're anything but that. I don't get rich people. I never will."

"You get people just fine," said Sarah, yawning as she rose to go to bed. "But you be careful, and don't let yourself get reeled in. Rich people have powerful friends, and powerful friends tend to squish people like us like bugs when we get underfoot."

"I'm a pretty big bug to squish," he said as he followed Sarah down the hall to retrieve Daniel.

"That just means you'll make a bigger splat, that's all," said Sarah as she lay down. She was asleep before her head hit the pillow.

Walter held Daniel in one arm while he finished cleaning the kitchen with the other. The little boy seemed to enjoy the movement, and Walter loved the feel of him in his arms.

"I think we'll keep you after all, little guy," said Walter.

Tomorrow would be another long day, but he wouldn't think about that now. He was happy, and at peace.

6

WALTER COULD COUNT the number of times he'd been to Fairfield County, Connecticut on the fingers of one hand, and the only times he'd ever stopped there had been to get gas and, once, to change a tire after they'd gotten a flat on the way up to New Haven to visit one of Sarah's aunts.

Unmarked police cars relegated to part-time use don't come equipped with navigation systems, so after he got off of I-95 at the Delavan Avenue exit he paid close attention to the GPS app on his iPhone as busy, well-marked streets gave way to smaller country lanes. He turned left where a sign said, "Coven Cove." There must be a story behind that, he thought.

The Schuyler estate was approximately the size of a minor European duchy, but Walter never would have known he'd arrived had it not been for the presence of a servant in livery flagging him down at the end of a well-hidden driveway. A sign off to the left side of the driveway entrance said, "Welcome, Friends, to Innisfree." A smaller sign hanging just underneath that one said, "Trespassers Will Be Prosecuted."

The servant hopped into a golf cart emblazoned with what looked to be a coat of arms on the back and led Walter up the long driveway and finally, under a large *porte-cochère*.

The Braxtons' home in Placid Hollow had been a cottage after all, thought Walter, as he gazed up at the facade of the house. It bore a strong resemblance to the White House, except it was larger.

He was led through the house, feeling like he was being escorted to a throne room. He felt awkward, like an oversized tap dancer, his size 14D shoes clicking on the wide, marble-floored hallway as he was escorted out through a double doorway in the back that opened up onto an Olympic-size swimming pool surrounded by a flagstone patio furnished with enough tables, chairs and *chaises longues* to accommodate dozens, if not hundreds, of guests. At the far end were what appeared to be a formal dining area and a restaurant quality kitchen. The water sparkled in the unseasonably warm May sunshine.

Two young women were swimming in the pool, but they hopped out as soon as he appeared. As he expected, one was Caroline Schuyler, who wore a one-piece bathing suit that, though relatively conservative, did nothing to hide her spectacular physique. She turned away from him as she toweled off and Walter had to concede that Eduardo had been right.

The other young woman, to Walter's great surprise, was Virginia Braxton, who wore what was probably technically a bikini, but was for all intents and purposes nothing. Her slender body, while not possessing the athletic litheness of Caroline's, was far more voluptuous.

Caroline quickly grabbed a terrycloth robe and donned it before walking over to Walter to greet him. Virginia picked up a similar robe but made no move to put it on before marching up to Walter with an impish smile on her face.

"Well, if it isn't our great big Lieutenant Hudson," she said. "What a pleasant surprise."

"Ginny, for God's sake put something on," said Caroline, hurrying over. "You're positively indecent."

"Yes, and we most certainly don't approve of indecency, do we," said Virginia, looking pointedly at Caroline as, to Walter's great relief, she wrapped the robe around herself.

"It's a pleasure to see you again, Ms. Braxton," said Walter with all the equanimity he could muster. He turned to Caroline and said, "Ms. Schuyler, I'm Detective Lieutenant Walter Hudson of the NYPD. It's a pleasure to meet you. Thank you so much for agreeing to see me on such short notice. I'm afraid I arrived a little bit early. I'm not familiar with the area and I didn't want to be late." Stop your babbling, he thought. You sound like a seventeen-year-old picking up his date for the junior prom.

"No problem at all, Lieutenant. Thank you for making the long drive," said Caroline. She turned to Virginia and said, "Virginia is actually here for an appointment with my father. Aren't you already a little late, Virginia?"

"Oh, your Daddy won't mind if I'm a little late, Caroline," said Virginia. "Besides, I'm sure he wouldn't want me to be inhospitable to one of your guests. But Caroline is right, Lieutenant," she said, turning to Walter. "I must get going. But don't be a stranger, ok?"

"Ah, sure," said Walter, stupidly, but Virginia was already walking away.

⸺⚜⸺

"Sorry about Ginny," said Caroline, after making a quick visit to a cabana to don shorts and a shirt before returning to the patio and leading them to a table with two chairs and an umbrella for shade. Her long, blond hair was still wet but carefully combed. "She can be a bit forward."

"No need to apologize," said Walter. "Are you sure you don't want your attorney present, Ms. Schuyler?"

"Arthur Hurley is not my attorney, no matter what he'd like to believe. I decide whom I talk to, and I'm entirely comfortable talking to you. Am I being clear?"

"Yes, you are, ma'am."

"Good."

"Have you known Virginia for a long time?" said Walter, not wanting her to have any time to change her mind.

"We've known each other all our lives," said Caroline as a uniformed waiter arrived with a pitcher of iced tea and two glasses filled with ice. She poured Walter a glass without asking him if he wanted any, but he was thirsty after the long drive and it tasted good.

"I take it then that your parents were close?"

"Our two fathers met when they were both just out of school. They were birds of a feather, and they apparently hit it off right away. Judge Braxton was my father's personal attorney until he accepted the judgeship, and Dad was Teddy's, uh, the Judge's, personal financial advisor."

"You said they were 'birds of a feather,'" said Walter. "In what way?"

"They both came from nothing, Lieutenant. Judge Braxton grew up in the South Bronx, and he was an orphan by the time he was fifteen. Dad grew up in Hell's Kitchen when it was still, well, when it was still Hell's Kitchen."

"Wow," said Walter. "I'd somehow gotten the impression that they were both blue bloods."

"Not by a long shot," said Caroline, laughing a deep, throaty laugh.

"How did they get where they got, then?"

"The hard way. Dad went to CCNY at night while working in a warehouse in East New York full-time. The Judge got his law degree from the Rockland College of Law, which operated out of an abandoned movie theater in Pearl River, New York, while he was working as a janitor at Lederle Labs, which was a chemical products company across the street from the law school."

"I've never heard of the Rockland College of Law," said Walter.

"There's a good reason for that," said Caroline. "It opened only a couple of years before the Judge started there, and it closed only a couple of years after he graduated. But it was there long enough for the Judge to get his law degree. It was cheap, and it offered night classes. That was all he cared about."

"But I thought I read in his obituary that he had a degree from Yale."

"That's an LL.D., Lieutenant, an honorary degree he bought with a ten million dollar gift to the Yale Law Library. It's the only degree he ever mentions in his biography. You can probably understand why."

"But he was obviously a brilliant lawyer in any case."

"Actually, Teddy was not what I would call a brilliant lawyer. He had an adequate grasp of the law, but not much more than that."

"I guess I don't understand," said Walter. "The man had an unbelievably successful legal career, and then he went on to become a federal judge."

"Lieutenant," said Caroline, "Teddy Braxton was only an average lawyer, but he was the most brilliant self-promoter, showman, and courtroom strategist I have ever known. He was also utterly, devastatingly, charming. That's how he made Braxton & Pierce the single most successful law firm in the country. You can always hire an outstanding legal mind, Lieutenant, and Teddy surrounded himself with plenty of them, including, at the risk of sounding immodest, me; but you can't send someone to school to get what Teddy had, and you can't buy it. He was one in a million."

"And what about your father? Was it the same with him?"

"Not at all," she said, smiling. "My father is many wonderful things, but charming isn't one of them. He is, though, brilliant, and probably the hardest working man I've ever known. After CCNY he got a job in the mailroom of Salomon Brothers, which back then was one of the most prominent investment banking firms in the world, while a whole lot of young men his age from Ivy League schools were sitting upstairs in the trading room. But Dad caught on fast. He's a true financial genius, and he was a partner at the firm before he was thirty. By that time all those Ivy League kids were either working for him, or he'd fired them along the way."

"So the Judge and your father did well by each other."

"Yes, and they both would have been multimillionaires in any event, but that's not the whole story."

"Then why don't you fill me in," said Walter, his mind starting to reel, the ice in his tea melting as it sat on the table, forgotten.

"Do you recall the dot.com bubble of the late '90s, when every scruffy twenty-something kid in the country who could create a webpage was getting rich before their businesses, if you could call them that, had turned their first penny?"

"Only vaguely."

"Well, we were all young then," said Caroline, "but being my father's daughter I lived and breathed it, even though I was barely in middle school. Investors made billions, at least on paper, when they participated in the IPOs of these companies."

"IPO?"

"Not important," said Caroline. "The point is, all those companies were fundamentally worthless, and Daddy, who was an independent financial consultant by then, knew it, so he quietly took massive short positions in dozens of them while all of his colleagues were still going crazy, pouring more and more money into them and ridiculing Daddy for missing the boat."

Walter was going to interrupt and ask what a "short position" was, but he decided it would be futile.

"Anyway, when the bubble burst, all those paper billions evaporated, but a great many of them turned into real billions for Daddy. He's now somewhere between Bill Gates and Warren Buffett on the richest people in the world listings."

"And how was the Judge involved in all this?"

"First, he did a brilliant job of making sure that everything Daddy did was legally airtight," said Caroline. "But most importantly, he was one of the few people who agreed with Daddy's view of the markets, and he was willing to say so. So Daddy took Teddy along for the ride with him. He didn't make nearly the money that Daddy did, but it turned him from a multimillionaire, which is what his law practice had made him, into a billionaire. I figure he was worth close to two billion dollars at the time of his death."

And that's two billion reasons for someone to want him dead, thought Walter.

"But Lieutenant," said Caroline, "I don't think you came here for a family history. I am still, I assume, your prime suspect in Judge Braxton's murder."

"The family history wasn't my main reason for wanting to talk to you, that's true," said Walter. "But you're a lawyer, so I don't have to tell you that most murders of this nature are committed either by a family member or someone who was close personally to the victim. So I consider all this information to be extremely relevant to my investigation."

"And I," said Caroline, looking him in the eye with a hint of a smile on her pretty face, "being Teddy's lover, am a particularly likely suspect, especially since I was, after all, holding the presumed murder weapon when the police arrived."

Walter didn't know how to react to any of that, so he remained silent.

"Oh, please, Lieutenant, let's cut the shit," said Caroline. "Of course I was Teddy's lover. I had been for the past year. And as for the gun, I'm sure that by now your clever investigators know all about my experience and training with firearms."

"Barbara Braxton told me yesterday that she was absolutely sure that you were not having an affair with the Judge."

Caroline hesitated. "Mrs. Braxton is a wonderful woman, perhaps the finest woman I have ever known. I have known her practically all my life, and I care for her deeply."

Walter waited for her to continue, but after a few seconds he realized that she was going to say nothing more on the subject. He decided to move on.

"I know about your training as a biathlete, Ms. Schuyler," he said, finally finding his tongue. "But I also know that handling a silenced .45 is a lot different than handling a small caliber rifle."

"You are correct, of course," said Caroline. "But I am expert in the use of a wide range of firearms. My father is, in addition to everything else, a huge firearms enthusiast and he is heavily involved in 2nd Amendment issues. If you look down behind the pool area you will find an excellent firing range. He also maintains an extensive collection of firearms, all of them in perfect working order and most of which I have fired at one time or another in my life. The rule at Daddy's parties was that no one got a drink until everyone had target practice. No exceptions. I've been shooting since I was five."

"So you are not denying that you could have fired the weapon accurately enough to kill the Judge?"

"Why would I deny it? You know my background with weapons and, for better or worse, you and a great many other law enforcement officers have had the chance to examine my physique in the past few days. I don't mean to brag, but I could shoot the eye out of a sparrow at fifty feet with that pistol."

"Thank you for your honesty," said Walter, not knowing what else to say. The woman was making absolutely no attempt to deflect suspicion from herself. "You said, 'presumed murder weapon' a little earlier. Is there any reason, in your opinion, to believe that it was not the murder weapon?"

"Haven't you done the autopsy yet?"

"It's scheduled for this afternoon."

"And you haven't personally examined the body?"

"Not yet."

"Well then," said Caroline, "you'll know soon enough. I just remember looking down at poor Teddy and thinking that there was no way he was shot with a .45."

"Why not?"

"Lieutenant, I'm sure you've seen what a .45 shot at point blank range does to a person. The bullets would have blown right through him, leaving gaping wounds, and there would have been a massive amount of blood on the floor. There was none of that. I think, no, I'm sure, that he was shot with a smaller caliber weapon, and I think that you will find the bullets in poor Teddy's body."

"The silencer would have slowed the muzzle velocity of the bullets, of course. We'll find out soon enough either way," said Walter.

"Yes, you will," said Caroline.

"But that doesn't make any sense, does it," said Walter. "I mean, why would there have been a .45 lying on the floor when you came into the room if it wasn't the murder weapon?"

"You've got me there," said Caroline. "I know a lot about firearms, but I decidedly do not know much at all about murder. That, I believe, is your area of expertise. All I can tell you is what I told Officer Sanchez on the night of the murder. It was a large suite, and I was separated from the living area by two closed doors while I was showering and changing. Still, you would think that if there had been any shouting or violent physical struggle I would have heard at least something, but I didn't. You can make what you want of that."

"Fair enough," said Walter. "Can you tell me if there is anything else that you saw when you entered the living area that might help us with our investigation?"

"Not that I can think of, Lieutenant. I'm very sorry."

"Ms. Schuyler," said Walter, picking up a manila folder that he had been carrying with him in his notebook, "I've brought with me copies of some of the photos that we took of the crime scene. Would you mind taking a look at them and telling me if you notice anything remarkable in them?"

"I guess I can try," she said.

Hudson laid out four of the photos on the table, and Caroline looked down at them. After only a few brief seconds, though, she looked away and focused her eyes instead on Hudson.

"I'm sorry, Lieutenant," she said, "but I'm afraid that I'm not prepared to look at these. Perhaps I will be more helpful at another time. I'm very sorry."

"Please don't apologize, Ms. Schuyler. It must be very upsetting. I understand."

"Thank you."

"Okay," said Walter, "I think I've taken up enough of your time for now, but I do have one final question."

"Fire away," said Caroline. "Oops, I guess that was inappropriate."

Walter waved that off and said, "Was anyone else aware of the fact that you and Judge Braxton were having an affair?"

"Oh, please!" came a voice from behind them, followed by a laugh. They both looked around to see Ginny Braxton standing behind them, wearing a short skirt and a tube top that was only slightly more modest than the bikini. With her dark brown hair pulled back in a ponytail and some light makeup, she looked closer to twenty than the thirty years old Walter knew she was.

"What Ginny is trying to tell you in her own inimitable way," said Caroline, "is that our relationship was no secret, either within or outside of the family."

"But you know, Lieutenant," said Virginia, "in our circles these things are accepted. Almost *de riguer*, you might say. We keep our mouths shut and carry on. We let others worry about the condition of their immortal souls. Right, Caroline?"

Caroline glared at her, but said nothing.

"Did you feel as though you were pressured into the relationship in any way because of the fact that you worked for Judge Braxton?" said Walter, trying to ignore Virginia.

"Absolutely not," said Caroline. "The relationship was purely voluntary. As I have said, Teddy Braxton was an extraordinarily charming, attractive man. I simply found him irresistible. You should also know that I was by no means the first woman to succumb to Teddy's charms."

"But you certainly were the last, weren't you?" said the dead man's daughter.

"Yes," said Caroline in a quiet, small voice, "I most certainly was the last."

As Walter rose to leave Virginia said, "I'm heading back to the city myself, Lieutenant. How would you like to save me some train fare and give me a ride?"

Walter hesitated, thinking that on the one hand it would give him a golden opportunity to crosscheck what Caroline had told him. She had been extremely convincing, but a woman that bright could be a damn good liar, and Virginia, as her lifelong friend, might be a valuable source of information to help him decide if she had been completely honest with him, especially since Virginia had a big mouth. On the other hand, the woman made him uneasy and, more importantly, he could almost see Sarah scowling at him in disapproval.

"Sure," he said, the cop in him winning out.

"Oh, goody," said Virginia. "Can we use the siren?"

7

"**L**OOK, I'M SORRY, OKAY?" said Young Ted Braxton as his wife, Alicia, threw the bedcovers back and stormed naked into the bathroom.

Although he was not yet thirty-five, Ted had been having problems with erectile dysfunction for almost three years now, and no amount of Viagra or Cialis seemed to help, despite his doctor's repeated assurances that there was nothing physically wrong with him.

Personally, he didn't miss the sex that much, but he knew Alicia did. When they had first been married she'd been insatiable, but over the years her appetite had seemed to fade. For a long time the reduced frequency hadn't seemed to bother her, especially once his performance issues started to surface. But over the past year her appetite had once again increased as, he surmised, she had become increasingly eager to start a family. She'd gone off birth control over a year ago, but so far they'd had no luck, mostly due to his failure to perform.

He quickly dressed while Alicia was in the bathroom to save himself the humiliation of having her stare at the flaccid evidence of his failure. He headed into the kitchen to make some coffee, hoping that she'd be willing to talk about something else once she came out. Thankfully, they had the Cottage to themselves today, a rare occurrence.

She arrived in the kitchen shortly, her blond hair combed neatly, wearing a pair of cream colored denims that fit her like a pair of tights, along with a crimson linen blouse. At thirty-two she was a damned attractive woman who could still pass easily as a twenty-something, and he felt a sharp pang of regret that he couldn't satisfy her in bed.

To his relief, she acted as though his latest failure hadn't occurred.

"Well, this ought to be an interesting visit," she said.

They sat down in a small, informal dining alcove that looked out on the barn. "How's the house coming along?" he said, as she poured herself a cup of coffee, added a little cream and took a sip, giving herself a small nod of approval. They had purchased a house less than a mile from the Cottage two years ago at a bargain price due to its dilapidated condition and had been renovating it ever since. In the process they had learned the hard lesson that there is no such thing as a "bargain price" in the Westchester County housing market. Ted was hoping to see a nearly finished home when they went to look at it today.

"The house is coming along just fine," she said, spreading some cream cheese on a bagel and handing half to Ted. "We should be able to move into it by Labor Day."

"What's the latest cost estimate?" he said, fearing the answer.

"About double the last estimate they gave us six months ago, which was about double the original estimate," said Alicia.

"Jesus," said Ted, putting down the bagel before he'd taken a bite, "how are we going to afford that?"

"I don't know," said Alicia. "Have you talked to Brad about increasing your partnership share at the firm like you said you would?"

"That just isn't going to happen, Alicia, you know that."

"I know that it's not going to happen as long as that loser Brad Pierce is running the firm," said Alicia. "It's about time that you started to assert yourself more there, Ted, while there's still time."

"Lord knows I've tried," said Ted, "but Brad's stubborn, and in the end I'm not the answer either. Let's face it, the firm hasn't been the same since Dad left, and I'm not my father."

"No, you're not," said Alicia under her breath. "Well, I assume you'll be coming into a healthy inheritance now that he's dead, right?"

"I don't know, Alicia," said Ted as he watched her face go pale.

"What do you mean, you don't know?" she said, her voice gone suddenly hoarse.

"Alicia, Dad acted as his own attorney when it came to his personal estate. Carlton Schuyler managed all of his money for him, but his will and all of the legal aspects of his estate he kept strictly to himself."

"But for God's sake, Ted, he must have left you something."

"With Mother still alive we can't be sure. For all I know, he may have left it all to her and it won't be distributed to Ginny and me until Mother dies."

Ted could almost see her mind spinning behind her eyes. "My God, Ted, that woman's going to live to be a hundred! What are we going to do?"

"Alicia, please, let's not get ahead of ourselves."

"Someone has to take the bull by the horns around here, dammit," she said, with a look that robbed him of any residual sense of masculinity that he had been clinging to. "You're going to have to get her to gift your share over to you. At least part of it."

"Well, at least we won't have to worry about the bank foreclosing on the mortgage like they've been threatening to do," said Ted, trying to change the subject.

"Why, do you think that the lawsuit will be settled?"

"I don't know if it will be settled, but with Dad's death the entire matter will have to be revisited by another judge, and I can't think of another judge in the Southern District who shared Dad's legal view of the situation."

"I just can't believe your father would have ruled against the town of Placid Hollow and let the federal government seize all that property through eminent domain just so they could build low cost housing. It's just so disloyal."

"I don't know what he would have done," said Ted, picking up the bagel and taking a bite. "Dad was funny about things like that. Remember, he came from nothing and he had a lot of mixed feelings about inherited wealth, which is another reason I'm worried about his will."

"I still say that bitch, Caroline Schuyler, had a lot to do with shaping your father's opinion. Her with her billionaire daddy--what does she care?"

"I never liked Caroline," said Ted, "but she was Ginny's best friend so I stayed out of that whole mess."

"Mess is right," said Alicia. "So when will you find out about your father's will?"

"Probably not for a couple of weeks," said Ted, "unless they accelerate the probate process because of the unusual circumstances of his death."

"Speaking of his death," said Alicia, "have you been asked to speak at the memorial service tomorrow afternoon? It would be a wonderful opportunity to raise your profile as the new face of the Braxton legal empire." She wanted to say, now that your father is out of the way, but she wisely bit her tongue.

"Yes, I have, but I've declined."

"But why?" said Alicia, her face falling.

"Because by the time Brad and Mother have finished speaking there will be nothing left to say, and, anyway, I don't give a damn about raising my profile."

"I know you don't, Ted," said Alicia. "I know you don't."

8

"**SO CAN I SEE YOUR GUN?**" said Virginia as she settled into the passenger seat of Lieutenant Hudson's unmarked car. Her already short skirt was hiked up so high that if it rode up any further on her bare thighs her underwear would start showing, thought Walter, assuming, as he desperately hoped, she was wearing any. She was turned toward him in a way that stretched the halter top tightly over her breasts and left little, perhaps nothing, to the imagination. He was trying not to look, and he knew that was just what it must have looked like to Virginia, who was smiling smugly.

"No, you may not," said Walter, as he tried to concentrate on merging into the heavy southbound traffic on I-95.

"Do you have a uniform?"

"All New York City police officers have uniforms," he said, trying not to sound impatient.

"Do you ever wear it?"

"Very rarely," he said. "Detectives usually wear plainclothes."

"Too bad," said Virginia. "I bet you look hot in it."

"Let's get one thing straight, Ms. Braxton," said Walter. "I agreed to drive you back to New York in order to question you about the case that I am working on, which just so happens to be the murder of your father, so I would hope that you would take it seriously. Also, for your information, I am a very happily married man with three young children and I don't appreciate this kind of banter, so please cut it out."

"Yes, sir," said Virginia, soundly suddenly chastened. She straightened herself out in her seat and did her best to pull her skirt over her thighs.

"Thank you," said Walter. "Now, Caroline Schuyler told me that you two have known each other all your lives. Have you been close friends or just acquaintances?"

"We were very close," said Virginia. "Caroline and her family lived less than a mile from us when we were growing up, and we were constant companions. Starting in 7th grade we went off to Miss Porter's School in Connecticut together where we were roommates until we graduated. Then we both went to Yale and roomed together there for all four years. I went off to Harvard for my MBA while Caroline stayed at Yale for law school, but even then we remained close."

Walter turned and stared at her.

"Surprise, surprise, Lieutenant. I'm not a mindless bimbo after all."

She had scored a point, and Walter decided not to argue about it.

"It must have affected your friendship when she began the affair with your father. Were you angry with her? Disappointed in her?"

"I guess it shocked me more than anything," said Virginia after a moment's hesitation.

"Why? I've gotten the impression that this was not your father's first affair by any stretch of the imagination."

"I wasn't shocked because of my father, Lord knows. I was shocked by Caroline. At Yale she was known as the 'Snow Queen,' and let's just say it wasn't because she was a terrific skier."

"Really?"

"Yes, really, Lieutenant," said Virginia. "Caroline, unlike so many of us, grew up in a strict, very religious household. I think they were Dutch Reformed or something like that."

"Was that her mother's influence?"

"No, I always got the impression that Caroline's mother, rest her soul, wasn't all that enthusiastic about religion, that she just went along with it because that was what her husband wanted."

"When did her mother die?" said Walter.

"When Caroline and I were both ten."

"Did her father ever remarry?"

"No, he didn't. He was very strict about that. And Caroline was an only child, so he is the only family she has, which, I think, is one of the reasons she was always so close to my family. She didn't really have any of her own. And after her mother died my mother took over most of the hostess duties for Mr. Schuyler's parties and social events, so she and Mother became very close. And I always came along with Mother, so I was at her house quite often, too."

"Did Caroline's father know about the affair?"

"He found out eventually," said Virginia. "Of course, they both tried to keep it from him, but our social circle is a relatively small one and it leaked out. It was inevitable."

"How did he react to it?"

"In a word, badly. He was furious. It basically destroyed the forty-year friendship between him and Dad. He continued to do Dad's financial work for him, but that was it. I don't think they'd spoken a word to each other since Carlton found out. I basically acted as their intermediary. My company, Avista Asset Management, is a subsidiary of the Schuyler Group; a very successful subsidiary, I might add. All of Dad's financial assets are invested with Avista."

"Is that why you were meeting with him today?"

"Yes it was, at least in part. We discussed Dad's estate, but we also discussed a range of other subjects. We meet at least twice a week."

"Did Mr. Schuyler try to convince Caroline to terminate the affair?"

"Yes, he did, but she refused even to talk about it with him, and that infuriated him even further."

"Why do you think, after living such a conservative, disciplined life, she suddenly embarked on an affair with your father?"

"Lieutenant," said Virginia, "if you haven't already heard this, you'll hear it many times before your investigation is concluded: My father was a charming man. He was more than charming. He was charismatic. Everybody wanted to be near him. Everybody wanted to be noticed by him. Caroline was simply incapable of resisting his charms and she was by no means alone in that regard."

"If you say so," said Walter, shaking his head.

"If you had ever had the chance to meet him you would know exactly what I'm talking about."

"You realize your mother denied any knowledge of the affair, or that it was even going on. She had to know that I'd find out eventually."

"That doesn't surprise me in the least. First of all, please don't take this wrong, Lieutenant, but that is a topic that she simply would not discuss with you, even in the context of a murder investigation. But it's more than that."

"What do you mean?"

"I don't know quite how to explain," said Virginia, biting her lower lip pensively, "but in a very real way she wasn't lying to you, because that is the world as she sees it; that is what she actually believes. And, in its own way, it's true. Mom and Dad loved each other. They were devoted to each other, and they were very kind and considerate to each other. Despite everything, it was a genuine love story. Daddy's aberrant behavior simply had to be ignored in order to see the world as it really was. I'm sorry, I don't know if that made any sense."

Walter looked over at her with a new respect in his eyes. "It actually made all the sense in the world to me. Thank you."

"I told you, Lieutenant, not a bimbo," she said, looking as if she'd just received an "A" from a demanding professor.

"And what about you, Virginia?" said Walter.

"What about me?"

"How did you feel? I can't help but notice that you don't seem to be exhibiting a lot of grief. I mean, for Heaven's sake, your father was just murdered four nights ago while he was in the middle of engaging in an affair with your best friend since childhood, and you're acting as if nothing happened."

Virginia turned away from Walter and stared out the window for a long time, saying nothing.

"Virginia?"

"Lieutenant," said Virginia, finally turning back to him, "I come from a very prominent family that lives a very public life. New York society at our level is simply vicious, and the first thing you have to learn if you're going to have any chance of surviving in it is that you can never show them anything real, you can never let them see *you*. Because once you do, they will turn it all against you and they will destroy you. I don't mean to sound condescending, but I'm not sure you're capable of understanding that. But please do not doubt for a second that I am devastated by his loss. He was my father, and I was his only daughter and......"

Walter looked over at her when she suddenly stopped talking. She seemed to be on the verge of tears and her breathing was becoming labored. He knew she needed some time to gather herself. But he was a cop. He had one more question to ask, and every cop instinct in him told him that he had to ask it now before she closed up again.

"Virginia, you must have been extremely angry with your father for the way that he behaved."

She looked at him, almost in disbelief. A tear streamed down her cheek but she made no attempt to wipe it away.

"Why do you ask, Lieutenant? Do you actually think that I could have killed my father?"

"Please understand, Virginia, I'm not accusing you, or anyone else for that matter, of anything at this point. I'm just trying to do my job. Please don't take it personally. If anything, your honest answers will help me clear you of any suspicion."

"Thank you so much," she said, slowly and quietly. "You don't quit, do you? I'm just another object to be investigated, and nothing gets in the way of your almighty investigation, right?"

"I'm just trying to do my job, Virginia," said Walter, keeping his eyes on the road, more as an excuse not to have to make eye contact with her than anything.

"How convenient for you."

"Please."

"Okay, you want to know?" said Virginia, sitting up straighter in her seat. "I'll tell you. Yes, I've been angry at my father ever since I was old enough to understand how he lived his life. I am not my mother. I couldn't simply ignore it. And it just got worse as I got older and his conquests started to become my age, or even younger."

"Were you angry because of the pain he inflicted on your mother?"

"Oh, stop it, Lieutenant. We just had that discussion. My mother is entirely capable of taking care of herself, and she put up with it for her own reasons." She paused, as if to gather strength, and then continued. "Listen carefully because I'm only going to say this once. I always wondered why I wasn't enough. I was right there, his only daughter, always loving him, always ready to do anything to please him. But no. It was always one girl, then another, then another. And I was always left standing there saying, 'What about me? What about me?'" A sob escaped her, and she turned away from him again.

"Virginia, I'm sorry."

"So to answer your fucking question, Lieutenant Hudson: Yes, I was angry. I was way beyond angry. Did it ever cross my mind to kill him just to get him to stop? You're damned right it did, especially when he started up with Caroline, which was a line I never thought he'd cross. But now he's gone forever and I can't get him back, even if just to kill him myself. And I'm a screwed up mess because of it all, and I don't know how I can ever heal myself now that he's escaped. Is that what you wanted to hear? Are you happy now, Lieutenant Hudson?"

She covered her face with her hands and sobbed, the pain-sodden grief so deep, so raw, that Walter could barely stand to hear it. They drove on in silence, until after a while the sobbing stopped and she was quiet, her hands still covering her face. Walter handed her his sport jacket, which he had folded and placed on the front seat. She eventually took it and covered herself, looking tiny under the 50-Long.

"Thank you, Virginia," said Walter.

"Shut up and drive," she said.

—⊸⊷⊶⊷⊶—

Walter insisted on driving Virginia to her apartment, although she protested that she could take the train from midtown. He was legendary for being one of the most ruthless interrogators on the police force. He was usually proud of that reputation, but not today, and he wanted to do whatever he could to make it up to her.

He didn't know Tribeca well at all, but he eventually found her place. Virginia was halfway out of the car and Walter, unable to think of anything apt to say, was about to mumble an awkward "goodbye" when his phone rang. He listened for a few seconds, and Virginia, seeing the expression on his face, sat back down. He hung up without saying more than, "Okay, I'll be right there."

"What is it, Lieutenant?"

"It's Caroline," said Walter.

"What about Caroline?"

"She was in an accident on the Hutchinson Parkway. They're taking her to Mount Sinai Hospital."

"Oh, my God," said Virginia, "is she all right?"

"I don't know," said Walter.

"Give me two minutes. I'm coming with you," said Virginia as she raced into the building. She reemerged not much more than two minutes later wearing a pair of dark wool slacks and a bulky but fashionable sweater. She got into the car without saying a word.

Walter turned on his emergency lights and siren and headed north, but Virginia didn't seem impressed.

⸻

Walter hated hospital rooms. They reminded him of when his father had died, the priest standing over him and murmuring prayers as the patient in the next bed and his family looked on. Even this spacious private room, with sunshine pouring through large windows, depressed him, the odor of death and sickness seeming to seep through its brightly painted yellow walls like sweat through a clown's makeup.

"I'm sorry, Lieutenant, but there's not much I can tell you," said Caroline Schuyler. She was sitting up in her hospital bed looking and sounding alert. She had a few bruises on her face and arms and she was attached to the usual array of monitors, but otherwise she seemed fine. Virginia, pale and trembling as she stood beside her bed, looked worse.

"Were you unconscious for long?" said Walter.

"I was never unconscious at all," said Caroline. "My Porsche Boxter doesn't look like much, but it has a very strong frame and a great roll bar, even with the top down. It flipped a couple of times, but it landed upright on the median. I was more stunned than anything. It all happened so fast."

"What made you lose control of the car?" said Walter.

"I didn't lose control of the car," said Caroline, "I was forced off the road."

"Can you tell me how that happened?"

"I was traveling in the left lane. I wasn't speeding and I wasn't passing anybody, but I don't like the short ramps on the Hutch, so I usually avoid the right lane when I'm on it. There wasn't much traffic, so I was driving along, not paying a lot of attention to anything when this big, black SUV came roaring up beside me. My Boxter sits pretty low to the ground and it looked like a great big, black wall had just sprouted up next to me."

"Did you notice anything about the vehicle? In state or out of state plates, make or model, that kind of thing?"

"Sorry, Lieutenant, but no. It was just a great big tank with tinted windows. They're everywhere, I know, so that's not exactly a lot of help."

"So what happened next?"

"Nothing for a few seconds. It just sat there beside me. It wouldn't pass me but it wasn't falling back, either, so I gave my car a little gas so that I could get ahead of it. But as soon as I started to pull ahead the thing just roared up beside me again. I mean, the damn thing sounded like a rocket taking off. So I gave my Boxter some more gas and I started to pull ahead again. By that time I was going about ninety, but that tank just caught right up with me again. And then, before I had any more time to react, it just pulled over into my lane, made contact with my car, and just pushed me off the road. My little car didn't stand a chance. The next thing I knew I was flying."

"Jesus, Caroline," said Virginia, looking even more shaken, "you could've been killed."

"Don't remind me," said Caroline.

"So this wasn't just some jerk in a hurry," said Walter.

"No, Lieutenant. Whoever was driving that SUV was trying to kill me."

9

THE LOCAL EPISCOPAL CHURCH IN PLACID HOLLOW was nowhere near large enough to hold the huge number of mourners wishing to attend Judge T. Franklin Braxton's memorial service. Besides, the Judge hadn't attended services there in years and hadn't even met the current priest, complaining that the priest, and the Episcopal Church in general, had become nothing more than a nest of Marxist agitators. So the family decided that the prudent thing to do would be to hold a non-sectarian service at Carnegie Hall in midtown Manhattan. The Judge had never been a big fan of music and had never attended a concert there, but it was generally concluded that he would have approved of the venue. More importantly, Bunny Braxton was a longtime board member who had donated heavily to the Hall's Foundation over the years, and the Hall had been made available on extremely short notice, perhaps coincidentally, after a generous special donation had been received from the grieving family.

Lieutenant Hudson did not want to bother the family, and he did not want to be noticed, so he quietly slipped into a seat in a back corner of the uppermost balcony. No one noticed him except, of course, Virginia, who turned her head and spotted him so quickly he felt like he was wearing a cowbell. She gave him a brief, mischievous smile and then turned back. Her mother frowned at her.

Walter had no idea what he expected to learn, if anything, as he scanned the packed hall. He only knew that a memorial service was a good place to catch people in unguarded moments. And he was also fairly sure that the Judge's murderer would be in attendance.

Walter knew that a federal district court judge was an important person, but he was shocked to see that Mayor Deborah Kaplan, United States Senator Robert Shields, and Congressman Susan Hardwick were not only in attendance, but that they all spoke at length as well.

He was also surprised that the only member of the family to speak was the Judge's widow, Barbara. Having gotten to know Virginia he hadn't expected her to speak, but he was more than a little surprised that Young Ted had declined also.

Caroline Schuyler was not in attendance, nor was her father, the Judge's lifelong friend, Carlton Schuyler. Walter wondered how many of the people there were surprised by that.

The Master of Ceremonies and the man who delivered the eulogy was Judge Braxton's lifelong law partner, Bradford Pierce. He was a tall, distinguished-looking man dressed in a dark, bespoke suit, white shirt, and somber tie. He had a thick head of silver hair and a resonant baritone voice that vaguely reminded Walter of Edward Everett Horton, the distinguished actor and narrator of his childhood favorite, "Fractured Fairy Tales." Walter remembered what Caroline had told him about the Judge's and her father's backgrounds, and he wondered how this man fit in.

Brad Pierce delivered his eulogy directly to the family, rarely looking up at the rest of the attendees. It was moving, deeply personal, and frankly religious; and for the first time Walter saw expressions of genuine grief on the faces of the Braxton family. All of them, including Virginia, openly wept, even though Pierce, a masterful speaker, had made no apparent attempt to elicit any pathos. Even Walter, who had never met the Judge, was moved. If he hadn't known otherwise, he would have guessed that Bradford Pierce was a preacher, not a lawyer.

Despite the ostensibly secular nature of the ceremony, a youth choir from the Cathedral of Saint John the Divine sang a medley of hymns. Carnegie Hall is reputed to be the most acoustically perfect music hall in the world, and the music sounded almost other-worldly as it resonated through the magnificent old building. Even high up in the balcony, Walter had the uncanny sensation that the children were singing directly into his ear. The crowd applauded at the conclusion of the singing, which Walter, a Catholic, found shocking.

At the closing of the ceremony Barbara Braxton once again took the stage to invite everyone to a "brief reception" on the new open-air courtyard atop the building. A sizable crowd seemed to head in that direction, drawn, no doubt, by the prospect of first class booze at the expense of one of New York's wealthiest families.

Walter had questions, but he knew that a memorial ceremony was not the place to ask them. He glanced at his watch and thought that he just might get home in time to help Sarah with dinner and the kids for once if he left right away. Sarah had always been uncomplaining about his long and irregular hours, but he knew that the baby had her just about at the end of her tether, and he was eager to get back to her.

He was almost out the door when he felt a light tap on his shoulder. When he turned he was unsurprised to see Virginia standing behind him, looking peeved.

"Weren't you even going to say goodbye, Lieutenant?" she said. She was wearing a dark, conservatively tailored woolen suit, a gray silk blouse and a simple chain of Tahitian pearls around her neck, but she still managed to look provocative.

"I just didn't want to intrude on your family's privacy, that's all," said Walter, moving toward the door.

Instead of trying to stop him, Virginia followed him out the door.

"Get me out of here," she said. "These people give me the creeps."

"Don't you think you should stay and socialize for a while?" said Walter, sensing he was on the verge of being trapped yet again with this unnerving young woman.

"No, I don't," she said. "Besides, knowing you, I bet you have all kinds of prying, inappropriate questions you'd like to ask. You always do."

"I really need to get going," said Walter, "but I'll probably call you in the morning."

"Just walk with me for a couple of blocks," said Virginia. "I really need to get away from there. Then I'll leave you alone. I don't want to be a burden or anything."

"You're not a burden," said Walter, wondering how Virginia managed to make every conversation with him seem intimate.

"Good," she said, taking his arm in hers and pulling it uncomfortably close to her breast. "So, what did you think of the service?"

"I thought it was very touching, actually," he said as they strolled south on 7th Avenue. "I thought Bradley Pierce did a magnificent job."

"Oh, yes, dear old Brad," she said. "I'm afraid he missed his calling."

"What do you mean?"

"Oh, nothing. I'm just agreeing with you, that's all. He's very good at that kind of thing."

Walter thought she meant more, but he decided to let it drop.

"I was surprised to see all of those prominent people in the audience," he said. "I knew that your father was an important judge, but there were some real big shots in there."

"Oh, that had nothing to do with Daddy being a judge," said Virginia.

"So what was it, his money?"

"Not as much as you'd think. Remember, Daddy had only been a judge for five years. Most of the connections he made with the people you saw in there were made while he was still practicing law."

"So he was their legal advisor at one time or another?"

"You are a naïve one, aren't you, Lieutenant?" she said, turning to him and giving him an artful smile.

"What do you mean?"

"Powerful people are like most other people, except more so. Like most powerful people, almost everyone you saw at that service today has been in trouble at one time or another in their lives. Money trouble, legal trouble, spouse trouble, kid trouble. You name it. Daddy was legendary for being the best fixer in New York City. He fixed their problems and buried the bodies for them, and they remained eternally grateful."

"I'm assuming you meant the 'buried bodies' part figuratively."

"Mostly," said Virginia.

"Mostly?"

"The point is that not one of those people would be where they are today if it hadn't been for Daddy."

"And I imagine he must have made some serious enemies along the way."

"You're damned right he did," said Virginia.

"Despite what people have been trying to tell me."

"Despite what people have been trying to tell you."

Walter looked up and was shocked to see that they were in Times Square, a full fifteen blocks south of Carnegie Hall. He thought that they'd only walked a couple of blocks. Virginia saw the bewildered expression on his face and gave him another beguiling smile.

"Time flies, doesn't it ?"

"Look, Virginia," he said, "I have to get on the subway here. Thank you so much for your time. You've been a great help."

"I'll walk with you over to Grand Central if you want."

"That's all right, I can pick up the 7 Train right here. It's quicker."

"So you live out in Queens, then?"

"Yes, in Fresh Meadows."

"Oh, that's a lovely area. I teach the occasional graduate finance seminar at Saint John's, so I'm quite familiar with the neighborhood."

"You do?" he said, failing to keep the shock out of his voice.

"Now, Lieutenant," said Virginia, "you do recall our 'I'm not a bimbo' conversation, right?"

"I'm sorry, Virginia, I didn't mean….."

"Oh, stop it, Walter," she said, laughing and giving his arm a playful tug. "Now, you get back to your lovely family while I get back to my crazy one. I truly enjoyed our walk. I'm sure I'll be seeing you soon."

She turned and headed back up 7th Avenue. His eyes followed her as she walked away, and he somehow knew that Virginia, without looking back, knew that.

It wasn't until he was at the subway entrance that he realized that she had called him "Walter" for the first time as they parted. He shook his large head once, like a horse that knows it's being led to the wrong barn, and walked down the steps to the subway.

10

"**I**F YOU DO ANY MORE INVESTIGATING, LIEUTENANT, pretty soon every man, woman and child in this entire damn city is going to be a possible suspect," said Police Commissioner Sean Michael Patrick Donahue. He had come to New York from Ireland as a seven-year-old child, but he still spoke with a faint brogue. He was a massive man, almost as tall as Walter, with an abundant shock of white hair, a florid complexion, and an enormous girth that made him appear older than his 53 years; but he exuded power, both physical and official, and there was no mistaking who was in charge when he was in the room. He went by the name of "Sean," but his close friends called him "Mike." NYPD detective lieutenants called him "sir."

They were sitting in Commissioner Donahue's pride and joy, a small room tucked away down a narrow hallway from his formal office at One Police Plaza, accessed by only one unmarked door. It was furnished to look like an Irish Pub, replete with a bar hand-carved from solid mahogany and a half-dozen barstools made of unfinished oak. There were also four tables with chairs, but they were rarely used. Those lucky enough, or unlucky enough, to be summoned to this inner sanctum for the first time were said to have "earned their splinters." Captain Amato had warned him to expect this, but he thought he'd have at least a little more time to put his case together. At least this wasn't his first meeting with the commissioner, and they'd seemed to get along in their previous meetings. But Walter also knew that his past meetings with the commissioner had gone well because Walter had solved his case. He had no illusions about what would happen if he failed to solve this one.

"It'll be Bushmills for you, right, Lieutenant?" said the commissioner as he moved with practiced ease behind the bar. If Walter hadn't known better he would have thought that he was back in the pubs of his youth in Greenpoint, Queens, and that Commissioner Donahue was the neighborhood barkeep. The man could weave a spell that put even lowly detectives at ease.

"That's right," said Walter, although Donahue had already reached up and plucked the bottle of Bushmills from a shelf lined with dozens of bottles.

"Good man."

"I apologize for the lack of progress, sir," said Walter, "but this case is turning out to be a lot more complicated than I thought. I mean, I thought it was solved the night of the murder when we discovered Ms. Schuyler standing over the body with a gun in her hand."

"But we're never that lucky, are we?" said Donahue as he slid a lowball glass with at least two fingers of the neat whiskey over to Walter. Walter actually disliked Bushmills, in fact he rarely drank at all, but Bushmills was the commissioner's drink of choice, so Walter went along with it.

"No, we're not. Especially now that the autopsy confirmed exactly what Caroline Schuyler told me, which is that the gun that killed Judge Braxton was a .38, not a .45. At least we've recovered the bullets intact, but they're not much use unless we find the gun. We're not disclosing that information to the public, by the way."

"Of course not," said the Donahue, sipping his drink, "but that is a head-scratcher, isn't it."

"Yes, it is. And Lord knows how many enemies the Judge made along the way with his womanizing. I don't think anyone will ever find out the identities of all of the women he had affairs with, all of whom he must have dumped at one point or another. And I have to think that some of them had angry spouses."

"Although he did seem to go for the young, single type, didn't he?"

"Yes, but that doesn't mean he never got tangled up with a married woman. And I haven't even begun to dig into the enemies he must have made as a lawyer and a judge, never mind all of the 'fixing' his daughter referred to."

"The man did cut a wide swath," said Donahue, smiling as he sipped his drink.

"Did you know him, sir?"

"Of course I did. Anybody who was anybody in this town knew Teddy Braxton."

Walter had never heard of the man before the night of his murder, but he decided not to point that out.

"I was especially surprised to see the mayor at his memorial service."

"Well, you shouldn't have been," said Donahue. "Deborah Kaplan would not be the mayor today had it not been for Teddy Braxton."

The comment echoed what Virginia had said to him, so Walter decided to press him on it.

"Can you explain that to me, sir?"

"Sure," said Donahue, pouring them each another generous two fingers of whiskey. Walter always had a headache the morning after he met with the commissioner, but he'd never seen the man appear even the slightest bit inebriated or hung-over, despite his propensity for drinking Bushmills like it was apple juice. "Teddy Braxton was one of the first people to see Deborah

Kaplan's enormous potential. He was good at that. But she suffered a terrible loss twenty years ago when her husband died while racing to the scene of a medical emergency."

"He was a doctor?" said Walter.

"Yes, he was, and a fine one, but he never made a dime off it because he was always taking care of the poor, and he didn't have the heart to ask for payment. He knew they'd try, and take food out of their children's mouths in the process."

"Sounds like the type of man Mayor Kaplan would have married," said Walter.

"Doesn't it, then," said Donahue. "So there was Deborah Kaplan, widowed and penniless, with a fourteen-year-old son to take care of. The poor boy had worshipped his father, and he was absolutely devastated by his loss. He wound up acting out and getting himself into trouble, as young boys are apt to do under those circumstances. One night the cops were called to a liquor store on Staten Island, where Deborah and her son were living at the time. Three boys were arrested for attempted robbery. One of the boys was Matthew Kaplan. Another one of the boys was carrying a gun."

"Was anyone hurt?" said Walter.

"Thank the good Lord, no," said Donahue, "but it was an armed robbery nevertheless."

"There's not much you can do in those situations," said Walter.

"That's not how Teddy Braxton saw it. He heard about the arrests from a contact inside the police department and immediately called Deborah and told her he'd take care of everything."

"Pretty bold statement, considering the circumstances."

"Not for Teddy it wasn't. He did all the things other lawyers wouldn't have done. He learned the backgrounds of the other kids and discovered they were all like young Matt: good kids from good families with nary a jaywalking fine among them. He learned who the presiding judge would be and found out that the judge's own son had gone through a bad patch himself once. He also had the weapon thoroughly examined and discovered that it was not only unloaded, but completely non-functional. The firing pin had been removed and it looked like it hadn't been used or serviced in a decade."

"But still....."

"So he got the judge, the arresting officer, and the prosecuting attorney together and explained the situation, as only Teddy could do. By the time he was done he had the charges reduced to misdemeanor petty larceny, a suspended sentence, and accelerated rehabilitation, at the end of which all records of the incident were expunged. Deborah Kaplan's life would have been ruined forever if not for Teddy Braxton, not to mention young Matthew, who is now a fine physician in his own right."

"Amazing. How did he do all that?"

"Son, I'm Irish and Teddy Braxton wasn't, so this is difficult for me to say, but he was the most charming, persuasive man I have ever met in my life."

"I've heard that before," said Walter.

"I'm sure you have," said Commissioner Donahue. "And now you know why I'm taking a personal interest in this case and making your job harder than it already is. This is personal for the mayor, and she wants this case solved. Call me directly if there is anything I can do to help you."

"Yes, sir," said Walter. "If I may ask, sir, how did you come to know about that incident? It sounds like it was pretty well buried."

"Well, son," said Donahue, "I was the arresting officer that night, and I was the cop who called Teddy."

But no pressure, thought Walter. None at all.

11

THE PLACE STANK OF MONEY, thought Walter, as he was shown into "The Library" of the Amsterdam Club, the oldest gentlemen's club in New York City. It was located on Maiden Lane, near Wall Street, and its membership, be they old-moneyed New Yorkers or freshly minted hedge fund billionaires, were rich beyond the comprehension of the average New Yorker, which, in the considered opinion of the members, was the whole point. Although the Club declined to discuss such matters publicly, rumor had it that those lucky enough to be invited for membership after a decade on the waiting list paid a $2.5 million initial membership fee, plus an annual $250 thousand in annual dues for the privilege.

The walls were lined with mahogany bookshelves filled with old, leather-bound volumes of the classics that looked like the only time they were ever touched was when they were dusted off once a month by the help. Members of this club, thought Walter as he perused some of the titles and authors, had no time for the likes of Jonathan Swift and James Fenimore Cooper. Neither did he for that matter, but he thought, as he had thought once while watching a program on PBS with Sarah, that we might all do well to make the time.

It was five o'clock and the room was still two-thirds empty, although Walter imagined it would be filling any minute, now that the markets and the banks had closed for the day. Membership was technically open to women, but none had ever applied. If they were made to feel as unwelcome as he was, he thought, he understood why.

The members stared at him in his blue, size 50-Long, Men's Wearhouse suit as if he'd walked in wearing a clown outfit, with expressions conveying a profound sense of tragedy that the Club's standards had fallen so low. Guests who can't manage to purchase their suits from Savile Row or Turin, their eyes said, were not true gentlemen, and should be invited elsewhere if one had to deal with them at all.

Bradley Pierce, at least, seemed glad to see him, although he immediately ushered him out of the Library and into a small private sitting room, probably expressly constructed for awkward situations like this.

"Welcome to the Club," he said to Walter, holding out his hand. "I'm having a Glenlivet. Would you care to join me?"

Walter was pretty sure that Glenlivet was a Scotch whiskey, and he was positive that it was one he'd never had. "That would be great," he said.

The drinks arrived, and they each took a taste. It was surprisingly good, thought Walter, certainly better than the Bushmills that the commissioner served. Smoky, and not as sweet.

"It's a pleasure to meet you, Lieutenant Hudson," said Pierce in the same rich voice that he recalled from the memorial service. "I'm an attorney, but my particular area of practice does not afford me the occasion to meet too many of New York's Finest." Pierce looked older up close than he had from the balcony of Carnegie Hall, but still looked distinguished and fit.

"Thank you so much for agreeing to talk to me, Mr. Pierce," said Walter. "This must have been an awfully difficult week for you. I'm told that you and the Judge had known each other for almost forty years."

"Yes, Lieutenant, it was a terribly difficult week, but the family behaved magnificently, don't you think? I'm a lifelong bachelor, so I've always looked upon Teddy's family as my own. They were a genuine source of strength to me, and I'm sure many others. Bunny Braxton is the heart and soul of the family, of course, and she was, as always, an inspiration to all of us. She is a truly great woman."

"It's my understanding that you and the Judge came from somewhat different backgrounds, Mr. Pierce. Can you tell me how you met?"

"It's a story I love to tell," said Pierce, a nostalgic expression lighting up his eyes. "You are correct, of course, that Teddy and I followed different paths to our partnership. I grew up in New York, but I went off to Harvard for college after I'd graduated from Phillips Exeter, as had five generations of Pierces before me. But then I broke with family tradition to go to Yale for my law degree."

"Why did you do that, may I ask?" The first glass of Glenlivet had gone down disturbingly smoothly, thought Walter, as a waiter appeared with refills for both of them. Walter gratefully noticed that Pierce handed the waiter a credit card. The last thing he needed would be a third drink before going home to Sarah and the kids for what would undoubtedly be another long night.

"My dream since childhood," said Pierce, after a thoughtful sip of his drink, "had been to become an Episcopal priest. Yale had, and continues to have, a fine divinity school which educates students in the Anglican tradition that I dearly wanted to attend. My family agreed, on the condition that I also complete my legal education. So I worked out an arrangement with the University to attend both the Law School and the Divinity School."

"At the same time?" said Walter.

"Yes, Lieutenant."

"That must have been awfully difficult." Walter himself had completed his bachelor's degree in criminology after five excruciating years of night school at Hofstra.

"I had always been academically gifted, but more than that, it was a labor of love. I recall those days as the happiest of my life. It was also during that time that I met Bunny deGroot, the future Mrs. Barbara Braxton."

"You mean that you knew Mrs. Braxton before she and the Judge were married?"

"I introduced them, Lieutenant," said Bradley Pierce, looking amused at Walter's surprise.

"I'd love to hear about that," said Walter.

"It's all part of the same story, actually," said Pierce. "I met Bunny deGroot at a party during her sophomore year at Yale College, where she was majoring in Comparative Literature. She was a member of the first Class to admit women. She was brilliant and beautiful, and I was quite taken with her. We developed a lovely friendship."

"Were you just friends or were you, uh, romantically involved?"

"We had what used to be called an 'understanding.' We came from similar family backgrounds, although the deGroot family was a fine, old Dutch Hudson River family that had roots going back to the 17th century. My family didn't arrive in this country until the late 18th century."

"Well," said Walter, "my family showed up in the steerage section of a tramp steamer in 1910 with no money and an Eastern European name a foot long, so I guess you're both way ahead of me."

"Really," said Pierce. "Then how did you come to be known as 'Hudson'?"

"When that steamer arrived in New York, my great-grandfather was told that the river we were sailing up was the 'Hudson.' It was the only English word he knew, so when the immigration agent at Ellis Island asked him for his name, he didn't understand the question, and he just said, 'Hudson.'"

"Fascinating," said Pierce, sounding not awfully intrigued.

"So, anyway," said Walter.

"Yes," said Pierce. "Bunny and I would talk endlessly about the future, about how we would minister to the less fortunate in the world, I as a priest and she as an educator. We both had trust funds coming from our families, at least we thought we did, and we would be able to depend on them for sustenance. We spoke of undertaking missionary work in Asia."

"You said, 'at least we thought we did,'" said Walter. "What happened?"

"Two months before my graduation, I received a letter from my mother. It seemed that Father had suffered some terrible financial reversals, and the family was now bankrupt. To make things worse, Father had illegally drained my trust fund in a last desperate attempt to salvage the situation, and it was gone."

"That's awful," said Walter. "Is that why you went into the law instead of the ministry?"

"Yes, eventually," said Pierce. "For a while Bunny and I thought we could keep our dream alive. After all, she still had her trust fund, and we thought we could survive on that. But a month after I received my letter she received a similar one, but even worse. Her father had drowned in a yachting accident on the Hudson River, at least that's what they called it at the time. In fact, it turned out that he had tethered himself to the anchor and jumped overboard. When the executor of the estate performed his audit he discovered that it was practically bankrupt due to years of chronic mismanagement. There was still something left of the family fortune, but only enough to hold onto the family property, at least for a while, and provide a modest living for her mother. Bunny was told that she would not be receiving her trust fund, and she would have to withdraw from Yale."

"She must have been devastated," said Walter.

"She behaved heroically, Lieutenant. It was her finest hour, and I couldn't have been prouder of her. I never saw her shed a tear, and I never heard her complain. I went back to New York to wrap up my father's affairs and take the bar exam while she returned home to look for a job. We promised to stay in touch."

"So what happened after that?"

"I guess you could call it serendipity. I had just completed the last day of the bar exam and had slipped into a small pub for a drink with some of my Yale classmates. I saw a young man sitting by himself, looking miserable. I guess it was the minister in me, but I'll never really know. On an impulse I went over and said hello to him. It was, of course, Teddy Braxton. We had a drink together and he told me that he was convinced that he had failed the exam, and he didn't know what he was going to do."

"He didn't have a backup plan?"

"He had a job as a truck driver for a dairy company."

"So what did you do?"

"Well, there wasn't much I could do, but I sat and talked to him. We went over some of the questions on the exam and I told him he may have done better than he thought he did. I told him I thought he would pass the exam, if only by a point. He laughed and thanked me. And then he looked at me and said, 'You know what? I think this is the beginning of a beautiful friendship.' We exchanged phone numbers and he promised to call when he got his exam results."

"What did you think of all that?" said Walter, completely absorbed in the man's story, his drink forgotten.

"I didn't know what to think, Lieutenant," said Pierce, his countenance still taking on an expression of wonder as he looked back through the years. "I was Yale Law Review, headed for a distinguished career with a respected law firm and then maybe the judiciary or an endowed chair at Harvard or Yale. Teddy simply was not at my level. But on the other hand, after just that brief meeting with him, I realized that he was simply the most magnetic, charming human being I had ever met, and I couldn't get him out of my mind."

"So he wound up passing the bar exam, I assume?"

"It was the craziest thing. He called me up the day the results came out and he just about shouted over the phone, 'You're a genius, Brad!'"

"'What do you mean?' I said."

"'I passed the bar exam by one point, just like you predicted!' he said. 'How did you do?'"

"'I passed, too,'" I told him. "I didn't tell him that I had attained the highest test score in the state, and that I had five job offers from blue chip firms waiting for me."

"'Brad, you and I were made for each other,'" he said. "He told me that I should chuck all the offers that I must have gotten from all those stodgy law firms and go into practice with him. He said, 'We'll make a fucking fortune and have some fun along the way.'"

"And what did you do?"

"How was I supposed to say 'no' to an offer like that?" said Brad, chuckling. "I said 'yes,' of course. The person who could say no to that man was never born. The rest is history."

"And Mrs. Braxton?"

"When Teddy and I formed the partnership," said Pierce, his smile turning rueful, "Teddy proposed that we celebrate. He was dating some cute young thing at the time, and he asked me to bring along a date, so I gave Bunny a call."

"Did you still have your 'understanding' with her then?"

"At that moment, yes I did, Lieutenant."

"So, what happened?"

"I've never seen anything like it before or since. Those two took one look at each other and that was that. They only saw each other from that moment on, and no matter what you've heard or been told it stayed that way until his death. I escorted Teddy's cute young thing home, and that was the end of Bunny's and my 'understanding.'"

"You must have been awfully angry," said Walter. "I mean, that's a hell of a way to start a partnership."

"Oh, I knew I didn't stand a chance against Teddy, so there was no sense in being angry. And besides, I couldn't help but be happy for Bunny."

"So you just put it behind you?"

"I did more than that," said Pierce, his smile now turned ghostly. "I was ordained an Episcopal priest the same day I was sworn in to the Bar."

"You were? That's amazing," said Walter in genuine admiration.

"Thank you, Lieutenant. I remain a licensed member of the clergy to this day. And so I did really the only civilized thing I could do under the circumstances."

"What was that?"

"I officiated at their wedding, of course."

12

BARBARA "BUNNY" BRAXTON LIKED WHAT SHE SAW as she stared into the full-length mirror in the bedroom of her Park Avenue townhouse.

She was naked, wearing only the simple string of pearls that the man currently in the shower had given her years ago. She knew that she was still an extraordinarily attractive woman, and she was proud of the fact that it was mostly the result of her own self-discipline and her good de Groot genes. Of course, there had been lifts and tucks over the years to her face, breasts, and buttocks; but they had been minor and subtle. What she saw in the mirror was unmistakably her. She had lost a couple of pounds recently, but with recent events that was to be expected, and she was probably the only one who would notice.

She recalled ruefully the years long past when she'd been the only woman Teddy Braxton had wanted. She had delighted in satisfying the needs of that remarkable man, even as he had worked endless hours building his law firm and accumulating the wealth that meant so much to her, while she had borne his children and raised them. They were the best years of her life.

But good genes, exercise and expensive plastic surgeons have their limits. All the money in the world can't buy youth. And the one thing that Teddy Braxton had wanted more than anything as the years passed was youth; to be close to it, to touch it, to possess it. As if by bedding an endless succession of increasingly younger women he could create his own personal Fountain of Youth, a private bubble in which he could live forever and never grow old. She had tried to talk to him, to reassure him that she could still satisfy him that she still wanted to satisfy him. But it was no use, especially as those young women succumbed to his charms as readily as everyone else in his world.

She continued to love him until the day he died. He had continued to be kind and generous to her, and she simply couldn't help herself. But she had left his bed forever twenty years ago, knowing that if she didn't she would lose any sense of her own self, and that she would not do for anyone, even Teddy.

For a while she thought that she could live without an intimate life of her own. But she learned early on that there were men in her world who did not share her husband's obsessions, and who not only found her desirable, but who also made no secret of the fact that they wanted her.

Eventually she had succumbed, but on her terms. For twenty years it had been only one man, and that man had been single. She could live with her own infidelity, but she would not impose that heartache on another woman.

She heard the shower being turned off, but she made no effort to move or cover herself, and when the door opened she got her reward for all those years of looking after her appearance. His eyes locked on her and saw nothing else, and even after all these years he was immediately aroused just by the sight of her.

"I take it you like what you see," she said.

"When haven't I?" he said. "My God, you're beautiful."

He crossed the room and took her in his arms, kissing her lightly on the neck, and then full on the mouth. They lay down on the bed, not bothering with the covers. They would create their own warmth.

"I think it's wonderful," she said, "that we are finally not adulterers, just lovers."

"You know that's what I've always wanted," said the man. "I would have married you at a moment's notice if you had ever been free."

"I know that," she said, "but you know how complicated things were."

"But they're not complicated anymore, are they, Bunny dear? We can get married any time we want now."

"And we will, you know that, but we mustn't marry right away, of course," she said. "That would be…..inappropriate. And we don't want tongues to start wagging, now do we?"

"Of course not, dearest," he said. "I don't mean to be impatient, but I've been waiting for so long."

"In due time, my love, in due time," said Bunny Braxton, "but let's not talk anymore, okay?"

"I can't resist you for another minute," said the man, letting his hands roam.

"Then don't," she said, melting into his familiar arms as she felt his excitement grow.

She had long ago shed any childish notions that it was possible only to love one person at a time. She loved this man; she loved him deeply and passionately, and his love for her had been a constant in her life for so long that she had no fear of ever losing him. That meant the world to her. But still, even as his arms enveloped her and their mutual passion mounted, she couldn't keep her mind, and her heart, from whispering the constant refrain: "Why did it have to come to this, Teddy? Why couldn't this be you?"

13

"**I** HAVEN'T REALLY GIVEN IT MUCH THOUGHT LIEUTENANT," said Caroline Schuyler. "I still have some things to wrap up here, and I want to focus on that before I spend a lot of time dwelling on what my next career move might be."

They were sitting in her cramped office in the Daniel Patrick Moynihan United States Courthouse on Pearl Street in downtown Manhattan. She was dressed casually, but expensively, in a pair of oatmeal colored slacks and a navy blue blouse. Her hair was pulled back in a ponytail and she wore little makeup, but there was no concealing the fact that Caroline was a striking young woman. She showed no apparent ill effects from her recent traffic incident.

"I guess I'm confused," said Walter. "Now that the judge is, ah, no longer with us, I thought that your job would be finished here."

"Not really. In fact, for the next few weeks, or even months, my role here will be rather critical."

"Sorry, I guess I don't follow. I thought you worked directly for Judge Braxton."

"I did. I was his lead clerk. In that role, I did most of the legal research for his major cases, and I wrote all of his major opinions."

"Really?" said Walter. "He was the judge. Didn't he write his own opinions?"

"Not Teddy," said Caroline. "Many judges take great pride in their writing ability and write all or at least most of their major opinions, although they leave the less important ones to their clerks."

"So why not Judge Braxton?"

"I do not wish to disparage the man now that he is dead," said Caroline, "but as I told you at our first meeting, Teddy was not a legal scholar, nor did he consider himself one. He was also not a very good writer. As you know, his early education and his legal training were both sketchy at best. That's why he and Brad Pierce were such a good match for each other professionally. Brad was, still is, a brilliant legal theorist, and he did all of the hard legal work-research, writing all the documents, whatever-while Teddy was out drumming up the cases and promoting the firm."

"I don't mean to get off the track here," said Walter, puzzled, "but why, then, did he ever want to become a judge, and why would anyone ever want to make him one?"

"I think you already know the answer to your second question," said Caroline. "There were any number of powerful people in this world who were eager to do Teddy a favor. You probably saw quite a few of them at his memorial service."

"I most certainly did."

"The other answer is a little more complicated. I never discussed it with him so I'm merely speculating, but I think he wanted the judgeship because he wanted to be remembered as something more than a slick lawyer who got rich cashing in on mass tort claims and defending wealthy clients when they got their peckers caught in their zippers. But I also believe that he was growing bored with the judiciary, and if he had lived I think he would have left it and gone back to the practice of law."

"You mean, he would have gone back to his old firm?"

"Perhaps."

"Did he ever discuss it with you?"

"A little. Off and on. The only point that I was trying to make, Lieutenant, before we veered off course, is that I will be needed around here for a while to provide some continuity as the Judge's cases are handed over to others."

Walter's instincts were shouting at him that he was being carefully manipulated by this woman; that she was gulling him into thinking that she was being open and helpful, while she was actually making sure that he only learned what she wanted him to learn. Walter was good at this game, but Caroline Schuyler, he was quickly learning, was a master. But even masters make mistakes, and he felt that she had just made one. The offhand comment about Teddy Braxton leaving the judiciary was loaded with implications, and he wasn't surprised that she wanted to change the subject. But his instincts also told him that now was not the time to press the matter.

"OK," he said, "so tell me, had the Judge handed down any decisions lately that would have caused anyone to want to do him harm?"

"None that I can think of," said Caroline, appearing relieved at the change of subject. "Besides, once a decision is handed down, what's done is done. There would be no sense in harming him after the fact."

"Unless the decision was overturned by an appeals court and sent back to him," said Walter, eager to show Caroline that he knew at least something about the judicial process.

"My decisions are airtight," said Caroline, slicing the air with her right hand for emphasis. "They don't get overturned. I mean, the Judge's decisions, of course."

"Of course," said Walter. "But what about current cases? Anything controversial there?"

Caroline hesitated for a few seconds, then said, "The only one that I can think of that has aroused any controversy is *Westchester County Homeowners Association v. FHA.*"

"Never heard of it."

"Most people haven't," said Caroline, "it's a local issue, so it hasn't gotten wide coverage."

"What's it about?"

"Two years ago the Federal Housing Administration issued a rule that said that Westchester County was effectively discriminating against minorities by not having an adequate supply of low and middle income housing. Westchester County is rich and overwhelmingly white. All of the low and middle income workers, no matter what color, are forced to commute, sometimes great distances, from other counties. It ordered the county to build an adequate supply of affordable housing to balance things out. It also said that, since there is essentially no undeveloped public land left in Westchester County, the county would have to exercise its eminent domain authority to take whatever property it needed for that purpose."

"Can they do that?"

"In case you haven't noticed, Lieutenant, federal agencies can do just about whatever they damn please."

"But I thought that only Congress could pass laws."

"It's rather touching that you still believe that, but you might as well believe in the Easter Bunny."

"I'm sorry, but I don't get it."

"You are technically correct that only Congress can pass laws, but the average senator or congressman is generally too drunk, lazy, greedy, or stupid to pay much attention to the process. All they want to do is raise enough money to get reelected. So they pass sloppily written but nice sounding laws that they can brag about back home. Then they add in a little clause that says that the executive agency responsible for implementing the law shall have the administrative authority to write any rules it deems necessary to do so. So the bureaucrats in those agencies now effectively rule the country and there's not much that anyone can do about it."

"That just doesn't sound right," said Walter.

"You and I can argue all day whether it's right or wrong, but it is what it is."

"So what does this all have to do with your case?"

"Well, the one thing people can do to fight back is bring a lawsuit against the federal agency, arguing that the agency has clearly exceeded the boundaries of the law or that people's constitutional rights are being infringed."

"And that's what this lawsuit is all about?"

"Precisely. The people of Westchester County are suing the Federal Housing Administration saying that they are interpreting the Fair Housing Act far too broadly and that neither the Congress nor the Constitution ever intended for people's private property to be taken for such purposes."

"I would assume," said Walter, "that the Judge would rule against the FHA. After all, he was a property owner in Westchester County."

"That's what everyone thought at first, but as the trial proceeded, comments and rulings he made from the bench began to make people nervous. I guess you can say they got more than nervous; they became frightened and angry."

"Were any threats made against the Judge?"

"There were no specific threats, but the president of the Westchester County Homeowners Association, the plaintiffs in this case, a guy named Randall Brandt, is a real hothead, and he began making remarks that were, if not direct threats, at least highly inappropriate."

"Can you give me an example?"

"He said that if the Judge thought that he could just make a ruling and then wash his hands of it, he had 'another thing coming.' Things like that."

"Was Judge Braxton concerned?"

"No. He just laughed them off."

"So, if anyone felt threatened by how the Judge might rule, they would also feel threatened by you, right?"

"Not necessarily, Lieutenant," said Caroline. "Not many people knew how the Judge operated. Most people are just like you; they thought since he was the judge he was the only one who would render the opinion."

"But some people must have known."

"Possibly," said Caroline.

"How about this guy, uh, Randall Brandt?" said Walter, looking down at his notes.

"Possibly," said Caroline. "He was at the courthouse every day and he paid very close attention to the dynamics. He also made a somewhat threatening comment to me outside the courthouse one day."

"What did he say?"

"He said, 'Don't think I don't know all about you, missy.' Then he just turned around and left."

"This sounds like a guy I might want to talk to," said Walter. "Is there anyone else who may have known how much influence you had on the Judge's opinions?"

"Not that I can think of," said Caroline, but in a way that made Walter think that he was getting stiff-armed again. But again, he decided not to press the point, at least not for now. He folded his notebook, stood up, and prepared to leave.

"Thank you once again for all your time and help," he said.

"No problem," said Caroline. "I'm just as eager to find Judge Braxton's killer as you are."

"By the way," he said, "which way was the Judge going to rule?"

"I'm really not at liberty to say, Lieutenant. And anyway, it's no longer relevant. A new judge will be assigned to the case and he'll make his own decision."

"Won't it take a long time for him to come up to speed on the case?"

"Yes, there will undoubtedly be a lengthy delay."

"But he'll have you to help, right?"

"Yes," said Caroline, a little warily. "I won't leave this position until I've done everything possible to assist the next judge. It has been a lengthy, complex trial, and I would never just abandon him."

"So that means that you'll have a lot of influence on the outcome, right?"

"Maybe," said Caroline, "maybe not. It depends on the new judge."

"Please be careful, Ms. Schuyler."

"Thank you for your concern," said Caroline, standing up, seeming suddenly anxious to terminate the conversation, "but I'm really not worried, and I think I can take care of myself."

"Ms. Schuyler, someone has already tried to kill you."

"I'm aware of that, Lieutenant. Thank you for your concern."

14

IT WOULD HAVE BEEN NICE IF SHE'D TOLD ME THE GUY WAS AN OLD PARAPLEGIC IN A WHEELCHAIR, thought Walter Hudson as he took a seat in Randall Brandt's living room. Its high-timbered ceilings and floor of wide maple planks gave it more the feel of a rustic lodge than a high-class home in Westchester County.

The sun shining in through the window gave the man's skin a translucent aspect, and the wispy white hair that remained on his head seemed to wave and flutter in a breeze that only it could feel, making him appear far older than his years, which Walter guessed was somewhere in his early sixties. Something had made this man old before his time, thought Walter. On the walls were portraits and pictures of a much younger Randall Brandt, with an attractive wife and two children. Images of weddings, graduations and family vacations told a story of a full life lived in this now quiet home. A caretaker set a pot of tea and some cups on the table in front of them. She poured two cups, adding milk and sugar to one, and looked at Walter questioningly.

"Just milk, please," he said. She handed him his cup and left, nodding her head when he thanked her.

"It's just me here now," said Brandt, seeing Walter's eyes wandering over the photos. His voice was surprisingly youthful and strong. "The kids moved out West and down South, anywhere that was more affordable than here. I lost my wife last year after a very long illness."

"I'm sorry to hear that," said Walter.

"So am I," said Brandt. "This is a wonderful house, but without Evelyn and the kids it doesn't feel much like a home anymore."

"How long have you lived here?"

"All my life. My grandfather built this house in 1920, and the Brandt family has lived here ever since, one generation on top of another."

"It must have been a wonderful way to grow up and raise a family," said Walter.

"It was the best," said Brandt. "But all good things come to an end one day, don't they?"

"Are you going to sell?"

"Well, Lieutenant, I'm kind of between a rock and a hard place. When my granddad got older, my father was here to help with the cost and the effort of maintaining the home and property, and I did the same thing when my dad got older. But as I said, my kids are gone, and I just can't manage the place anymore, either physically or financially. I hung on during Evelyn's illness because I didn't have the heart to take her away when we both knew she was dying. But now I'm out of money, the hospital is still hounding me for more, and the place is falling down around me. I made a lot of money in my life, but I plowed it all right back into this property and to Evelyn's end of life care. It's the only asset I possess."

"So, besides the emotional attachment, which I completely understand," said Walter, "what's keeping you from selling?"

"The place is worthless," said Brandt.

"What?"

"You heard me, Lieutenant, worthless. Ten acres of beautiful property and a meticulously maintained, 4,500 square foot house. Worthless."

"I would have thought that it would be worth a million dollars, minimum."

"Five years ago it was--$2.2 million to be precise. But then along came the damn FHA and destroyed everything."

"That's what the lawsuit, *Westchester County Homeowners Association v. FHA*, is all about, right?"

"That's right. This house and property were identified early on as one of the properties that the county was ordered to take by eminent domain. The plan was to tear down the house and build low income housing units on all ten acres."

"But certainly they'll have to pay you?"

"Pennies on the dollar, Lieutenant, pennies on the dollar, and you can spend the rest of your life appealing their valuation and probably never win. The government, as usual, does what it damn pleases and no one can stop them. Not the country I grew up in, but there you have it."

"And that's why you became active in the homeowners' association?"

"Not really. I did that mostly for Evelyn," said Brandt. "I didn't want her to die in despair."

"So you're not holding out much hope for the lawsuit?"

"I'm holding out no hope whatsoever."

"But why not?"

"Lieutenant, I may not look like much now, but in my day I was an extremely successful and influential attorney. They used to call me 'high powered,'" he said with a self-effacing smile that took years off his appearance. "I retired from active legal practice prematurely in order to take care of Evelyn and spend every moment I could with her before she passed," said Brandt. "My specialty was property law."

"That's great," said Hudson. "You'd be just the right person to fight this thing, right?"

"It means that I am just the right person to tell you exactly what's going to happen: If we prevail in the district court, the government will appeal to the circuit court. That process will take at least two to three years. If we prevail in the circuit court, the government will appeal to the United States Supreme Court, taking another two to three years. And there we will lose."

"Why do you say that?"

"Because the United States Supreme Court has always interpreted the Takings Clause of the U.S. Constitution, the one that describes eminent domain, in favor of the government; and this case will be no exception."

"So you're telling me that whatever the district court rules in this case will ultimately be irrelevant."

"That is correct. And as a practical matter, the homeowners' association is running out of money, which the federal government never does. Even if we were to get a favorable ruling out of the district court, we will probably have to abandon the case sooner rather than later."

"So you don't think that Judge Braxton's murder will affect the outcome of the case?"

"It most certainly will not. Frankly, in my innermost heart, I was hoping that the Judge would rule against us and get the whole thing over with. I know for a fact that we would not appeal, we can't afford to, and then at least we could accept our pathetic pieces of silver from the government and get on with our lives."

"I have to admit I'm surprised," said Walter. "I came up here thinking that this case may have been a likely motive for his murder."

"And you thought maybe I might be a likely suspect?" said Brandt, smiling again.

"I'm sorry, sir, I didn't know about your condition."

"I lost the use of my legs just after I lost Evelyn," said Brandt, "so I barely noticed, really. But I'm afraid you will have to look elsewhere for a murder suspect."

"So you don't think this case had anything to do with his murder?"

"I didn't say that, Lieutenant. I may be a cripple, but I still have a clear head and I continue to possess an outstanding legal mind, if I do say so myself. There are undoubtedly others who do not have the legal expertise or intellectual clarity to see things as I do. I cannot say what those people may or may not have done."

"What about the Braxton family?" said Walter. "Even though Judge Braxton was presiding over the case, they own significant property in this area."

"Oh, don't worry about the Braxtons," said Brandt.

"Why not?"

"First of all, you must know by now that the Judge was a billionaire, so no matter what happens to the family property, they'll be just fine. Once you amass that kind of wealth, even the government can't harm you. And of course, deGroot Farm was never identified as a property to be taken the way my home was."

"Do you think some kind of fix was in between the FHA and the Judge?"

"It would be fun to think that," said Brandt, "but I doubt it. It just isn't in a part of town that the FHA targeted. I'm not sure that you can say the same thing about the house that their son and daughter-in-law purchased, however, but you would have to ask them about that. I'm not really sure."

Brandt was clearly tiring, and when the caretaker came in to clear the tea tray she gave Walter a dirty look. So despite the fact that he found the man fascinating and wanted badly to continue the conversation, he rose to leave.

"Thank you so much for your time, Mr. Brandt," he said. "You've been extremely helpful."

"If that's the case, I'm glad," said Brandt. "And please give my regards to Bunny if you see her."

"I didn't realize you knew the Braxtons personally," said Walter.

"I don't know the Braxtons well at all," said Brandt, "but of course I've known the deGroot family all my life, even though they were in another social stratum than we were. They were always friendly, especially Bunny. And Bunny was wonderful to my Evelyn during her illness. I'll never forget that."

"I'll be sure to tell her you said hello," said Walter. "She seems to be a very nice woman."

"She's more than that, Lieutenant," said Brandt with unexpected vehemence. "She's a great woman."

"You are not the first person to tell me that."

"And I won't be the last, I assure you."

"Can you tell me what it is about her that makes people think so highly of her?"

"That's easy, Lieutenant. Barbara Braxton is the most selfless person I have ever met. She is always thinking of others, always focused on what she can do to benefit others, and she doesn't just think that way, she acts on it. I repeat, Lieutenant, she is a great woman."

"Yes, sir," was all Walter could think to say as he rose to leave. "Thank you again for all your help. Goodbye, sir."

"Goodbye, young man," said Brandt.

Randall Brandt stared out the window and watched Walter Hudson's police cruiser back down his driveway and head back toward town and the Saw Mill River Parkway. He then stood up and walked to the small wet bar at the far end of the room and mixed himself a martini.

The wheelchair was not a prop. He had indeed suffered a stroke just after his wife's death that had left him unable to walk, and he was just now regaining his mobility, able to stand for only brief periods of time. But he didn't feel that was any of young Detective Hudson's business, at least not right now. He'd worry about that later.

He reached inside his sweater and pulled the envelope out of his pocket that had just arrived in the mail today; the envelope holding the brief letter that he had already read half a dozen times, but would read a dozen more before dinner. It was hand written in a firm, clear hand, and it was brief:

"Dearest Randall,

I wish that I could have done this before your dear Evelyn passed away, but under the circumstances existing at the time that was impossible.

Now, however, those circumstances have quite unexpectedly changed. I hope you accept this gift in the spirit in which it is given, in thanks for wonderful memories of a magical childhood shared long ago, and in loving memory of your dear departed Evelyn.

With all my best wishes,

Bunny

A second typed page contained the details, including passwords and access instructions, of a numbered account established in a Belize bank. The account had a balance of five million dollars.

He and Bunny had had long talks on those days when she had come over to visit with Evelyn. While Evelyn dozed they would chat endlessly about their childhood years and the marvelous experiences they had shared. But they'd also talked about his dire financial condition, and Bunny had been quite clear that she would have loved to help, but of course Teddy would hear nothing of it.

But now Teddy was out of the way, and Bunny, dear Bunny, had done just as she had said she would. She was, indeed, a great woman.

Detective Hudson had impressed him as a bright enough young man and a thorough investigator, and he may yet have to deal with him. But, as he had told the lieutenant, he still possessed a fine, clear mind, and he would make sure that the earnest young policeman would never find out about the five million. It was none of his business. But he would think about all that another time.

Right now, he had a life to live. He rose on shaky legs, went to the bar and mixed himself another martini.

14

***

"THE WOMEN IN THAT FAMILY DO SEEM TO BE LEADING YOU ON A MERRY CHASE," said Leviticus Welles, unable to suppress a smile. With his closely cropped, thinning hair going gray and his slight build, Levi looked more like someone's mild-mannered uncle than a highly respected member of the NYPD's Intelligence Division; but the man's analytical capabilities were razor sharp, and right now Walter needed all the help he could get.

"They certainly are," said Walter. "I've got the widow looking at me with a straight face telling me that she had the perfect marriage. I've got her kooky daughter telling me all this Freudian stuff about her relationship with her father, which you'd think she'd keep to herself, while at the same time she's looking at me like I'm tonight's pot roast while she's already got a napkin stuffed in her collar and a fork in her hand. And now Caroline Schuyler sends me off on a false lead when I know she's holding back, too. Still loving that coffee, Levi?"

They were sitting in Walter's tiny cubicle in the detectives' squad room of the Midtown South Precinct. As an employee of the Intelligence Division of the NYPD Levi had no formal role in the Braxton case, but Walter trusted his judgment implicitly and went to him often for informal conversations. Walter's coffee cup sat empty before him, but Levi's was still almost full.

"The best thing I can say about the coffee here is that it never gets worse," said Levi.

"Not exactly what Julie makes for you at home?"

"Not exactly."

"So what am I supposed to do?" said Walter. "The hotel security apparatus is worthless, the one weapon we found in the hotel room isn't the murder weapon and is clean as a whistle, and we haven't been able to pick up even a trace of physical evidence from the room itself. And after all these conversations I feel like I've learned an awful lot about Judge Braxton and his family, but absolutely nothing that will help me solve his murder. In the meantime I've got Commissioner Donahue and the mayor breathing down my neck, and that just never feels good."

"The gun came back clean, huh?"

"No prints, all the markings were expertly removed, and it looked like it hadn't been fired in years."

"And the hotel room itself?"

"The Judge was the first occupant, and every single print we lifted belonged either to the Judge, Caroline Schuyler, or the hotel staff, and we've cleared all the hotel staff."

"And the women are running you in circles."

"Yes, and it's all making me crazy."

"I think that should tell you a lot right there," said Levi.

"What do you mean?"

"First of all," said Levi, pushing the coffee away with a grimace, "they are three extraordinarily intelligent women. I know you're a terrific investigator and you're a lot smarter than you want to admit to yourself, but be careful. I'm positive that at least one of those women, if not all of them, are lying to you. And I'm also positive that any one of them could be the killer."

"The problem is," said Walter, "that whatever lies they're telling me are buried inside a lot of truth."

"Or they're giving you a lot of valid information so that you won't notice what they're not telling you," said Levi. "Remember, there are a lot of ways to tell a lie, and these women seem well-schooled in all of them. And don't let your problems with the women divert your focus away from your other suspects."

"What, you mean the Right Reverend Pierce and poor old Randall Brandt?" said Walter. "Neither one of them looks like a stone killer to me."

"Walter, if all murderers looked like murderers, your job would be a lot easier."

"You're right, you're right," said Walter wearily.

"I haven't heard you talk about Ted Braxton, Junior yet. Have you spoken to him?"

"No, I haven't," said Walter, "except for the few words we exchanged when I went up to 'the Cottage.' I have an appointment to see him tomorrow."

"Nice place, is it, 'the Cottage'?"

"Very."

"You know that it was Teddy's 10th anniversary gift to his wife."

"That's news to me," said Walter.

"What was left of the deGroot family trust was just about exhausted by then. The place was in disrepair and Bunny's mother was nearly destitute. Teddy's ship had come in by then, so he bought the place for an extremely generous price, had it completely refurbished, and put the title to the property in Bunny's name. The money from the purchase was used to replenish Mrs.

deGroot's trust so that she could live out her remaining days in comfort. He also established a property trust whose sole purpose is the perpetual maintenance of the home and the property. Bunny is the sole director of the trust."

"So that property is not included in the marital assets?"

"No, it is not."

"Wow."

"And the other 'wow,'" said Levi, "is that almost the entire marital estate goes to Bunny upon Teddy's death."

"How do you know that?" said Walter. "I didn't think they'd read the will yet."

"I'm in Intelligence, remember? But just so you know, the will is being read as we speak."

"Sorry. You said, 'almost.' Does that mean that Ted Junior and Virginia got at least something?"

"They will each receive one hundred thousand dollars."

"That's it?"

"That's it."

"But why? Did Teddy have some kind of falling out with his kids?"

"No, he just didn't believe in inherited wealth. Remember, he was an orphan who grew up poor, and he had to fight for everything he got. He believed that was the making of him, and he wanted his kids, at least to some extent, to earn their own way in the world, too."

"But can't Bunny just hand over some of the money to them once it's hers?"

"Yes, she can," said Levi, "but from everything I've heard she agreed completely with Teddy on the matter. The rumor is that she's going to set up a charitable trust with her fortune, and the kids will once again get little or nothing."

"Ouch."

"Yes, ouch."

"Were the terms of the will known to the family?" said Walter.

"That I don't know," said Levi.

"For once you don't know something? I'm shocked."

"Sorry to disappoint you, Walter," said Levi, smiling as he rose to leave. He hesitated for a moment and then said, "And Walter?"

"Yes, Levi?"

"I know it's none of my business, but watch out for Virginia. It sounds like she's trying to get into your head. You've got to ask yourself why; and on top of that, you just don't need that right now."

Walter sat back with a sigh. "Don't worry, Levi, I'm not that kind of man, you know that."

"And that's why a woman like Virginia will come at you out of nowhere," said Levi, "because you're just not the type of guy to be looking for it. I know things are rough at home these days. And don't forget that her behavior just might be a ploy to divert any suspicion from herself. It's a ploy that's been known to work. Again, I apologize for sticking my nose into your personal life."

"Oh, come on, Levi, you're a good friend and I appreciate the concern. But seriously, don't worry, okay?"

"Okay," said Levi as he rose to leave. "Say hello to Sarah and the kids for me."

"I'll do that," said Walter, "and you say hi to Julie."

The problem was, Walter thought as he sat back in his chair, Levi was right. Virginia Braxton wasn't just trying to get into his head; she'd moved right in and taken up residence. Walter Hudson was a faithful man, and he had never so much as touched another woman in his entire life. It had never been much of a matter of discipline to him; it simply never entered his mind. He had met Sarah when they were both eighteen and he had been perfectly content with her ever since. More than content: devoted and passionately in love. He desired her as much now as he had as an inexperienced teenager, maybe more.

Walter was an attractive man, and Virginia was not the first woman to express interest in him, but he had just not been interested in return. Women soon got that message loud and clear and moved on.

So what was it about Virginia? She was surely stunningly attractive, but this was New York City, for heaven's sake. You couldn't walk a city block in Manhattan without seeing at least ten Miss America candidates, but Walter's head had never turned. She had clearly been severely emotionally damaged by a dysfunctional relationship with her father, and she was smart and sophisticated in a way that Walter could never hope to be. Danger signals flashed at him from all directions. But still, there she was, ensconced, and she was showing no signs of going away.

But he would just have to deal with all that. He had an important investigation, and she was not only a potential suspect, but a prime source of information about the Braxton family and about her father. He would simply have to compartmentalize any other feelings and move ahead. He was a happily married man and a professional cop, damn it, and he would just have to deal with it.

He sat up and reached for his phone. After a few rings the call was picked up at the other end.

"Well, hello, Lieutenant," came the voice that seemed to lick his ear. "I thought you'd never call."

16

ONE WAS AS BLACK AS THE OTHER WAS WHITE, but that had never mattered to Marshawn Hill and Patrick Reilly. They'd been fast friends since they had met in kindergarten, and now that they were approaching the age of twelve they showed no signs of changing. They shared each other's homes and families just as they shared each other's mitts and bats in pickup ballgames.

But the most important thing that they shared was their love of adventure and mischief, which is what brought them, on this warm spring morning, to the banks of the Harlem River at the southern tip of the Bronx. This part of the river, just where it branches off from the massive Hudson River, is still known by its old Dutch name, Spuyten Duivel, the "Devil's Spout," and the name is well-deserved. The currents are unpredictable and treacherous, and Patrick and Marshawn had been warned time and again by their parents to stay away from that area and from the Harlem River in general, where, despite restrictions and precautions from families, friends, and the City of New York, at least a few people drowned every year.

That, however, was just an added enticement to the two adolescent boys, who only considered something truly fun if they knew they weren't supposed to be doing it. The sense of fun and danger was enhanced by the massive structure of the Henry Hudson Bridge that loomed over them under the clear blue sky like some monstrous alien spaceship.

They stood at water's edge, mesmerized by the sun's reflections off the eddies and currents that swirled along the shore, carrying the bits of debris that floated by close to the shore, then back out to the middle of the river, then farther downstream. They discussed the tales told by other boys at school of the bodies that had been seen floating by on this river, at this very spot- -stories they didn't quite believe, but that were too much fun to disbelieve.

"C'mon, Patrick," said Marshawn, "we ain't gonna see any dead bodies today."

"Nah, you're right," said Patrick. "The other guys have all the luck. Besides, we gotta get back. My old man picked up tickets to the Yankees game today at the Stadium, and he said he was gonna call your Dad to see if you could come along."

"Cool," said Marshawn, "but it ain't gonna be the same watching the Yanks without Jeter at short." Derek Jeter had been the Yankees' shortstop for far longer than the two boys had been alive. Following his exploits, either at Yankee Stadium, on the television, or in the *New York Post's* Sports section, the best sports page in the world, had been a constant in their lives as enduring as their friendship.

"Yeah, but, hey, it's still the Yanks."

"Yeah, and it's the only time my old man lets me get Cracker Jacks."

"Yeah, mine too," said Patrick as they turned away from the riverbank.

"Hey, look at this," said Marshawn, suddenly stopping and staring down at the soft, muddy ground at the water's edge. Patrick stepped closer to see what Marshawn was staring at, eager to see what was interesting enough to divert his attention from the Yankees and Cracker Jacks.

"Holy shit," he said, spontaneously using the expletive that they'd been self-consciously trying out on each other before they started using it with their other friends at school.

"Holy shit is right," said Marshawn, as he reached down to pick up the object of their attention.

"Don't do that!" said Patrick.

"Why not?"

"Because it probably belongs to murderers, that's why! They probably just got finished dumping a body in the river and they must have dropped it by mistake."

"Holy *shit*," said Marshawn, awestruck. "I can't wait to tell the guys."

"Yeah," said Patrick, "if the murderers don't come back looking for it and kill us first." They both looked out at the river, imagining their own bodies floating by. Man, would they be heroes at school or what?

"C'mon, let's leave it there and get outta here," said Marshawn, starting to move away.

"Aw, man, we can't just leave it here."

"Why not?"

"Because then who's gonna believe us, that's why. We can give it to our dads. They'll know what to do with it. They both work for the city."

"Patrick, our dads work for the Sanitation Department."

"Still, c'mon."

"Okay, then pick it up and let's go."

Patrick hesitated, but he didn't want Marshawn to think he was a chicken or, even worse, a douchebag, so he reached down and picked it up. It was cold and damp, and it was heavier than he thought it would be. He stuffed it into the front pouch of his hoodie.

"C'mon," he said, "let's get outta here before we get killed."

"Holy shit!" they shouted in unison as they ran off.

It was the first time either one of them had ever touched a gun.

"Where the hell did you boys get that? What the hell have you been up to?" bellowed Terrell Hill, Marshawn's imposing father, as they stood around the kitchen table staring at the gun. The boys were suddenly wondering if it would have been wiser to take their chances with the murderers.

"Terrell, how many times do I have to tell you not to use that language in front of the......Oh, my God!" shrieked Audrey Hill, Marshawn's equally imposing mother, as she strode into the kitchen.

"Audrey, please, calm down," said Terrell.

"Calm down?! You're telling me to calm down? I told you this is what was going to happen if we didn't move these boys out of this damn city!"

"They did the right thing, Audrey. They found it down by the river underneath the bridge. They didn't want to just leave it there. If it's loaded, someone could've gotten hurt."

"How many times do we have to tell you boys not to go down by that damn river!" said Audrey, "We told you and told you. And now look at what you've done. Did you say *loaded*?"

"I don't know, Audrey. Please, I'll take care of it."

"What are you going to do?"

"I'm going to take it to the cops, that's what."

"Oh, that's right. I can't wait to see that. A big black man walking through the South Bronx with a gun in his hand? My only question is: who'd shoot you dead first, the cops or the gangbangers?"

"I'm not going to carry it openly, for heaven's sake. I'll put it in my lunchbox or something."

"So now you'll be a black man walking into a police station with a concealed weapon. I'm sure all those armed cops would give you the benefit of the doubt."

"Audrey, most of the cops in this precinct are black."

"And when was the last time that made a difference?"

"Okay, okay. I'll call them and ask them to stop by and pick it up. Is that okay?"

"That's the best idea you've come up with so far," said Audrey. "All I'll have to do is spend the next week explaining to every neighbor on this block why we had the cops at our front door on a Saturday morning, but that's better than identifying your body at the morgue. I guess." She turned and glared at the boys. "I hope you're both proud of yourselves."

"Audrey, please," said Terrell, but the woman he loved was already storming out of the room.

"So, Dad?" said Marshawn.

"Yes, son?"

"Does this mean that we can't go to the ballgame?"

17

"SO WHAT HAVE YOU GOT FOR ME, EDUARDO? I'm running on fumes here."

Walter was sitting in a chair beside Eduardo's desk in the crowded squad room of the Midtown South Precinct. It would have been at least slightly more comfortable to meet him in his cubicle, but he needed to get up and move around, perhaps just to stretch his legs and give himself the illusion of doing something useful.

"I don't know, Lieutenant," said Eduardo, looking uneasy. "I've got a lot, but in the end it all seems to add up to nothing."

"Eduardo, I don't need cryptic right now," said Walter, leaning forward in his chair.

"I know you don't, sir. I'm sorry."

"That's okay. Why don't you just tell me what you've got."

"On the surface, everybody's alibi seems to work out," said Eduardo as he reached for a notebook lying on a far corner of his desk. "Ted Junior did indeed work late at his law office. They don't have any sign in or sign out, but the night security guard remembers saying 'good night' to him, and the video camera in the lobby had a pretty good image of him leaving at about ten o'clock. And I was able to confirm that his wife, Alicia, was at a fundraising dinner uptown. The restaurant had her on the reservation list, and I talked to two other attendees who confirmed that Alicia was there."

"Then they both claimed that they went back to the Park Avenue duplex, right?"

"Yeah, and that's where the problems start. First of all, they have no video security system in that building."

"You've got to be kidding me."

"No, can you believe it? The owners' association rejected a proposal to install one because they said it was too expensive."

"These guys are all billionaires, right?"

"I know. It's amazing the things that people get cheap about. At the same time they rejected the camera system they approved funding for a new, all season rooftop infinity pool that cost about ten times what the security system would've cost."

"Did the security guard remember anything?"

"He says he did, but I don't believe him."

"Why not?"

"I dropped by at seven at night to see him. He was already out of it, and I spotted an empty pint of vodka in the garbage can under his desk. And on top of that, he claimed that they both walked in together at ten-thirty, but they both told me that they arrived separately, since Alicia's dinner didn't break up until eleven, which the maître d' at the restaurant confirmed."

"What about the staff at the duplex?"

"Albert and the cook had both travelled up to Placid Hollow with Barbara Braxton, and the maid is not a live in, so there was no staff there that night."

"So for all we know, either of them could've gotten to the hotel in time to murder the Judge within the timeframe we've established."

"Yessir," said Eduardo, staring at his notebook.

"How about Virginia?"

"Actually, she might have the best alibi of them all," said Eduardo, perking up a little. "Just like she said, she was at a dinner with a bunch of Asian investors from seven-thirty until one on Friday night at a place called 'Chez Vous' at 34th and 6th."

"It's 'shay voo' Eduardo, not 'shez voos.'"

"Yeah, yeah."

"And that seems like an awfully long dinner. Are you sure about the timing?"

"It's one of those places with an outdoor bar at the back of the restaurant that opens out onto the inner square of the block where smoking is allowed. Virginia took them there because these Asian guys were all heavy smokers and, by the way, heavy drinkers. You should see the bar tab. Anyway, I talked to the bartender from that night and he remembered these guys pretty clearly, which doesn't surprise me, given the number of drinks he served them."

"Did he remember Virginia?"

"Yeah. He says he didn't recall her drinking anything, but he clearly remembered her herding them all out of the bar about one o'clock."

"He was clear about that?"

"She gave him a five hundred dollar cash tip, Lieutenant. He also said she was the type of woman who was tough to forget, you know?"

"Yeah, I know," said Walter. "So what about Barbara Braxton and the staff?"

"That's tough," said Eduardo, staring at his notebook again. "They all say that they drove up to Placid Hollow together and spent the night there, at least until they got the call about the Judge. The problem is, there are no independent witnesses. They can all confirm each other's story, but why wouldn't they?"

"So everybody's got an alibi and nobody's got an alibi, with the exception of Virginia, and I couldn't see her for this anyway."

"So what are you thinking then?"

"That's the problem. It's like the alibis. It could be any of them, or it could be none of them."

"Do you really think that it could be none of them, Lieutenant?"

"No, I don't, but what am I supposed to think? And I just can't let myself believe that this was a robbery gone wrong, or committed by some old enemy of the Judge. If that's the case, I'm never going to solve this murder, and I just can't face that."

"So, what are we going to do?"

"We're going to keep digging, Eduardo. Because somebody's alibi has a great big hole in it, and we're not going to stop digging until we find it."

18

VIRGINIA DIDN'T WANT TO COME UP TO THE PRECINCT HOUSE. She said she was working from home, as usual, and that the trip uptown and back would take up an entire morning she couldn't afford to waste. Walter, on the other hand, refused to accept her invitation to come to her apartment to talk, not wanting to know how he would find her attired if he accepted, and unwilling to trust her behavior behind closed doors. He was almost successful in dismissing any doubts about his own behavior. They settled on meeting at a small coffee shop a couple of blocks from her apartment: public enough to ensure propriety and just noisy enough to afford them the necessary privacy for their conversation.

Walter was waiting for her when she arrived wearing a pair of skin-tight designer jeans and a snugly tailored blouse. It was warm, and she wore no sweater or jacket. She gave Walter a knowing grin as she watched him tear his eyes off her body and attempt to establish eye contact. She wore only light makeup, and her hair fell loosely over her shoulders. Walter himself wore his usual dark suit and white shirt, keeping his suit jacket on despite the warmth to conceal his service revolver. He felt large and awkward around this petite woman in a way he never did around Sarah, even though the two women were about the same size. They each ordered coffee and a small pastry and found a table in a back corner that looked out onto the busy sidewalk,

"Well, Lieutenant, to what do I owe this honor?" said Virginia. "Or did you just miss me?"

"Virginia, please, don't get started," said Walter, but it didn't matter. She had already managed to make him feel like he was participating in an illicit rendezvous instead of conducting a professional interrogation. "I wanted to talk to you because I know that the will was read yesterday, and I was hoping you could give me some details and perhaps fill me in on how everybody reacted."

"Why didn't you call my mother or my brother?"

Why, indeed? thought Walter

"I actually have an appointment with your brother this afternoon, and I plan to follow up with your mother, too. I think it's important to get everyone's perspective."

"Okay, have it your way," said Virginia, giving him another smile. "What would you like to know?" She took a sip of her coffee and sat back.

"My sources," said Walter, "tell me that your mother received essentially the entire estate, and that you and your brother were effectively cut out. Is that true?"

"That is for the most part true," said Virginia, suddenly serious. "Dad left some small bequests to some of the servants, and a couple of relatively insignificant gifts to some charitable institutions. But he was clear in the will that any large acts of charity would be up to my mother once he died. You are also correct that he, for all intents and purposes, cut my brother and me out of the will. A hundred thousand apiece out of an estate that amounted to $2.5 billion is a pittance."

I'd take it, thought Walter.

"How do you feel about that?" he said.

"I don't feel much of anything about it," said Virginia with a shrug. "It didn't surprise me in the least. Dad always told us from the time we were kids that it was up to us to make something of ourselves. He said we already had a head start in life because we were born with good minds and healthy bodies, and he'd made sure that we both got a first rate education. He said that it would only weaken us if he gave us a free ride through life."

"So you're not angry?"

"Let me ask you a question, Walter," she said, leaning her over coffee cup. "How old are you?"

"I'm thirty-five."

"And look at you, already a detective lieutenant in the finest police organization in the world. That's quite an accomplishment, isn't it?"

"I think it is."

"Is your father still alive?"

"No, he passed away when I was twenty-five."

"I'm sorry, Walter, that's too young to lose a parent."

Walter nodded his head but said nothing. He still missed the man every day.

"When he died, how much did he leave you?"

"He left me nothing. But he didn't do that by choice, like your father. He just didn't have anything to give. He worked hard all his life, but we always lived paycheck to paycheck."

"But what if he had? What if he'd left you, say, ten million dollars? Do you think you'd be an NYPD detective lieutenant today?"

"I think," said Walter, laughing, "that I'd be a beach bum on some remote Caribbean island, drinking too much rum and chasing the local women."

"And I'm sure catching your fair share, but you get my point."

"Yes, I do, Virginia."

"I'm thirty years old, and I'm worth a little more than fifteen million dollars. Not exactly billionaire territory yet, but I'm getting there. I'm fine. I don't need anybody else's money and I don't want anybody else's money, especially not my father's. My father did some pretty crummy things in his life, and I don't have to tell you that he left me pretty messed up in a lot of ways, but leaving me out of his will was the kindest thing he ever did for me."

"I'm glad you feel that way, and I'm not surprised either."

"But just think, Walter," said Virginia, the smile returning to her face. "If Daddy had promised me a pile of money, I may have actually become that bimbo you first thought I was. Maybe I would have been one of those girls you'd be chasing on that remote Caribbean island of yours. How would you have liked that?"

"I think I like you the way you are," he said, immediately regretting it.

But instead of returning the compliment with the flirtatious response that he expected and feared, the smile fled her face and she suddenly went silent, her eyes cast down, staring at her coffee for a few long seconds. When she looked up she had tears in her eyes.

"Virginia, I'm…"

"Please, Walter, don't say a word, okay?" She was silent for a few more seconds as she regained her composure. "Now, I'm afraid I have to get back to my non-bimbo job or I'm going to have some angry clients. Perhaps you can walk me back to my apartment. We can finish up our conversation along the way." She snatched up the check before Walter had a chance to react and paid it at the counter.

They left the coffee shop and headed south on Church Street. The sun was shining and the air was warm; the smell of salt water wafted in from the Hudson, reminding him of his teen years when he and his friends used to spend long summer days at Jones Beach. There was no better place in the world than Manhattan Island to take a walk with a pretty girl on a day like this, and Virginia, as if reading his mind, hooked her arm through his. He thought he should remove it, but now was not the time to make an issue of it, as he continued to get remarkable insights into the dead judge's family from this mystifying young woman. And besides, it felt good. A guilty pleasure was still a pleasure, as his uncle used to say.

"So did your brother react the same way that you did?" he said.

"My brother and I are not close," said Virginia, seeming, unusually, to choose her words carefully. "You said you were going to see him this afternoon, so maybe it would be better if you asked him."

"Why? Did he appear upset or surprised when the will was read?"

"I don't really know. I wasn't really paying much attention to him."

"I guess I'm surprised," said Walter. "When I visited all of you up at your home in Westchester, I got the impression that you were a very close knit family."

"That's because you were listening to my mother. It means a lot to her for people to have that impression of our family. She's not necessarily being dishonest. She wants to believe that as much as she wants the rest of the world to believe it, so in her own way she was being completely sincere. But again, you should probably talk to Ted directly."

They had just turned the corner onto Thomas Street, which was the address of Virginia's building, and Walter was about to ask her one last question when she suddenly stopped. He felt her arm tighten around his, and when he turned to look at her he saw that her eyes were locked on something straight ahead, and her face had lost color. Walter looked in the direction of her stare and saw a man, probably Virginia's age, perhaps six feet tall, walking rapidly toward them from about halfway down the block. He was wearing what looked like khakis and a short sleeved shirt and, at least from that distance, looked fit and strong.

"What's wrong, Virginia? Do you know this guy?"

"He's just a guy I met in a local bar a few weeks ago. His name is Mark Glidden, or Gladden, I really can't remember."

"Is there some reason for you to be afraid of him? Because it sure looks like you are."

"He was hitting on me and I made it clear that I wasn't interested, but he's apparently not the kind of guy who takes no for an answer. This is the third time I've come home and found him hanging around on my block."

"Has he been violent or threatening toward you?" said Walter, feeling his body tense.

"He hasn't been violent," said Virginia, still not moving, "but the last time I saw him I tried to walk by him and he grabbed me by the arm. He's awfully strong, and it scared me. He finally let me go, but he said, 'This isn't over between me and you,' and when I told him that there wasn't anything between us in the first place he said, 'That's what you think,' and really squeezed my arm hard. It hurt."

"Okay, let's just keep walking. Maybe because he sees you're with someone he'll just walk on by."

"Maybe, but I wouldn't count on it. This guy doesn't seem to be the type to give up, and if you ask me he's kind of crazy."

"Don't worry about it, okay? Just keep walking."

She looked up at him with frightened eyes and tried to smile. "Okay," she said.

The man seemed to walk faster as he got nearer, and Walter realized that he would probably have to deal with a confrontation with the man, but still, hoping against hope, he kept his eyes straight ahead to avoid any provocative eye contact.

"Hey, hey!" the man shouted as he approached.

"Mark, please," said Virginia, "just leave me alone, okay?"

"Leave you alone?" said the man, reddening. He grabbed her arm. "I called you five fucking times in the last two days and you never answered me once. What the fuck is that all about?"

"Mister," said Walter, "nobody wants a confrontation here. The lady wants you to leave her alone, so why don't you just move along?"

"And why don't you just stay the fuck out of this, Tarzan. This is none of your fucking business." He squeezed Virginia's arm even harder, and Walter saw her flinch.

"Mister, I'm going to ask you one more time. Let go of the lady and move on."

"And you listen to me, asshole. If I want to talk to this stupid cunt it's none of your fucking business, so just buzz the fuck off. I'll hurt you if I have to, and don't think I can't." He jerked Virginia's arm to move her away.

Walter's right arm shot out and his enormous hand wrapped around the man's throat. The man's face immediately started to swell and redden. He tried to struggle but it was to no avail.

"That's no way to talk to a lady! Do you hear me! This is a lady you're talking to! Do you hear me, motherfucker!" Walter heard himself shouting, as if from a distance. He lifted the man off his feet with one hand and slammed him up against the side of the brick building they were standing in front of.

"I asked you a question, motherfucker! Answer me!" In the red fog of his fury it would have been so easy for him to squeeze just a little bit harder, so easy to crush the man's trachea, so easy to watch him die. He felt the man's body going limp.

"Walter! Walter! You're going to kill him! Put him down, please!" Virginia's voice was faint, and sounded even farther away than his own.

"For God's sake, Walter, please!"

The voice finally penetrated his consciousness as his rational mind began to reassert itself. He loosened his grip and the man collapsed to the sidewalk like a marionette with its strings let go. Walter stared at the inert form curiously, as if he wasn't sure how it had gotten there. He noticed that the man still seemed to be breathing. He felt that he should be relieved, and he probably was.

"Thank God," he heard Virginia say from behind him.

The man regained consciousness, and, after a few long minutes, struggled to his feet, staring at Walter with a petrified expression.

"You so much as look the wrong way at the lady again and I'll chase you down like a rat and rip your heart out. Do you understand?" said Walter with clinical calm.

The man was unable to speak, but he nodded his head.

"Good," said Walter, "now get the fuck out of here." The man turned and stumbled down the street, tripping and falling twice. He never looked back.

Virginia grabbed Walter by the arm and walked him to the next door, which was hers. She pulled a key out of her pocket, unlocked and opened the door and pulled him in behind her. They were in a large, well-lit foyer.

Before Walter had the chance to react or protest, she flung herself at him and wrapped her arms around his torso. A sob escaped her as she reached up, pulled his face down to her and kissed him fiercely. He felt his arms go around her, seemingly independent of his conscious will.

"Thank you," she said, "oh, thank you. You took care of me. Thank you."

Walter knew he should let go of her and pull away, but his arms wouldn't obey his mind's commands. She seemed to melt into him.

"I'm a professional," said Walter after a few long seconds, "and I should be ashamed of myself. I've been trained to handle situations like that, and I have, dozens of times. I could have killed that man. It's the most unprofessional thing I've done since I got my shield."

"And you did it for me," said Virginia, kissing him again and again.

Her mouth was soft, her breath was warm and sweet. He felt her body pressing against his in all the right places. Oh, God, he thought. He forced himself to pull away from her as his arms finally obeyed his mind.

"Virginia….."

Her breathing was still heavy, and her eyes blazed at him. For a moment he thought she might lunge at him again, but then she seemed to calm herself. "I know, I know, you're a married man."

"Yes, I am."

"Now you listen to me, Walter Hudson," she said, staring at him with those hypnotic eyes. "I know you're a married man, and I know you have a lovely family, and I know you're a Catholic who believes that adultery is a sin. I don't care. I fell in love with you the first time I ever laid eyes on you. I have never in my life felt for any man what I feel for you, and I never will. I don't understand that, I can't explain it, and I don't care to. All I can tell you is that for the first time in my life I feel whole when I'm with you. I don't want to hurt your wife, who I'm sure is a lovely woman, and I certainly don't want to destroy your marriage or harm your family. I will take you on any terms that you offer, do you understand? And don't lie to me, and don't lie to yourself. You care for me, too. You just proved that. And you want me as much as I want you. You just proved that, too."

"Virginia, I have to leave now," said Walter. "I'm not going to say anything because I don't know what to say. I just know I have to leave now."

"Yes, you do, and you'd better leave quickly before I throw myself at you again," she said, the beguiling smile returning to her face.

She walked him to the door and kissed him lightly on the lips before opening it.

"Goodbye, Walter. I love you. Please never forget that."

He turned and left without saying anything.

19

"IT SOUNDS LIKE YOU GOT OUT JUST IN TIME, WALTER,"
said Leviticus Welles as he stared across the table at his friend and colleague. They were in a small Greek restaurant in midtown where Walter had asked him to meet him. The cheerful murals of the Greek Islands and the Acropolis that covered the walls seemed to mock Walter as plates of food, ordered by the linguistically gifted Levi in perfect colloquial Greek, a language he had been studying for only a month in preparation for a vacation that he and Julie would be taking in the summer, sat on the table, untouched.

"It doesn't feel that way to me," said Walter, looking miserable. "Levi, I've got to go to Captain Amato and get myself taken off this case."

"Walter, don't do anything that you're going to live to regret," said the older man, frowning and putting his fork down. "Give yourself some time."

"I don't deserve any time, Levi. I've got to get off this case before I do any more damage. I don't know how I'm going to look Sarah in the eye when I get home tonight. What am I going to say to her?"

"Listen to me, Walter," said Levi, leaning across the table toward him, "you're not going to say anything to anybody, not right now. You know Amato. That man is pure politics, and the only thing he sees when he looks at you is long-term competition. You will effectively be destroying your career with the NYPD if you open up to him. Do you want that?"

"Oh, c'mon, Levi, I'm just going to ask him to relieve me of one case."

"Not just one case, Walter. This case. This is one of the highest profile murders this city has seen in a long time. The mayor and the commissioner are both following it on a daily basis, and they both asked for you, personally, to take it on. You're being looked at as potential future commissioner material. What are you going to do? Tell them that a suspect got inside your head temporarily and that you can't manage that?"

"I don't think Virginia is a suspect, Levi."

"Well, you'd damn well better start thinking she is. What, is your male ego so eager to believe that you're God's gift to her that you can't acknowledge that what she's probably doing is manipulating your feelings to divert your attention from her as a prime suspect? For heaven's sake, Walter, snap out of it. You're a professional cop. Act like one."

"Maybe you're right, Levi."

"Not 'maybe,' Walter; I am right and you know it. At least you'll know it once you get your testosterone levels under control."

"But what about Sarah?"

"Well, you have a choice, don't you? I guess you could go home and spill your guts to her about feelings you may or may not have for another woman, and things that you didn't quite do but really wanted to do for a brief moment. I think right now, when she's exhausted and stressed, when she's probably feeling inadequate and unattractive as your wife, would be the perfect time to unload that on her. Don't you?"

"I guess I didn't think about it like that."

"No, I guess you didn't."

"So, what do I do?"

"Here's what I would suggest: We're sitting here with all this great food in front of us. I propose that you eat a good meal. Then, since you're a good Catholic and Saint Patrick's is just around the corner, you're going to go to Confession and bare your soul to a priest instead of your wife. That's what the priest and your faith are there for. You will then complete your shift like the excellent cop you are and go home and be the wonderful husband and father you are. Finally, you will take your beautiful wife to bed. What you do after that is none of my business. How does that sound?"

"That sounds good, Levi. That sounds awfully good. Thank you," said Walter, reaching for the *spanakopita*.

"I'm glad you think so," said the older man, dishing up a large serving of *spetsofai*. He ordered more bread from the waiter, joking with him and making him smile.

The meal and the company made Walter feel better, but long after he left the restaurant his mind remained haunted by Virginia Braxton.

20

※※※

"COME IN, ALICIA," said Barbara Braxton to her daughter-in-law. "Help yourself to some coffee. I assume you've already had your lunch."

They were in the large "sun room" of the family duplex on Park Avenue. It was on the second floor and, since they were twenty-two floors up, they had a beautiful view of Central Park two blocks to the west. It was adjacent to what was technically Barbara's and Teddy's bedroom but was, in fact, hers alone. They hadn't shared a bedroom in many years, and the bedroom in which he actually slept was on the first floor, also overlooking the Park.

The sunroom was decorated with a feminine sensibility; Barbara used it as her personal office as well as a sitting room where she received guests both socially and, since she was one of the most influential philanthropists in New York City, for business purposes. It was decorated with a contemporary furniture ensemble placed at the end of the room nearest the front windows, but a Georgian period *escritoire* at the other end, a large-screen Apple Macintosh incongruously occupying most of its surface. They sat facing each other on the matching sofas like two chess masters, tensed for a deadly battle of skill and wits, the coffee sitting before them on a stainless steel and glass table top.

"Yes, I have, thank you," said Alicia. An objective assessment would probably conclude that she was prettier than either Virginia Braxton or Caroline Schuyler. Her rich blond hair hung in natural waves that no stylist could improve upon. Her skin was pale and smooth, and her sea-green eyes were large, limpid, and intelligent. She was tall and fashionably thin, and she had perfected the art of accenting her generous, well-shaped breasts, untouched by a surgeon's scalpel, while still maintaining a demure image. The perfect Manhattan housewife. But somehow it all fell a little short, and she tended to fade into the background whenever she was in the same room with the other two women.

"Alicia," said Barbara, "it won't be long before Detective Hudson calls on you for a more in-depth interview than the one he conducted up at the Cottage, and I thought it important that we at least make sure that our testimonies are as consistent as possible."

"Yes, you're probably right, Mother," said Alicia. "I thought because a few days had passed since the murder that maybe his investigation was going in a different direction, and I wouldn't be bothered. Perhaps that will still be the case."

"I doubt it," said Barbara. "Remember, he's the police investigator who uncovered all that disagreeable business with the president and that horrid Henry Kellar last year."

"That's right, him and that odd man, Leviticus something."

"Yes, so I doubt that he'll fail to dot his 'i's and cross his 't's on this investigation."

"I suppose you know that he is visiting Ted this afternoon, in just a half hour, I believe," said Alicia, looking down at her watch, a rose gold Jaeger le Coulture.

"No, I wasn't aware of that," said Barbara, paling only a little.

"Don't worry, Mother," said Alicia. "Ted, as you would expect, is oblivious to just about everything of any relevance, so it is unlikely that he can inflict any serious damage on the situation."

"I presume 'everything of relevance' is your convenient euphemism for the fact that you spent two years of your married life fucking my husband, until dear Caroline assumed that happy duty for you."

Alicia reddened noticeably. "I didn't know you were capable of being that crude, but if that's the way you want to put it, yes."

"I can't think of any other way to put it, can you?" said Barbara. "I have found it fascinating in the course of my life to discover just what people are capable of. I should think that you would have developed that same fascination by now, if only in the process of self-discovery. So I think we should dispense with that odd habit of yours of calling me 'Mother.' There's a bit of an incestuous whiff to it, don't you think?"

"I wasn't sure you knew," said Alicia.

"Oh, please, do you want the complete list of my late husband's conquests in alphabetical or chronological order? Both?"

"I'd rather not."

"I'm sure," said Barbara. "But that's all beside the point, isn't it? The issue at hand is how do we deal with the matter when Detective Hudson comes calling. It's a tidbit I'm sure he'd find uncomfortably germane to his investigation."

"I really don't see how it's any of his business," said Alicia. "My first concern, whether or not you choose to believe it, is to protect my husband from learning what went on between his father and me. I'm afraid it would destroy him, and I don't want that on my conscience."

"How belatedly thoughtful of you. Are you sure he doesn't already know?"

"At a certain subconscious level, I think he does," said Alicia after a brief pause. "There have been signs of that ever since I began the affair."

"I can guess what they are," said Barbara, "but I'd rather not. The fact that you are not pregnant after more than a year of trying probably tells me all I need to know."

"But I am certain," said Alicia, ignoring her mother-in-law's all too accurate implication, "that he has no conscious knowledge, and I want to keep it that way. He has always been kind to me. I love him, and I wish him no harm. I intend to take that secret to my grave, and if he ever asks me, I will look him straight in the eye and lie about it."

Barbara deGroot Braxton stared long and hard at Alicia Chadwick Braxton with the same detached respect that a general would as he stared at his opponent across the field of battle.

"I do believe you," she said, "but I'm not sure we can take the same approach with the impressive young detective."

"With whom, by the way, your dear daughter seems to be completely infatuated."

"Ginny's infatuations come and go, and I'll leave it to Lieutenant Hudson to handle her. My concern is how *we* handle *him*."

"Yes, I believe you're right," said Alicia. "What do you propose?"

"I propose that we volunteer nothing, but if he raises the subject we should be completely honest with him and implore him not to reveal his knowledge to Ted. I don't know what else to do. He's too smart to lie to. He'll figure it out, and once he does it will just raise his suspicions and bring unwanted focus to the private lives of our family."

"I completely agree with you."

"Good," said Barbara, starting to rise from her chair. "I'm glad we understand each other."

"But, of course, there's one more thing to talk about."

"And what would that be?" said Barbara, settling back into her chair.

"Your son's and my financial welfare, of course."

"I'm not sure I understand."

"Of course you do," said Alicia, feeling control of the conversation shifting to her for the first time. "Ted and your old flame Brad Pierce—oh, yes, I'm familiar with the family lore—have made a fine mess of the once proud firm of Braxton and Pierce. Between the two of them I doubt they could manage a lemonade stand successfully."

"I haven't been paying that much attention to the firm. I guess I assumed that Teddy had left it on a firm footing and it was continuing to prosper."

"Oh, really, Barbara. What did you think would happen when the firm was left to my poor, feckless husband and your Reverend Pierce? This is Manhattan, for God's sake, the most treacherous legal jungle in the world. The competition knew the situation, and they were licking their chops before your husband had zipped on his judge's robes for the first time."

"So you're telling me that the firm is struggling?"

"I'm telling you that the firm is broke. It is bleeding associates and clients at such an alarming rate that I doubt it will survive the year, and it will bring Ted and me down with it. You have to help us."

"I'm not sure I understand."

"I'm not sure how you can't. You and I, Barbara, share similar backgrounds. We both come from fine, old, respected families who managed to lose all of their wealth just as we were about to inherit it. I married your son on the assumption that he would be my financial salvation, if not my family's. Of course, I had no illusions about his personal skills, but I did have faith in your husband's genius, and I always assumed that you and he would never let your son fail. I did not marry Ted just to sink back into genteel poverty, and I do not intend to do so now. Only you can help us."

"Which is why, I suppose, you wound up in my husband's bed."

"Not at all. Your husband charmed me into his bed, and I guarantee you that money had nothing to do with it, though I'm sure you would like to believe otherwise."

"What I believe or wish to believe is hardly any of your business."

"Precisely."

"So what do you want of me?"

"I want you to let go of your husband's ridiculous notions about his children making it on their own, and gift over to me and Ted at least a portion of our eventual inheritance."

"It is presumptuous of you to assume that you ever had an 'eventual inheritance' coming to you. I have no obligation to leave you anything, and Teddy and I had long talked of taking our fortune in its entirety and establishing a charitable trust with it."

"Well, Teddy's dead, and you can cut the crap. Unless you wish to witness the spectacle of the firm's failure and the dirty family laundry that it would expose, I suggest that we come to an understanding."

"I'm sure you have something to propose."

"Yes, I do. I would propose that you gift over to Ted and me an after tax sum of one hundred million dollars. We can let the tax attorneys work out the details. That is about the minimum amount required in order to live well in Manhattan these days, and I don't think it's greedy at all. Then, you will establish your beloved charitable trust, the Braxton Foundation or whatever, name Ted president and chief executive officer, and put me on the board, both at generous salaries. Of course, you will have to find someone who is truly competent actually to manage the trust, but I'll leave that up to you. "

"But what about the firm?"

"I already told you. The firm is broke. Putting Ted in at least nominal charge of the foundation will give us an honorable excuse to wind down the firm without admitting its failure and without tarnishing Ted's reputation. Ted will simply be moving on to far more important work, that's all. You know the standard line: He'll be helping the family to 'give back' and all that nonsense."

"And what about poor Brad?"

"Poor Brad is broke. Teddy always made sure that the lion's share of the firms' revenue went to himself, and whatever capital Brad had in the firm has evaporated. I would propose that you give him a severance of, say, five million dollars, and then hire him as chief counsel to the foundation at a generous stipend. That way appearances will be maintained all around."

"That was never Brad's dream, you know."

"That's none of my business. He can take or leave the offer. I'll let you have any discussions with him about his dreams, since I imagine you've always been a part of them."

"You are in no position to be offensive, dear, so please watch your tongue."

"You are correct. In fact, I think you'll agree that neither of us is in any position to be offensive. So, do we have an understanding?"

"Yes, dear, I believe we do," said Bunny Braxton. "And by the way, I believe that you should continue to call me 'Mother' after all. People might notice otherwise. You know how people can be."

"I agree," said Alicia, rising and smiling warmly at her mother-in-law. "People can be simply awful, can't they?"

She saw herself out.

⊷⊷⊷

Bunny Braxton refilled her coffee cup and sat back on the sofa.

The conversation with Alicia could not have gone more perfectly. But then again, she wasn't surprised. As Alicia herself had observed, they were birds of a feather, and she would have expected that their minds would work so much alike. She hadn't needed to prompt Alicia at all. The foolish young girl had just sat there and proposed everything that Bunny had been planning for so long. And Bunny was perfectly content to give her the credit. The only thing that had surprised her about the conversation was that Alicia had so readily believed that she was unaware of the situation at the law firm. She was Bunny Braxton, after all; it was her job to be aware of these things. How could she protect the family otherwise? And family, of course, was everything. Even poor, flawed Teddy had understood that.

And now, she thought, came the truly challenging part of her plan, the conversation with her brilliant but troubled daughter.

Bunny had long ago found it in her heart to forgive her husband for his all-too-human failures. The vast chasm between their respective upbringings had made him a cipher to her in her youth, but over the many years of their marriage the scales had fallen from her eyes. She had come to understand him perhaps better than he understood himself, and that had afforded her at least a certain degree of peace of mind and, more importantly, a sense of control.

He should have known the damage that his behavior would inflict on his all-too-observant young daughter. But like every other consideration in his life that would have caused him to change his ways, he had simply refused to see it. And now, just as he had with Young Ted, Alicia, and Brad Pierce, he had left her to clean up the mess.

It was absolutely vital to her plans that they come to an understanding. Virginia, however, would not be as easily dealt with as the others, and the conversation would require all her skills, especially when the subject turned to Detective Lieutenant Walter Hudson. There would be no margin for error.

21

THE LAW FIRM OF BRAXTON AND PIERCE was located on the west side of Sixth Avenue, almost directly across from Rockefeller Center. The young associates liked the location because of its easy access to Central Park, where they could go for morning jogs and, in the warmer weather, eat their lunches al fresco in its peaceful surroundings.

It was also only a block away from Saint Patrick's Cathedral, where, obedient to Leviticus Welles's instructions, Walter Hudson had gone to Confession immediately after lunch. Many modern Catholics disdained that Sacrament and the confessionals in the cathedral were largely empty; but it was an important part of Walter and Sarah's religious life and, as usual, he had emerged feeling cleansed and renewed.

The proximity of the cathedral to the law offices meant that, despite the long lunch with Levi and the stop for confession, he arrived at the firm's reception desk precisely at two o'clock, the hour of his appointment.

The receptionist, an attractive, fortyish woman with dark hair and large glasses, reminded him of a desk sergeant at a precinct house: polite and efficient, but brooking no nonsense. After Walter introduced himself she made a quick, whispered call and escorted him down a long hallway to a large corner office, which the lettering on the door announced to be the office of "T. Franklin Braxton, Jr., Senior Partner." And, indeed, the man who reminded him so much, and so little, of his formidable mother, rose to greet him as the receptionist opened the door.

"Good afternoon, Lieutenant, welcome to Braxton and Pierce," said Ted, Jr., in a "hail fellow, well-met" manner that somehow fell flat as he rounded his desk and offered a handshake diminished in its intended heartiness by the clammy softness of the man's grip. "Can I offer you some coffee or tea?"

"Some coffee would be great," said Hudson, thinking that it would easily be an improvement on his usual afternoon cup at the precinct house. It arrived almost immediately, and Walter was surprised to note after a sip just how marginal an improvement it was.

"If you don't mind, Lieutenant," said Ted, "can you tell me how the investigation into my father's murder is proceeding? I don't mean to sound critical, but it's been almost a week since Dad's murder, and I'm afraid that by now the trail may be going cold."

"I'll be blunt, Franklin," said Walter, the man's chosen form of address still ringing false in his ear, "I, and the entire NYPD up to and including the commissioner, not to mention the mayor, are all frustrated. I normally would have collected a great deal of physical evidence at this point which would be leading to a strong suspect. But as you have probably heard, the crime scene itself was basically immaculate, and of course there were the well-publicized problems with the new security systems at the hotel."

"Yes," said Braxton. "I must say I'm puzzled that the hotel management hasn't fired their head of security yet. The man is clearly incompetent."

"He has been retained at the express request of the NYPD. We feel that most of the problems at the hotel were beyond his control, and that if anyone can help dig up any meaningful information from the hotel security system it would be him."

"And of course, he's a former NYPD cop. I understand how that works."

"You'll have to take my word that his former employment with the NYPD had nothing to do with the decision to retain him."

"I can only hope you're right, Lieutenant."

"I have, however, with the continued help of your family, been able at least to gain a good sense of your father's past, which is always helpful."

"That's all well and good, but I and my family expect my father's murder to be solved. All the good intentions and hard work in the world will not suffice." Braxton sat back in his chair, apparently pleased with his assertive tone.

"And I can assure you that they will not suffice with the NYPD, either, Franklin," said Walter, badly wanting to change the subject. "Perhaps you could help me."

"How can I help you, Lieutenant?"

"I heard that your father's will was read yesterday, and if my information is correct, you and your sister were pretty much left out of it. How did you feel about that?"

"I don't see how that has any bearing whatsoever on your criminal investigation. If those are the types of questions you are asking I'm not surprised that there has been no progress."

"I'd just like to know if you and your sister were aware of the terms of the will, that's all."

"Why? Do you think I would have murdered my father just to get at his money?" said Ted, his face red, his inadequate chin dimpling.

"Please try not to draw any conclusions from my questions," said

Walter, although that is exactly what he was implying, and he was getting just the reaction he expected. Young Ted was already getting rattled; he was clearly going to be an easier nut to crack than the hard-headed women in his family.

Ted was about to respond when there was a sharp rap on his door, and a secretary popped her head into the office.

"Your wife would like to speak with you, Mr. Braxton," she said.

"Is she here? My phone didn't ring."

"She called on my line."

"That's odd. Well, anyway, please tell her that I'm in a meeting and I'll call her back as soon as I can."

"She said it's urgent, sir, and that I'm to pull you out of any meeting you may be in."

Ted's face took on an expression of genuine concern. "If you'll please excuse me for a moment, Lieutenant; I'm sure it's nothing." He hurried from the office.

Walter used Ted's absence to let his eyes roam around the office. He hadn't spent much time in the offices of well-to-do attorneys, but it was about what he expected. The expensive desk and chair at one end of the room, a large table with chairs for eight at the other end. Both the desk and the table overlooked Sixth Avenue, the city itself lending an air of energy and vibrancy to the office. The walls were covered with photographs, mostly of Ted, Brad Pierce, and his father with one or another important-looking personage, none of whom Walter recognized, except one with Henry Kissinger. There was a large framed photograph facing away from him on the desk, which he assumed was of Ted and his wife.

But it was what he didn't see that struck him most sharply: the almost complete absence of any sign of work being done. His experience with lawyers was that their desks were uniformly piled high with folders and documents, the stock and trade of their profession; but Ted's desktop was clear, as were his inbox and outbox. Before he had any time to consider the implications, Ted returned to the office, and Walter noticed immediately that he was a changed man. Walter felt that he'd been on the verge of having him just where he wanted him: nervous, defensive, angry, and confused, the perfect target for an interrogation. Now he seemed relaxed and unconcerned.

"Everything all right?" he asked.

"Oh, sure. It was just a small matter with some contractors. Sometimes Alicia lets little things get under her skin," said Ted, with an attempt at one of those knowing, "You know how the little women can be," looks.

"I'm glad it was nothing serious."

"Oh, no. Please, don't worry. Now," he said rubbing his hands together and looking expansive, "where were we?"

"I was asking you about your reaction to the will."

"Oh, yes, the will," said Ted, with a dismissive chuckle. "Look, Lieutenant, I'm my own man. I can take care of my wife and myself quite well financially, and what my father chose to do with his money was my father's business. I long suspected that he would expect my sister and me to make our own way in the world, and I fully supported him, of course. The firm of Braxton and Pierce is thriving and so am I, although I may forge a new direction for myself in the future. In the meantime, I have complete faith in my mother to do the right thing with the fortune that my father made."

"So the firm has continued to do well since you father's departure?" said Walter, hoping he kept the incredulity out of his voice.

"My father was an outstanding attorney, and he built a fine firm, a firm built on a solid foundation that could easily withstand his departure, and it has. Brad and I, of course, feel a strong sense of stewardship, and at the risk of sounding prideful, I believe we have done an excellent job."

"It's just that I seemed to notice an awful lot of empty offices around here, and it doesn't seem very busy, that's all."

"Like my father, Brad and I believe in running a lean firm. We've never had a lot of partners or associates. And when you see what has happened to so many of the so-called 'mega-firms' over the past several years, I think you can see the wisdom of our management."

"One of the reasons I'm asking is that when I spoke to Caroline Schuyler recently she indicated that Brad Pierce was a brilliant lawyer, but that your father was the one who was the outstanding promoter and businessman. Should I assume that you took that role over from your father?"

"As I've said, the firm has done just fine under Brad's and my stewardship, and I'm not at all sure that Caroline Schuyler is the appropriate person to be rendering any opinions on the subject."

"Just one final question before I go, if you don't mind," said Walter.

"Please ask anything you wish, Lieutenant."

"I spoke to a man named Russell Brandt recently about the property lawsuit in Westchester County that your father was adjudicating."

"Ah, you mean *Westchester County Homeowners v. FHA.*"

"Yes, that's the one," said Walter. He thought he saw a shadow fall on Young Ted's face, but it passed quickly.

"What about it?"

"You mentioned to me when I visited your family at deGroot Farm that you and your wife had recently purchased a home in Placid Hollow and were in the process of refurbishing it. How will that house be affected by the lawsuit?"

"That's an astute question, Lieutenant, and I'm glad you asked. My wife and I are prudent investors, and of course we were aware of the lawsuit when we purchased the property and factored all the risks into our financial commitment. I have actually spoken to Mr. Brandt myself, since he was an acquaintance of my mother's. I'm not worried about the outcome of the case either way. And, of course, circumstances have changed with the tragic passing of my father. Mother has asked Alicia and me to take up permanent residence at the Cottage. The property is a big responsibility, and Mother would prefer to focus on her charitable work in the future."

"So what will you do with the other house?"

"It depends on the outcome of the lawsuit. If the government prevails, we will graciously accept what they offer us for the property and move on. If not, we will sell it privately. As I've said, that property is only a small part of our portfolio and we're really not all that concerned."

Hudson persisted in the conversation for a few more minutes, but it was apparent to him that he was not going to break through the wall of complacency that had somehow been erected while Braxton was out taking his phone call. But as he walked back toward the lobby, past the empty offices and meeting rooms, he knew that he was being lied to.

The only question was why. And Walter knew only one person who could help him answer that question.

22

"I'D FEEL BETTER IF WE HAD JUST ONE SHRED of physical evidence," said Lieutenant Hudson.

He was sitting, along with Officer Eduardo Sanchez and Leviticus Welles, in a small, windowless meeting room near his cubicle. It was normally used for interrogations, and it reeked of decades of stale coffee and flop sweat.

"Before we start dwelling on what we don't have," said Leviticus, "let's review what we do have."

"That'll be a quick conversation," said Eduardo.

"Maybe, maybe not. Let's see," said Leviticus. "The first thing we have is the .45 that Caroline Schuyler was holding when the police arrived at the scene."

"I don't know what good that does us, since it's not the murder weapon," said Eduardo.

"It almost certainly tells us that on the night of the murder, at least two people entered Judge Braxton's hotel room with the intent to kill him," said Leviticus.

"And it also tells us that at least one of them was a complete amateur, motivated more by emotion and opportunity than by long term thought and planning," said Walter.

"How do you get that?" said Eduardo.

"Because bringing a .45 to a hotel room to commit a murder is like bringing a howitzer to a duck hunt," said Walter. "Anyone with a plan would bring something smaller, lighter and more concealable, never mind easier to handle."

"You're right," said Eduardo, "and now that I think of it, it tells us something else."

"What would that be?" said Levi.

"That we probably have a person out there somewhere, in addition to the murderer him- or herself, who knows who killed the Judge, unless the two people with the guns never crossed each other's path, which I think is improbable."

"We also know that whoever fired the actual murder weapon was an excellent shot, judging from the grouping of the bullets. An amateur just couldn't do that," said Walter.

"And even a .38 packs a kick," said Eduardo.

"But I'm not sure we know anyone beside Caroline who is trained in firearms," said Levi.

"We actually know a lot of people, depending on how you define 'trained,'" said Walter. "Remember, Caroline told me that everyone who came to her father's parties took target practice. Which brings me back to my fear that we haven't even met the killer, despite the probability that it was one of the family. I just can't get Virginia's comment out of my head about all the enemies he made during the course of his life. You know, we keep on hearing about how he was the most charming, charismatic man that anyone had ever met, but at the same time, two people hated him so much that they wanted to murder him on the same night."

"OK," said Levi, "let's move on. We also have that curious smudge of lipstick on the Judge's cheek."

"I didn't ask Caroline about it," said Walter, "but I just assumed that was her lipstick."

"It's gonna be hard to tell," said Eduardo. "The lab report said that it was something called, 'Eros,' by some French company, 'Va Va Hoo Hoo,' or something like that. I was told it's the single most popular brand of lipstick in the world. They said if you did a random check of women's purses, 90% of them would have a tube of that stuff in them."

"Weren't they able to pull any DNA out of it?" said Levi.

"They're still trying," said Eduardo, "but they're not holding out a lot of hope. They said it must have been from a new tube and freshly applied. There might not have been enough saliva residue to get any DNA."

"Yeah, but hold on a minute," said Walter, laying out some of the crime scene photos. He studied them for a few seconds and said, "That's what I thought. You said that lipstick was a really pale pink, right? Look at this picture. Look at Caroline's lips." It was a photo of the crime scene, but Caroline was in sharp focus in the background, sitting forlornly beside Eduardo on the sofa before she had gone back to the bathroom to put her clothes on. He turned it toward Eduardo and Levi.

"I don't see what you're getting at, sir," said Eduardo.

"Perhaps it would help if you'd looked at her lips, Officer Sanchez."

Eduardo blushed deeply and the other two men burst out laughing.

"You see now?"

"Yes, sir," said Eduardo. "The lipstick she's wearing is a lot darker. It's really red, not pink at all."

"But she could have put that on when she was in the bathroom while the murder was taking place," said Levi.

"Let's see," said Walter, pulling out another sheaf of photos. "The hotel security cameras weren't working, but there was a fair amount of press covering the dinner, and we've been able to get quite a few photos. Of course, the *Post* was urgently covering all the good-looking women there for *Page Six*. And............here we are."

He pulled another photo out and turned it toward the other two. It was a picture of the Judge and of Caroline, looking stunning in a black gown with a plunging neckline.

"Same dark red lipstick," said Levi.

"But Lieutenant," said Eduardo, "any number of women could have kissed the Judge on the cheek during the course of the evening."

"You're right, Eduardo," said Levi, "but if you were about to hop into bed with your mistress, don't you think you'd wipe any stray lipstick off your face first?"

"I don't know," said Eduardo, looking around the small room guiltily. "I mean, how should I know? I never had a mistress. I wouldn't even think of it...."

"Eduardo, please," said Walter. "Angelina's nowhere near here."

"Sorry, sir."

"Walter," said Levi, stepping in to save Eduardo from further humiliation, "I know where you're headed here, but we can't get ourselves carried away. Does it place another woman in the room? Maybe. Does that mean that the murderer was a woman who somehow planted a symbolic kiss of death on his cheek? Maybe. But let's not forget that we're a long way from knowing that."

"I know, I know," said Walter. "All I'm saying is that it does increase at least the possibility that the murderer was a woman, a woman who may have been romantically involved with the Judge at some time in the past or, for all we know, currently."

"Which at this point makes at least fifty percent of the women in New York City possible suspects," said Eduardo.

"Don't remind me," said Walter. "I guess all we can do is hope the lab gets lucky and turns up some DNA after all."

"OK, then," said Levi, "is there anything else that either of you have noticed from the crime scene photos?"

"The only thing that I keep on noticing is the dead guy," said Eduardo.

"What about him?" said Walter.

"Well, look at him. He doesn't look like a real live dead guy, you know what I mean? He looks like a dead guy on a movie set, like an actor the director just told to lay down and play dead. His hands are folded over his stomach, his hair looks nice, his feet are together. You know, stuff like that."

"I hadn't noticed that before, but you're right," said Levi, "although it could just be coincidence."

"But it's something we should definitely keep in mind," said Walter. "If someone positioned him, it brings us back to our main theory that it was someone who knew him and was quite possible romantically involved with him. Good catch, Eduardo."

"Be careful about going too far with that theory, guys," said Levi. "Anyone who cared about him may have done something like that, not just someone romantically involved. I'm still betting on someone in the family, or someone very close to the family."

"But who?" said Walter. "The entire family has some kind of motivation. Ted Junior and Alicia were in big trouble with their house if the Judge's decision on the *Westchester County* trial went against them, no matter what he tried to tell me when I went to visit him. Virginia was an emotional mess because of all of his past behavior, and you never know when people like that are going to snap. Brad Pierce obviously had strong feelings for Bunny his entire life, and maybe the affair with Caroline was just the last straw. And again, despite what young Ted said, the law firm was failing, and who knows if one of them or both of them blamed the Judge for that? Even Caroline, despite her alibi, is still a suspect as far as I'm concerned. Who knows if he was about to jilt her? She doesn't impress me as the type of woman who would take that, ah, lying down."

"And then, of course, you have Bunny herself," said Levi.

"Yeah," said Walter, "except that, ironically, even though she was the classic wronged woman, she could have walked away from him anytime she felt like it over the past forty years, and with a pile of money to boot. She was probably the least emotionally damaged of all of them. So why would she kill him now?"

"You're probably right," said Levi. "It's the Hillary Clinton syndrome. The woman knows her husband is a rascal, but for a lot of practical reasons she decides that he's her rascal and chooses to stay with him anyway, and everyone moves on. I can see Barbara Braxton being just that kind of woman. The women who can't tolerate it tend to leave the marriage sooner rather than later."

"Good point," said Walter.

"And of course they all have alibis that check out," said Eduardo.

"I'm not so sure about that," said Levi. "Their alibis all check out if we're just looking at what they told us, but they all kind of run out of gas around midnight of the night of the murder, except Virginia's. And everyone's alibi but Virginia's tends to rely way too much on each other's for support. You've done a great job so far, Eduardo, but there's still more legwork to be done to confirm where they were at the time of the murder."

"Levi's got a good point," said Walter. "We've been kind of sloppy in the alibi department, and we have a lot more work to do. Heaven help me if the commissioner gives me a call before we have more solid info."

"I'll get right on it, sir," said Eduardo. "Sorry."

"Don't apologize, Eduardo, just get on it. And don't let the lab guys off the hook on the DNA analysis, you hear me? They're great guys, but they're busy, and I don't want them giving up on that lipstick."

"Yessir."

"Ok, guys, thanks," said Walter. "I'm going to visit Virginia and see if she can help me figure out what caused Ted Junior's miraculous transformation while I was talking to him at his office. And then I guess I'm going to keep hoping for a miracle. We really need a break here."

They were all standing to leave when Walter's cell phone started to ring. He said, "Hudson," listened for a few short seconds, then said, "Thanks," and hung up.

"It was ballistics," said Walter. "Some guy up in the Bronx handed over a .38 caliber pistol to the local police that his kids found the other day while they were out playing. The cops ignored it for a couple of days before remembering that the Judge was murdered with a .38."

"And?" said Eduardo and Levi simultaneously.

"And they brought it to ballistics, who ran it through some tests."

"And?"

"And it matched up with the bullets recovered from the Judge's body. We have the murder weapon."

"That's terrific," said Levi. "I guess it would be too much to ask, but did they find any prints or markings on it?"

"We're lucky, but not that lucky," said Walter.

"Where'd they find it?" said Eduardo.

"On the Bronx side of Spuyten Duivel, almost directly under the Henry Hudson Bridge."

"Holy crap," said Eduardo.

"Which side of the bridge was it on?" said Levi.

"I don't know," said Walter. "We'll have to find those kids and talk to them. Hopefully they'll be able to show us exactly where they found it."

"It appears that we have the break we've been looking for, gentlemen," said Levi.

"Yes it does," said Lieutenant Hudson.

23

"JESUS," said Alicia Chadwick Braxton, trying to catch her breath. "What was that all about?" She lay on top of the sheets of their bed, her naked body slick with sweat. It was late afternoon, and late day sunshine kissed by the warm spring air streamed through the open window of their bedroom at the Cottage. They had just finished making love for the second time in the last half hour.

"I don't know, but right now I'm not asking any questions," said Young Ted, lying beside her.

"Believe me, neither am I," said Alicia as she rolled toward him and lay her head on his chest. "It's been a pretty eventful day, hasn't it? It's a bit overwhelming, at least to me."

"You can say that again. I'm still trying to believe that all this has happened so quickly and how much our lives have suddenly changed. How did you ever get Mother to agree to all that?"

"It really wasn't all that difficult. Your mother is a very common sense woman and I think she realized that there wasn't much to disagree about. Face it, $100 million changes our lives forever, but it barely makes a dent in your father's estate, so she can still create her charitable trust, and we can all move on. There was just no reason to cause a family crisis."

"Yes, and you know my mother: She puts the welfare of the family before everything."

"She most certainly does. Do you think the financial settlement had anything to do with, you know, what just happened?"

"I'm wondering the same thing, of course," said Ted. "I mean, it's hard to believe it's a coincidence that on the same day that we get the best financial news of our lives my, uh, issues suddenly seem to evaporate."

"But you don't exactly sound convinced."

"I guess that's because I'm not."

"But why?"

"I know this is going to sound funny, Alicia, but I never really let the money issues bother me. It's not like I didn't lose any sleep over them; of course I did. But I always figured we'd find a way to make the dollars and cents work out. Maybe that was naive, but that's the way I felt."

"Then what do you think caused this, you know, change?"

"I really don't know how much I want to psychoanalyze myself, but I'll tell you something that I will never tell anyone else, so I want you to keep this to yourself."

"OK," said Alicia, not at all sure that she wanted to hear what her husband was about to say.

"God forgive me, Alicia, but the happiest day of my life was the day my father died."

"But Ted, you loved your father," said Alicia, feeling her heart start to pound and her mouth go dry.

"Of course I did. He was my father. But he was always looming over me, casting his huge shadow. The better man. More professionally successful, wealthier, more charming, more, you know, attractive to women. Every time I was with him I was reminded of everything that I wasn't."

"Did you always feel like that?"

"I guess to some extent, yes, but for some reason I'll never understand it became totally overwhelming a few years ago, and it just wouldn't go away. I'd have these nightmares, night after night. I could never remember what they were about, but I knew that my father was in them and I'd wake up every morning feeling depressed and exhausted. I'm sorry; I wanted to talk to you about it, but for some reason I just couldn't make myself do it. And then, starting the day after the memorial service, the dreams just went away, and I started waking up feeling really good and, you know, like this." He looked down at himself, and so did Alicia.

"I'd forgotten how, uh, impressive you were," said Alicia, reaching down to stroke him.

"So had I," said Ted, letting out a small gasp at her touch.

"Listen baby," she said, giving his ear a nibble, "I guess we can speculate for the rest of our lives about what happened and why, but I'd rather not waste another minute on all that."

"Neither would I," said Ted. "The past is the past and I'd like to leave it there and move on. We have so much to look forward to." He leaned down and kissed her generous breast.

"Good. Now, come and get me, big boy," said Alicia, rolling onto her back, knowing that all things happen for a reason.

24

THE TWO BIG COPS SEEMED TO FILL THE HOUSE as Marshawn Hill and Patrick Reilly stood, head down, in front of their parents in the tiny living room of the Reilly home on West 227th Street in the Bronx.

They had spotted the unmarked police car parked in front of Patrick's home from a block away as they were walking home from school. Two other friends who had been walking with them scattered at the sight of the car, yelling, "See you when you get out of jail!" as they ran. Images of life in the Big House filled their imaginations as they trudged the rest of the way home. Perhaps they could at least share a jail cell.

"Please, don't worry, any of you," said Officer Eduardo Sanchez. "We're here because we need your help, not because you did anything wrong." He knew he must look like Darth Vader to them standing there, all six feet and two hundred pounds of him in his full uniform, his service revolver hanging from his belt. Lieutenant Hudson wasn't wearing a uniform, just a dark suit, but his sheer mass would intimidate anyone. The boys stared at the immense hands dangling from the sleeves of his suit jacket, the size of Thurman Munson's catcher's mitt they'd seen at the Hall of Fame in Cooperstown the previous summer.

One of the men emitted a huge sigh of relief, although the mothers did not appear placated.

"Officer Sanchez is right," said Hudson. "You boys made an important discovery that could help us solve a major crime, a murder. And now we need you to help us some more, if it's all right with your parents."

The boys seemed to grow two inches as they lifted their heads, stared at each other and then at the two cops. From jailbirds to crime stoppers, just like that! The guys at school would never, ever, in their entire lives, be able to top this. Assisting the cops in an important murder investigation! Their legends would be permanently cemented at David Dinkins Middle School. Perhaps a plaque would be erected in their honor.

"Don't you worry, Officers," said Audrey Hill, her expression unchanged and not sounding impressed, "they will give you their full support." Walter almost laughed out loud. Mothers are the same everywhere, he thought, always ready to bring you down a peg. He could almost hear Martin Luther

King's mother saying, "I've heard you do better," after he gave the "I Have A Dream" speech.

"What we'd like to do," said Sanchez, "is bring them down to Shorefront Park and see if they can show us exactly where they found the weapon. The precise location is critical to our investigation."

"They'll do anything they need to do to help," said Terrell Hill, in his low rumble of a voice, "won't you, boys?"

"Yes, sir," they both replied.

"Thank you, folks," said Hudson. "We'll be sure to have them back before dinner. Then he turned to the boys and said, "Let's hop in the car, boys."

"Go to the bathroom first, both of you," said Patricia Reilly.

—⟨⟨⟨⟨⟨⟩⟩⟩⟩⟩—

The air was warm and the water sparkled brightly in the sun as the two police officers and the two awestruck boys walked toward the river bank. They had ridden in a police cruiser. They were helping the cops with an important murder investigation. Life would never be the same.

"It was right over here," said Marshawn, pointing to a spot only a few feet from the bank of the swirling river.

"Whoever threw it was obviously trying to dump it in the river," said Officer Sanchez.

"Yeah," said Patrick, "but I've been over that bridge plenty of times, and it's really hard to see the river from way up there." They all looked up at the massive structure.

"You're right," said Hudson. "That is a very good observation. What else do you notice?"

"Well," said Marshawn, "they must have thrown it off this side of the bridge, you know the, uh, east side."

"Which means," said Patrick, not to be outdone, "that they were heading north, away from the city."

"That's right!" said Hudson, genuinely impressed. Maybe the New York public schools weren't that bad after all.

"And there's another thing," said Marshawn.

"What would that be?" said Hudson.

"That's a tough throw if you're the driver," said Marshawn, "kind of like trying to turn a double play when you're facing the wrong way. You might not even get the gun out the window, especially since the guy would have to be keeping his eye on the road at the same time."

"Would it have to be a guy?" said Sanchez.

"Guess not," said Patrick, looking dubiously at Marshawn.

"Any other thoughts, guys?" said Hudson.

"Maybe that means there were two people in the car," said Marshawn, "one to drive and one to throw from the passenger side."

Hudson and Sanchez looked at each other. "I'm not sure I would have thought of that," said Hudson.

"Me either," said Sanchez. "Good work, guys. You're both gonna make great cops someday."

And from that moment on, both boys knew that was exactly what they were going to be.

25

VIRGINIA BRAXTON OPENED THE DOOR to her Tribeca townhouse. To Walter Hudson's great relief she was dressed modestly, in a bulky sweater and stylish but loose fitting charcoal gray woolen slacks. Her gleaming brunette hair was pulled back in a ponytail, and if she was wearing any makeup it was too subtle for him to detect. Still, just the sight of her struck him like a physical blow, and for what must have been the tenth time since he left the precinct house, he questioned the wisdom of making this visit.

Last night had not gone well at home. Walter and Sarah had hoped for a quiet evening, with perhaps some time for each other after the kids were put to bed. But little Daniel, after showing some signs of progress for a couple of days, had a terrible time, crying and throwing up the entire evening. Sarah had wound up in tears, retreating to the bedroom with Daniel while Walter served his two unhappy little girls hot dogs and baked beans out of a can. The girls had scampered off to bed without any prompting as soon as dinner was over.

Daniel had finally settled down, and Walter had slipped into bed beside Sarah, hoping to give her a little comfort. But she'd taken the gesture all wrong, and things had gone from bad to worse.

"Sarah, I just wanted to hold you for a little while, that's all," he'd said, but she would have none of it.

"You've been crawling into my bed for fifteen years now, and I know what you want and when you want it," she'd said, her eyes wild with anger and exhaustion. "How can you even think of coming chasing after me for a quick roll in the hay after the day I've had?"

"I'm sorry, Sarah," he'd said, wondering what he was apologizing for, and for the first time in their married life he'd left their bed and gone to sleep on the living room sofa. He'd been positive that she would come out and invite him back in, but she hadn't. Instead, she had remained in the bedroom, positive that he would come back to her. She got up at two to feed Daniel, but Walter had pretended to remain asleep, and when he got up at five to shower and dress she'd done the same. They had gone to bed angry and parted angry, something they had never before allowed to happen, and he felt awful.

"You look like shit, Lieutenant," said Virginia, without a trace of humor. "Please come in." As usual, she had refused to come to the precinct house, and she'd also told him that she was tired of coffee shops and hikes through the city. If he wanted to talk to her, she had told him, he could damn well come to her home and talk.

"Thanks for the compliment," he said. "You, on the other hand, look terrific." The thought had gone from his exhausted mind to his mouth so fast that it took him a second to realize that he'd actually said it.

"Well, thank you," she said, her eyes widening.

"Christ, I'm sorry," he said. "That was rude and unprofessional."

"No need to apologize, just come on in and sit down. I've got some coffee on. Would you like some?"

"That would be great, thanks. I guess I need it."

She showed him into a spacious living room that was twice the size of the tiny one in his and Sarah's home in Queens and went to the kitchen to fetch the coffee while he took a seat in a large, well upholstered chair. He looked around and felt a sudden, poignant sense of his own inadequacy as a husband and a father. The room reeked of success. There were paintings on the wall that, at least to his unpracticed eye, looked original. The furniture wasn't just comfortable; it was designer. The floorboards were original wood that had been painfully, and expensively, refinished. Why can't I be doing better, he thought, if this young woman has been able to achieve this level of comfort and success so quickly? Because I'm a cop who went to night school at Hofstra and got Bs, while she had sailed through Yale and Harvard and then moved up through the bare-knuckled, viciously sexist world of high finance before she was thirty by dint of her own sheer guts and brilliance, that's why. What could she possibly see in him?

Before he had a chance to sink further into abject self-pity, Virginia returned with two large mugs of steaming black coffee and sat in a sofa catty-cornered to his chair. She tucked her legs underneath herself and stared at him, looking like Venus on a half-shell.

"Walter, you look like you just lost your best friend," she said. "Is everything all right? Is there anything you want to talk about?"

"Everything's OK," he said, "just tired, that's all. The little one is still giving us fits with his colic, and we're all a little worn out right now. It'll pass."

"OK," she said. But as she looked at him, he knew that there was precious little that he could hide from the razor-sharp mind lurking behind those luminous eyes.

"I came here to talk about your brother," he said, before the conversation went completely off the tracks.

"Yes, you said. What about my brother? I told you that we're not all that close and never have been."

"I had a very odd conversation with him at his office on Monday."

"What made it odd?"

"Well, when I got there he was defensive, unsure of himself. He was sitting there in that big, empty office looking for all the world like a failure. I hate to say it, but he was just about the way I expected him to be when I first met him. Then his secretary poked her head in the door and told him that his wife urgently needed to speak to him. He was gone for only a few minutes, but when he came back he was a changed man. He was relaxed and confident. He talked about how well the firm was doing under his and Brad Pierce's management, although I've got to tell you, Virginia, it's not like I know a lot about this stuff, but that firm is struggling. Then he made some offhand comments about how, even though the firm was doing well, he might be taking his life in a different direction. And when I asked him about his and his wife's house up in Westchester and the problems with the lawsuit, he just blew it off like it was nothing. It's like someone just told him he'd won the Irish Sweepstakes or something."

"As usual, Walter, your perceptions are dead on," said Virginia, smiling. "He was, in fact, behaving exactly the way you'd expect someone to behave when he'd just been told that he'd come into a one hundred million dollar fortune, after taxes."

"Holy shit," said Hudson. "Excuse my language, but is that what happened?"

"I believe that's exactly what happened, and there's more. He is also going to become the chief executive of the Braxton Family Foundation that my mother is going to announce as soon as she can get the details wrapped up. He will, of course, be paid an appropriate salary for his services, say, a half million dollars a year or thereabouts. Mother will have to find someone who is actually competent to manage the Foundation behind the scenes while Ted and Alicia attend all the right cocktail parties, but that's just a detail."

"I don't get it, Virginia. Why would she have done such a thing? I thought your mother and father agreed that they were against passing their wealth on to their children."

"She did it because Daddy's dead, and she could see clearly what Daddy wouldn't: that Ted's a failure, and she wouldn't stand by and watch him fail. He's her son, after all, and she felt that she owed him at least that much."

"How do you know all this?"

"Because," said Virginia, pausing for effect, "my mother called me up that same afternoon and made me the very same offer. She only would have done that if she'd just made the same arrangement with my brother. You know, fairness and all that. Mother has no real desire to give me a penny, and I don't blame her."

"My God, Virginia. What did you say?"

"I was hoping by now that you would know me well enough not to have to ask," said Virginia. "I said, 'no,' of course. I don't want the money and I don't need the money, and for all the crummy things my father did to me, he did far worse to Ted. Mother knew that."

"What do you mean?"

"Lieutenant, I'm sure you would have discovered this in your own dogged way before you concluded this investigation, so I'll spare you the legwork. My father had a two year affair with Ted's wife, Alicia, before he picked up with dear, innocent Caroline."

Walter sat in stunned silence for a good half minute before saying, "While she was married to your brother?"

"Yes, while she was married to my brother."

"My God. Did Ted ever find out?"

"Not to my knowledge, no, at least not consciously; but as I said, I'm really not that close to him. You know how these things are, though. I'm sure on some level of consciousness he suspected something, but he truly loves Alicia, and his personality would have been destroyed if he ever actually found out; so his mind just wouldn't allow him to see what was fairly obvious, and I pray to God that it never does."

"So do I," said Walter, suddenly shivering at the idea of an unfaithful marriage. He wasn't at all sure that he could survive it any better than Young Ted. "I'd kill the man who ever tried to take Sarah from me."

"Yes, Walter, you would," said Virginia, after a long pause. "But then again, we both know that, unlike my poor brother, you are a fundamentally violent man. It's one of the things I find most attractive about you, if you care to know. Watching you pick poor Mark Glidden up by the throat with one hand and nearly killing him, and knowing that you were doing it for me, was without a doubt the single greatest sexual thrill of my life."

"Which is perhaps why you reacted the way you did."

"Which is definitely why I reacted as I did. I live a carefully self-examined life, Walter, and I've thought of that moment a lot."

"I know, I know. Not a bimbo, right?"

"Right."

"So, anyway, what did your mother say when you said 'no'?"

"She said the worst thing possible, of course," said Virginia, her composure suddenly crumbling as her eyes filled with tears. "She said, 'You're just like your father, aren't you?'"

"Aw, dammit, Virginia, that was awful. I'm sorry. You're not at all like your father was, and you never would have done the terrible things he did."

"You mean like invading the marriage of someone you supposedly love?"

"Yes," said Walter after a long pause. "I guess that's just what I mean."

"You're right, Walter. As always, you're right, damn you."

"Now, come here," said Walter, holding out his arms.

She crawled onto his lap and tucked her head underneath his chin. "Just so you know, all my self-examination hasn't changed my feelings for you. I still love you."

"There are lots of ways you can love a person, Virginia," said Walter Hudson, wrapping his huge arms around her. Angelina Sanchez would have warned him that this was a venial sin, a sin of commission. But what sins aren't?

"Yes, there are. I guess that's something I'll have to keep working on," she said, closing her eyes and melting in to him like butter on toast. But they both knew that whatever spell had come over them in the past week was broken, and that this would be the last time they would ever touch each other.

"So will I," said Walter, "so will I."

But he also now knew that the most charming man that anyone had ever met had in fact been a monster, and his model family had been terribly infected by his poison. And he still had to solve his murder, now more sure than ever that one of the members of that model family had committed the crime, possibly the young woman who was now curled up so warmly on his lap.

He prayed to his God that it wasn't.

26

*

IT WAS LATE IN THE AFTERNOON by the time Walter arrived at de-Groot Farm in Placid Hollow. He was exhausted, and all he really wanted to do was get home to Sarah and the kids. But he was also aware that twelve days had passed since the murder had been committed, and every additional day reduced the already slim prospect of ever solving the crime. He also knew that, in personal terms, his failure to solve such a high profile case would be a career breaker. After the "Points of Light" case last year he had been identified as a young cop on the fast track, future commissioner material. But that would all be over the instant he acknowledged to his superiors that he had failed to solve Teddy Braxton's murder. He had been polite, even deferential to Bunny Braxton in his past encounters. In fact, he had been polite to the entire family, having been gulled into buying into the portrait of the perfect family they had so carefully created. No more.

As he pulled into the driveway he once again saw Albert and Richard waiting for him at the front steps. Albert was, as always, unfailingly polite. Richard, however, seemed surlier than he had been the first time they'd met. He mumbled a barely audible, "hello," when Walter greeted him, and when Walter reached out his hand to give the keys to his cruiser to him Richard surprised him by snatching them away before Walter had a chance to let go fully. It was a high school stunt, but it worked, and the heavy keys scratched Walter's fingers painfully.

"Hey! Watch it!" he said as Richard turned away without apology.

"Sorry, sir," said Richard as he turned back slowly to face Walter, not looking apologetic at all.

"Having a bad day, are you, Richard?"

"No sir, at least not until a couple of minutes ago."

"Richard, really," said Albert, looking appalled. "This is not how we treat our guests."

"I'm not so sure he's someone we'd call a guest."

"Richard! For God's sake!"

"That's all right, Albert," said Walter. "Richard's right. I'm not a welcome guest, am I?"

"That is not for Richard or me to decide, Lieutenant!" said Albert. "Richard, please apologize!"

Richard backed down, but only a little. "Albert's right, of course, as usual, so, okay, I apologize. But that doesn't mean that I have to be happy about it."

"What is it, exactly, that's bothering you, Richard?" said Walter.

"It's pretty obvious, isn't it? Mr. Braxton's dead for almost two weeks, and all you can think to do is pester his poor family. Mrs. Braxton is a great lady, Lieutenant, and she has a wonderful family. They didn't kill Mr. Braxton; they all loved him, just like everybody else who knew him. In the meantime, while you're hounding them, the real killer is out there somewhere laughing his ass off."

"Richard, really," said Albert. "Please go and park the lieutenant's car before I have to report this incident to Mrs. Braxton."

Richard turned away, and as he did Walter said, "Thank you, Richard." Richard turned back around once more, an incredulous look on his face.

"Thanks for nothing, you mean."

"I mean, thank you for your honesty. I may be asking for more of it before I'm done." Richard turned away without saying another word and Walter said, "Okay, Albert, why don't you escort me inside?" It was comforting to know that he could at least get under someone's skin in this family, knowing from years of experience that honesty lives there.

⚜

Walter received his second surprise when he walked into the sun room.

"Good afternoon, Lieutenant," said Bunny Braxton, holding out a hand but not rising. "May I introduce you to my dear friend, Carlton Schuyler."

Carlton Schuyler did not look like a man worth something north of $50 billion, at least not to Walter. In his imagination, billionaires were all tall, good looking, and debonair; always dressed like the people in *New York* magazine, looking like they hadn't lifted anything heavier than their American Express Platinum Cards since Reagan was president. This man was none of that. Walter guessed that he was maybe five-ten or five-eleven. His headful of coarse, thick, salt-and-pepper hair, sitting atop a large square head with blunt facial features, stood up in unruly spikes, despite what looked like more than a few little dabs of Brylcreem massaged into it. He wore jeans that were Levis, not designer, and a plaid short-sleeved shirt that looked like it had been mail-ordered from LL Bean. Caroline had clearly gotten her looks from her mother.

But most of all, the man just looked tough. Walter guessed that he was around Bunny Braxton's age, perhaps early sixties, but his body was still lean, sinewy, and hard. Walter was much bigger and much younger, but as he glanced at Schuyler's still rippling forearms he got the distinct sense that he wouldn't want to tangle with this man, not unless he had to. He'd known kids built like that in his childhood neighborhood of Greenpoint, and he had learned from painful experience that they were the ones that you just didn't mess with. But his eyes sparkled in a way that betrayed the extraordinary intellect lurking beneath the crude exterior, and made his ugly face almost handsome.

"Pleased to meet you, sir," said Walter, reaching out to shake Schuyler's hand. It was one of the rare occasions that a hand as large as his reached out to return the handshake. The man's casual grip was dry, hard and powerful,

"Pleased to meet you, too, Lieutenant," said Schuyler in a surprisingly warm, rich voice, "although I gotta tell you that I'm not the kind of guy who's normally glad to see the cops."

The man's easy humor disarmed Walter, and he felt an immediate liking for him. They were two city boys from tough neighborhoods who understood each other without having to exchange many words.

"Please gentlemen, sit down," said Bunny. "I'll have some coffee brought in."

Walter was suddenly facing an awkward situation. He wanted to talk to Bunny alone, but he was in her home, and he had no right to make any demands. And he wasn't at all sure how to invite a man like Carlton Schuyler to leave a home where he was clearly a welcome guest. He didn't have to worry.

"Thank you, Bunny, but I really have to get going," said Schuyler.

"Oh, Carlton," said Bunny, "I was so hoping that you would be staying for dinner. The children are all busy in the city and I'm going to be here by myself tonight."

"You know how much I would love that, Bunny," he said, his intense eyes looking at her with what Walter could only describe as appetite; and in that instant Walter knew that these two compelling people were more than just friends. They were lovers, and he had interrupted their tryst.

"I really won't be long," said Walter.

"That's OK, Lieutenant; I need to be on my way."

"Actually, Mr. Schuyler, I'd like to have an opportunity to speak to you, too, whenever you have a chance."

"Any particular reason?"

"Only that your daughter was at the murder scene, and I've been told that you were close to the Judge," said Walter. Not to mention, he thought, that your daughter was having an affair with the man, you seem to be having an affair with the man's widow, and you're apparently a gun nut. He felt like a fool for not having chased Schuyler down sooner. More and more, he was beginning to suspect that his interactions with Virginia, and perhaps the tensions at home, had made him less relentless than usual in his investigation. He had some catching up to do, and fast, or he'd find himself being asked questions that he would have a hard time answering.

"No problem," said Schuyler, with an expression on his face that made Walter feel like he'd just had his mind read. "Look, I'm going to be in the city tomorrow. I'll stop by and meet you for lunch if that's OK. My treat. Midtown South, right?"

"That's right, but I can come and see you if it's more convenient."

"Thanks, but I'll stop by. It's near some old stomping grounds of mine and I'd enjoy the visit."

"OK, then, see you tomorrow." Schuyler left the room after giving Bunny a polite kiss on the cheek and murmuring, "Don't worry, I'll call," into her ear. Walter caught a glimpse through the window of Richard driving a monstrous, midnight blue Mercedes SUV up to the front entrance.

Coffee had arrived, and Bunny poured them both a cup as he sat down opposite her.

"Have you made any progress in your investigation?" she said. "I was hoping you had, and that was why you wanted to talk to me."

"Yes, we have," said Walter. "We've made significant progress, in fact."

"Please tell me, then," said Bunny.

"We have found the murder weapon, ma'am."

"But that's wonderful, Lieutenant, where did you find it?"

"We found it on the north bank of Spuyten Duivel, ma'am, almost directly beneath the Henry Hudson Bridge."

"What an odd place to find it," said Bunny. "Did it have any markings or fingerprints that would help you to find out who it belonged to?"

"No, ma'am, unfortunately all markings and fingerprints had been wiped clean, but we were able to establish without a doubt that it is the gun that fired the bullets that killed your husband."

"That's all quite well and good, but what good does that do you if you can't tie it to a potential killer?"

"You're right, ma'am, but we believe that where we found it is an important clue in itself, and that's what I wanted to talk to you about."

"I'm not sure I follow.."

"You see, the exact location where we found the weapon indicates that the gun was thrown from a car off of the east side of the bridge, meaning that the car was traveling north when the gun was thrown from it."

"What makes you think that it was thrown from a car at all? Why couldn't the killer simply have walked down to the river's edge and dumped it there? It wouldn't surprise me if the killer were some low life from that part of the Bronx."

"It just doesn't make sense to us that a killer would do that. He would have just thrown it in the river, where it never would have been found. It makes far more sense to theorize that it was thrown from a moving car, and whoever threw it simply missed the water. As you know, you really can't see the river from that bridge, and it's very narrow."

"Even so, it still doesn't surprise me that the killer would be some common thief from the Bronx. Are you telling me that you're surprised by that?"

"I'm not saying that I'd be surprised, but I also don't think that a common thief from the Bronx would have left a one hundred thousand dollar watch on your husband's wrist. I also couldn't help thinking that the route is on the way here, to Placid Hollow."

"Oh, Lieutenant, are you still on that witch hunt after my family? I believe we have all told you where we were that night, and I have no doubt that you have checked our alibis thoroughly. Why can't you just admit that your pet theory that it was one of us is wrong and broaden your search before the actual killer completely disappears, which I fear he may have done already? I don't think I need to remind you that I am not the only one who will be deeply disappointed if that is the eventual outcome. I believe Mayor Kaplan and Commissioner Donahue will be as chagrined as I."

"You are correct, ma'am, that all of you have excellent alibis that have so far stood up to scrutiny. We have some final details to pursue, but otherwise, I have nothing new to report relative to that subject. One of the reasons that I'm here is that we are performing a thorough review of all the alibis before we broaden our investigation. I would like to review yours, if you don't mind, ma'am, and I'd also like to talk to Albert and Richard before I leave."

"As you wish," said Bunny in a resigned tone.

"Thank you, Mrs. Braxton. I'm very grateful for your patience."

"Please, let's get on with it, then," said Bunny, sounding anything but patient.

"Please tell me again, in as much detail as possible, your activities and whereabouts on the day of the murder, if you don't mind."

"Lieutenant, what do my activities during that day have to do with anything? Poor Teddy wasn't murdered until very late that night, technically the next day."

"Please, ma'am."

"All right. I was up at nine, and I had breakfasted and was out the door by ten-fifteen for a ten-thirty appointment with my personal physician. Richard was driving me, of course."

"Have you been ill, ma'am?"

"It's really none of your business, now is it, Lieutenant. Even under these circumstances I believe that I am afforded the courtesy of doctor-patient confidentiality. But if you must know, it was just a routine visit. I am sixty, and I suffer from all the minor aches and pains that come with attaining that age."

"How long were you there?"

"Only thirty minutes. As I told you, it was merely a routine visit."

"So you left right about eleven?"

"That would be correct."

"And where did you go from there?"

"I went to the offices of Braxton and Pierce to meet with Brad Pierce. Two of my close acquaintances and I are kicking off an effort to fund an organization to support the performing arts in our local public schools. They are suffering terribly what with all the budget pressures. Brad was setting up a 501(c)(3) corporation for us so that all donations would be tax deductible. It's a terribly tedious process, I'm afraid, but necessary."

"And how long were you at the office?" said Walter. He seemed to recall vaguely something in the news about 501(c)(3) corporations, but he couldn't remember exactly what it was.

"We actually went out to lunch. Brad and I are old friends, as you know, and we thought we might as well enjoy a nice meal together while we waded through the minutiae of setting up the corporation."

"Where did you eat?"

"We dined at 'Pagliacci,' my favorite restaurant."

"I think I've heard of that," said Walter. "Isn't that one of those places where you have to make a reservation a year in advance to get a table?"

"I don't make reservations. The owner and I are old friends and I have had their executive chef cater some of my private dinners. I eat there several times a month, so I just sign the check and they send the bill around to the house every month. Would you like to know what I ate?"

"That won't be necessary, ma'am. So you paid for the meal, not Brad? Is that because the firm is struggling?"

"Really, Lieutenant, where *do* you get these ideas? Braxton and Pierce is thriving. So, no, I merely signed the check because I have an account there. It's so much more civilized than using a credit card or, Heaven forbid, cash."

It was the first lie she'd told, at least the first one that he'd been able to detect, but he let it go. "And when did you finish your lunch?"

"Right around two. We dropped Brad off at the office, then Richard and I drove over to the townhouse to pick up Albert before driving up. We arrived around four. It normally doesn't take that long, but you know Friday afternoon traffic in New York in the summertime. It seems like the entire population decamps to cooler locales."

"And you all stayed there the entire evening?"

"No, we did not. Albert and I did, but Fridays are Richard's night off. I give him the use of the car and he normally returns mid-morning on Saturday."

"That's something I hadn't heard yet. Richard was gone the entire evening? Do you have any idea where he went?"

"Oh, please," said Bunny, smiling at him, "you are the suspicious one, aren't you? Richard is gruff but harmless, and he was devoted to Teddy. And yes, I know exactly where he went. He has a girlfriend, for lack of a more refined term, over in Nyack, and he visits her almost every Friday night; and if you must know, yes, he spends the night with her. I have urged him to spare me the details."

"So you and Albert were stuck here without a car on Friday night?"

"Oh, dear, Lieutenant, you get more amusing by the moment. One is not 'stuck' here at deGroot Farm. We are sufficiently provisioned to survive the night. We could probably even manage a second if the need arose, harsh as the conditions may seem."

Walter was being needled, but he didn't mind. "So, if Richard was gone for the night, how did you get back to the city when you received the call concerning your husband early on Saturday morning? Richard still would have been in Nyack, right?"

"Yes, he was," said Bunny. "But of course I have his mobile number, and Albert called him. He was here in fifteen minutes."

Walter closed his notebook and stood up. "Thank you so much for your time, Mrs. Braxton. It was very helpful."

"I really don't see how," said Bunny, remaining seated, "but I'm glad you are satisfied. Perhaps now you can move ahead with your investigation."

"Yes, ma'am," he said, as his eyes wandered over the large collection of photographs that covered the walls, all featuring Teddy Braxton himself during the course of his long and successful career. "My goodness, is that Ronald Reagan?"

"It is, indeed. And that is Margaret Thatcher standing beside him. And this, of course," she said, moving him to another prominent photo, "is President Obama and the First Lady, a woman whom I do not particularly like. He was a beautiful man, my Teddy, wasn't he?"

"I guess I would say that you were a very good-looking couple," said Walter, not being the type of man who cared to comment on the beauty of other men. He continued to stare at the photos, mesmerized by the images of the Braxtons with the high and the mighty.

He was interrupted once again as if by some dog whistle of a signal, Albert appeared at the door.

"If you are leaving, Lieutenant, I will have Richard bring your car around."

"Actually, Albert, if you don't mind I'd like to have a few minutes of your time before I leave."

Albert's eyes quickly shifted in Bunny's direction, and Bunny said, "Please, Albert. As you know, we have promised Detective Hudson our full cooperation. Please spend as much time with him as he requires. I trust you will be completely forthright in your responses to his questions. Perhaps then he will be persuaded to cast his net somewhat wider in his search for the Judge's murderer."

"Yes, ma'am, of course," said Albert. "Please come with me, Lieutenant. Perhaps you wouldn't mind talking to me in my private quarters. That way we can leave Mrs. Braxton in peace."

"Thank you, Albert, that's a wonderful suggestion," said Walter.

<hr>

ALBERT LED HIM down a long hallway that led to the rear of the house. There was a door on the right side just before they got to the kitchen and Albert opened it.

"Please come in," said Albert, standing aside and ushering Walter in.

Walter wasn't sure what he had expected a servant's quarters to look like. Perhaps he'd watched too many episodes of "Downton Abbey" with Sarah, but it certainly wasn't anything like this. The door opened into a spacious living room, well-furnished in a style that evoked a comfortable old men's club, dominated by leather upholstery and dark, heavy-looking wood. The late springtime sun poured in through large windows and bathed it in light. Through an open doorway he glimpsed a spacious kitchen, decorated attractively, if a little incongruously, in French Country style. Another hallway led to what Walter assumed to be the bedroom. The walls were adorned with photos, once again dominated by Teddy and Bunny Braxton, but this time with a family theme. But what caught his attention the most were the older photos, of Teddy and Bunny as a young couple. Yes, Teddy had been a handsome man, Walter quietly conceded, but Bunny had been stunning. He wasn't surprised; at sixty she was still a head-turner. There were also much older pictures.

"Albert, I don't mean to be nosey, but is that a picture of you and Mrs. Braxton?"

"Please, Lieutenant, it's your job to be nosey, after all," said Albert, "and yes, that is a photo of Mrs. Braxton and me." Walter couldn't help but notice the expression of warm affection that softened Albert's face as he gazed at the picture.

"How old were you when it was taken?"

"I believe we were both fifteen in that photo."

"Albert–I hope you don't mind me calling you 'Albert,' but it just occurred to me that I don't even know your last name; how long have you worked for the Braxton family?"

"My family name is 'Montcrief,' Lieutenant, but I beg you to continue to call me 'Albert.' Very few people in my life have called me Mr. Montcrief, and they were uniformly people I didn't like. As for your next question, I don't mean to sound opaque, but I'm not sure I've ever 'worked' for the Braxton family. I have been a part of the deGroot household since the day I was born, and I have always played what I hope has been an important role in the daily life of the family. I have never considered it work, and I have always considered deGroot Farm my home, not my place of employment. Please don't misunderstand me; I have always had a great deal of admiration and respect for Judge Braxton. Indeed, this wonderful home would have been lost if the Judge had not saved it. He was a great benefactor to the entire deGroot family."

"I'm struggling here, Albert."

"Excuse me, I'm afraid I've been a bit obtuse, haven't I? My father was Mr. Matthew deGroot's personal butler, and my mother was Mrs. deGroot's personal assistant."

"And they were?"

"They were Bunny's, Mrs. Braxton's, parents."

"Matthew deGroot committed suicide, right?"

"That is correct," said Albert, still wincing at the memory. "My father was the one who identified his body. I'm afraid Father was never the same after that. I think he always thought that he should have been able to prevent it all somehow."

"I'm sorry," said Hudson. "So you grew up with Mrs. Braxton then?"

"Yes, I did. Of course, she went off to private schools when she was fourteen, and I attended the local public schools, but other than that, we were inseparable."

"It must have been a lovely way to grow up."

"Ah, it was. Westchester County was a different world back then, much quieter, far more rural in character. Of course, we always kept horses here on the farm, and Bunny and I would pass the summers riding through the countryside and sailing on the Hudson. It was positively idyllic."

"You must have developed a terrible crush on her," said Walter, taking a guess. "Judging from the photos, she was a beautiful young woman."

"I guess you could say I was the test model," said Albert, a rueful smile coming over his face as his mind's eye looked back through the years. "Mine was the first heart she stole, and mine was the first heart she broke. But of course there was nothing for it, given that we held such vastly different social positions."

"It must have been difficult to find someone who could take her place."

"As it turned out it was impossible, and I found myself unwilling to compromise. After all, it would have been unfair to the other woman, now wouldn't it? I don't think I could have kept it a secret that anyone else was just a second best. But I'm sure you didn't come here to learn about my ill-starred love life."

"You're right, Albert," said Walter. But I did, he thought. And now he'd identified at least three men—Albert, Bradley Pierce, and Carlton Schuyler— who would rather remain bachelors than try to love any woman other than Barbara deGroot Braxton. Apparently, her husband had been the only man in the world she couldn't hold on to. The question was, was one of them willing to kill for her?

He chatted with the man for another half hour, confirming Bunny Braxton's account of her activities on that Friday and also verifying Richard's alibi, including the woman's name and address.

"She's a rather odd woman, but she's nice enough," he said. "They've been together for years. And please don't draw any conclusions from Richard's untoward behavior. He's essentially a kind, utterly harmless man and, strange as it may seem, he was probably more devoted to Judge Braxton than anyone. The Judge found him working at a local garage for slave wages and brought him here. He would have died for the man and he never, ever, would have harmed him, never mind kill him."

"Thank you, Albert. I think I've taken up enough of your time."

"Not at all, Lieutenant."

As they were walking toward the door, Walter noticed a photo that hadn't caught his eye before.

"Is that you, Albert?"

"Didn't have me pegged for a soldier?" said Albert, smiling.

"No, it's not that...."

"Please, don't worry. I didn't either. I was drafted near the end of the

Vietnam War. They were the only two years I've ever spent away from this place."

"Did you serve in Vietnam?"

"Yes, I did."

"Were you infantry?"

"Actually, I was a sniper. It turned out that I was a good shot, which was surprising since I'd never so much as picked up a gun before I got to basic training, and I've never picked up one since. At the end of my two years they asked me to re-up and become an instructor, but I was too eager to come home."

"Did you ever actually kill anyone?" Walter knew veterans hated to be asked that question, but it was important for him to know.

Albert's face showed a brief flash of anger, but he controlled it and said, "The Army taught me duty, Lieutenant. I did my duty, nothing more, and nothing less."

When they walked out the front door Walter's car was there waiting for him, already running, as if Richard didn't want to give him any excuses not to leave immediately. Richard, however, was farther down the driveway, working on another, smaller car. It was painted yellow, and the late afternoon sunlight gave it an incandescent glow. Walter walked over.

"This is a beautiful car," he said. "What is it?"

"It's a 1975 Mercedes Benz 450SL," said Albert from behind him. "Do you like it?"

"It looks like it just came off the showroom floor."

"That's the original paint from the Mercedes factory," said Albert, "and look at this." He opened the driver's side door and asked Walter to look in. "Look at the odometer."

Walter looked. It was an old analog readout that showed 18,500 miles.

"Those are the original miles. Did you find a problem today, Richard?"

"No, just a rear brake light was burned out, that's all."

"That's funny," said Albert, "I never even noticed that."

Richard hesitated for a second and then said, "Well, anyway, it's fixed now."

"Parts for that car must be hard to find," said Walter.

"Not really," said Richard, looking up from his work, a friendlier expression on his face. "Mercedes keeps parts in stock for all their cars going back to the fifties because there are so many of them still on the road. They're just expensive, that's all."

"Do you still drive it?" said Walter, turning to Albert.

"Not much, though it's still in mint condition, and Richard keeps it running beautifully. When I first got it I'd take it out on the roads and let it perform, like a healthy thoroughbred, but now I only take it out in the warm weather. I don't think it's left the Placid Hollow village limits in twenty years. I've had a lot of offers for it, but I like it too much, and Bunny loves to ride with me into the Village with the top down in the summertime when she has errands to run. It's worth keeping it, just for that."

Walter looked at the man, saying nothing. Albert looked back, feeling Walter's eyes on him.

"Yes, Lieutenant," he said, "you don't have to ask. Of course I do."

AS WALTER HUDSON was leaving the village limits of Placid Hollow he reached for his mobile phone and dialed a familiar number. He knew he wasn't supposed to be using the phone while he was driving, but he figured there had to be some privileges to being a cop.

"Hey, Eduardo," he said as the phone was picked up at the other end.

"Hey, Lieutenant, what's up?"

"I have a couple of things I need you to check out for me."

27

POLICE STATIONS GIVE ME THE CREEPS, LIEUTENANT. Let's get out of here and I'll buy you a real lunch," said Carlton Schuyler. He was wearing what looked like the same jeans he'd been wearing the day before and a denim shirt. The shirt had a logo of a cowboy bronco riding a 1957 Chevy stitched into the left-hand breast pocket, with the name "Fred" sewn in just above it. It looked like it pre-dated the Bush presidency—the George H.W. Bush presidency. Walter decided not to ask.

They walked out of the precinct house and turned right on West 35th Street, then turned right again and walked up 9th Avenue. It was not the direction that Walter had expected to take. He'd worn his best shirt and tie and his newest Men's Wearhouse suit today, assuming that when a man worth more than most Central American nations invited him out to lunch, it would be someplace on the order of Delmonico's. But then again, he doubted even a man with Carlton Schuyler's clout could get into Delmonico's dressed as he was. They walked north on 9th Avenue until they reached 41st Street and then turned left--another shock. All the famous Times Square neighborhood restaurants and delis were east, over on Broadway and 7th Avenue. Walter noticed that the farther they traveled west, the more Schuyler seemed to hunch his shoulders and keep his head ducked in an instinctive defensive posture, his eyes furtively scanning the street. Hell's Kitchen was gentrifying rapidly, but there was still enough of the old neighborhood left to give Walter a feel for what it used to be like. About halfway between 10th and 11th Avenues, they ducked into a door that had "Hell's Diner" etched in faded orange paint on its glass pane.

The inside of the place was small, hot, and crowded. It had a counter with stools bolted to the floor along its length, and maybe ten small booths looking out onto 41st Street, only one of them empty. Walter felt ridiculous in his jacket and tie and began taking them off as they walked to the booth.

"Junior!" boomed a voice so loud it made Walter jump as they squeezed into the booth. It came from a surprisingly small black man standing behind the counter with a large spatula in his left hand.

"Deacon, my man!" said Schuyler, standing and reaching across the counter to high five the man.

"When did you start hangin' with the cops, Junior?" Luckily, the place was so noisy that few of the customers heard it. The few who did eyed Walter suspiciously. He was in mufti, and he hadn't worn his gun, but he didn't have to ask how he'd been immediately spotted as a cop. In neighborhoods like this, just like the one he'd grown up in, you learned how to spot a cop before you learned how to ride a bike.

"Walter, meet Deacon Jones, my oldest friend. His real name is Micah, but he's been Deacon since we were kids. Deacon, meet Walter Hudson, not a bad guy, all things considered."

"Pleased to meet you, Walter," said Deacon, holding out his hand. Walter reached out to shake the man's hand and he felt his arm go numb from the elbow down as his hand was enclosed in a crushing grip. Walter had always trained himself to be careful not to hurt others when he shook hands, and he'd never felt a grip like Deacon's. He could only imagine what it would have felt like if the man had actually squeezed.

"What can I get you gentlemen?" said Deacon. "I'm sorry to say that we're all sold out of paté de foie-gras."

"I would strongly suggest that you order the Reuben sandwich made with brisket, a side of fries, and a serving of slaw," said Schuyler.

"Sounds good to me," said Walter, thinking that Sarah would be appalled.

"That'll be two," said Schuyler. A waitress in a green uniform came by and gave them each a place setting and a glass of ice water. They each ordered a cup of coffee.

"Junior?" said Walter.

"Lieutenant, my birth name was Karl Schmidt, Junior. No middle name. Pop figured if he didn't have one we didn't need one either."

"Who's we?" said Walter.

"My older brother and me. My only sibling."

"What was his name?"

"Karl Schmidt, Junior. Pop didn't have much of an imagination."

"So what did you call him?"

"Everybody called Pop 'Smitty,' so we just called my brother Karl."

"He still live around here?"

Schuyler paused before answering. He looked out the window and pointed. "See that store across the street with the blue sign over it that says, 'Dry Cleaning'?"

"Yeah," said Walter, looking out.

"It wasn't a dry cleaner back then, but my brother was shot dead in front of that store. He was sixteen and I was twelve. I was standing on the sidewalk right outside this window."

"My God, that's terrible. Was it a gang shooting?"

"Nah. My brother wasn't very bright, but he wanted to be a big shot. So he took it upon himself to try to pimp out a couple of whores. Problem was, these ladies already had representation, so to speak, who were not too pleased with this development. They politely asked my brother to desist, and my brother politely told them to fuck off. End of Karl. End of story."

"I'm sorry. That must have been awful for your family."

"By that time Pop was already dead from drinking too much cheap booze, and Karl hadn't lived at home since he was fourteen, but yeah, it was tough on Ma. But what can I say? The guy was a jerk."

"But you loved him anyway."

"You're damn right I did."

Their lunches arrived, and conversation stopped as the men dug in. The sandwich was hot, greasy, and exploding with flavor. The fries were thick, crisp, and sizzling. Walter let out something like a groan.

"Heh?" said Schuyler, as Deacon looked on, smiling.

"This is amazing," said Walter. He looked over at Deacon and said, "You're a genius." Deacon's smile grew even wider.

"Always happy to keep New York's Finest satisfied," he said.

"I'll tell you what, Lieutenant," said Schuyler. "If you can find any restaurant in this city that serves you a bite of food that tastes better than that, I'll buy the place and give it to you."

"I won't even try," said Walter as he wolfed down the remainder of the lunch. "So you eat here a lot?"

"Oh, probably once a week. I'm a busy man, and I can't get here as often as I'd like."

"I take it you grew up around here somewhere."

"If you have a little more time," said Schuyler, standing up and throwing two twenties on the table, "I'll show you."

They waved goodbye to Deacon as they left, and Schuyler said, "Friday night?"

"Wouldn't miss it," said Deacon.

"Good. See you then. And be prepared to lose."

"That'll be the day," said Deacon Jones.

They walked to the corner of 41st Street and 11th Avenue, where an old six-story brick tenement stood.

"What's this place?" said Walter.

"Home," said Schuyler. "I own the whole building now. I've refurbished the first five floors, and I'm renting them out to Millenials for twenty-five hundred dollars a month. Apparently they love saying they live in Hell's Kitchen. The sixth floor was where I grew up, and I've kept it the way it was. The elevators won't take you there. It was a walkup then, and it's a walkup now. Think you can make it?"

"I think I can manage," said Walter.

By the time they got to the sixth floor Walter was winded but he tried not to show it, since Schuyler's breathing hadn't changed at all.

The apartment was obviously the attic when the building was first built. The ceiling was low and there were only two rooms, a kitchen/living/dining area and a small bedroom in the back. The furniture was old, but the tiny kitchen area contained a modern refrigerator and range.

"Can I get you anything, Lieutenant?" said Schuyler. "I don't drink myself, but I keep beer and wine here for the guys. I've also got water and soft drinks."

"Actually, a glass of water sounds good after that meal," said Walter.

"Me, too," said Schuyler as he took two glasses from the cupboard, put a couple of ice cubes in each, and poured water from the tap. They sat down, and Walter found the chair in which he was sitting surprisingly comfortable.

"I got the furniture reupholstered," said Schuyler, reading his mind.

"So I guess I don't have to ask you why you changed your name," said Walter. "When did you do it?"

"As soon as I turned eighteen. Ma died just before I graduated from high school. I knew I wanted to go to college, and I knew I wanted to work on Wall Street by then, and I wasn't sure Karl Schmidt, Junior from Hell's Kitchen would get me there."

"Did many of your friends graduate high school?"

"Not many, but it wasn't because they weren't smart enough. They just had to start working. I was lucky. School always came easy to me, so I was able to work full time to support Ma and me and still keep up with my studies. I think I got my brains from her. She was always reading books in German and Polish, heavy stuff: poetry and philosophy."

"What did your father do for a living?"

"He was a longshoreman when he was sober, which wasn't often. I don't think my father was a bad man, and I don't think he was stupid; he was just a drunk. Ma made me promise never to touch the stuff, and I never have. Not that I ever wanted to. Like I said, I had goals."

"Deacon mentioned something about 'Friday night,'" said Walter. "What's that all about?"

"Friday nights are poker nights. Deacon, me, and a few of the other guys from the old neighborhood get together here on Friday nights to eat pizza and play cards. We almost never miss a night. We meet here about nine, and we usually don't break up until around two or three."

"And you were here the night of the murder?"

"Yes, I was, and I've got four upright citizens who are willing to back me up."

"But they're your friends. They'd all probably lie for you, right?"

"They probably would, but they don't have to," said Schuyler as he retrieved Walter's water glass and brought them back to the kitchen. "Look, Lieutenant, I know you have every reason to suspect me. Teddy Braxton and I were old friends, but then he started that affair with my daughter, and I hated him for it. Hated him. You also know I'm a gun enthusiast, and, not to brag, but I'm a terrific shot. Not quite in my daughter's league, but damn close."

"And you're also in love with Bunny Braxton," said Walter.

Schuyler froze, but he never lost eye contact with Walter. He was silent for a few seconds, then Walter saw his shoulders almost imperceptibly relax.

"Yes, Lieutenant, yes I am."

"How long have you been having an affair with her?"

"A long time. You know that I lost my wife over twenty years ago."

"Yes, I do. And you were happily married, right?"

"Yes, we were. I was worth a few hundred million dollars when she was diagnosed with cancer, but I couldn't do a damn thing about it. It turns out that, unlike most people, cancer can't be bought off. Losing Doris almost destroyed me. Bunny saved me. She was so kind. She spent time with me, she listened to me, and eventually I listened back. By then she knew that Teddy was a serial tomcat and that he was never going to change. She was lonely and I was lonely. She was irresistible. She still is."

"Are you planning to get married now that the Judge is dead?"

"Yes, we are, but we feel as though there has to be a decent interval first."

"Did your daughter know that the affair was going on?"

"No she did not, and to my knowledge no one else ever did either. Unlike Teddy, we were very discreet."

"So despite everything," said Walter, "all those motivations, you still deny that you murdered Teddy Braxton."

Schuyler stood up and walked over to the window overlooking 11th Avenue. He stared out for a few seconds and then turned back to Walter. "Lieutenant, I had a violent upbringing in a violent place. I have committed acts of violence in my lifetime that discretion prevents me from sharing with you. But no, I did not kill Teddy Braxton. If I'd wanted him dead I would have done it much more efficiently than a shooting in a hotel room with my daughter present. He simply would have disappeared without a trace. I'm not bragging. I'm just telling you."

"I've got one last question, if you don't mind," said Walter, not doubting the man, but not wanting to admit it out loud.

"Go right ahead."

"Do these people in the neighborhood, Deacon and the others who come over here for cards, do they know who you really are?"

"Yes, Lieutenant, they do," said Carlton Schuyler, "which is why I still come here. They know who I really am."

28

❧

THE MAÎTRE D' AT PAGLIACCI did not look pleased to see Lieutenant Hudson come through the door only a few minutes before the restaurant opened for lunch. Just as he had with Deacon Jones at Hell's Diner, he felt like he was wearing a sign stuck to his forehead that said, "Cop," not to mention that his inexpensive suit and polyester shirt and tie labeled him as a less than lucrative customer and a lousy tipper.

"I'm sorry, sir," said the woman, whose nametag said, "Beth." She was wearing black slacks, a heavily starched white cotton shirt, a tightly knotted black necktie, and a vest as well as an expression on her otherwise attractive face that indicated that she was prepared to become unpleasant if necessary, "but we have not yet opened, and all our tables are taken for today's lunch hour."

"Good morning, ma'am," said Walter. "I am Detective Lieutenant Walter Hudson of the NYPD, and unfortunately, judging by the smells coming out of that kitchen, I'm not here for lunch."

"Then how may I help you, Lieutenant?" said Beth, her expression turning wary.

"Two weeks ago a regular guest of yours, Mrs. Barbara Braxton, came in to dine with a Mr. Bradley Pierce. I'd like to talk to the waiter who served them."

"And may I ask why?"

"No, you may not. As the maître d', and I'm sure a very good one, I'm sure you recall Mrs. Braxton's visit and who served her and Mr. Pierce. I'd like to speak to that person. Alone, please."

"Lieutenant Hudson, I'm not at all sure……"

"I'm not going to ask again, Ms.?"

"Gardner."

"I'm not going to ask again, Ms. Gardner."

He didn't have to say anything more. She knew what the drill would be if she didn't cooperate: Board of Health visits at awkward hours. Immigration officers storming in through the back of the kitchen at peak hours, leaving food burning on the stove and heaps of dirty dishes and cutlery by the dishwasher as half their staff fled through the front door in full view of the diners. And most importantly of all, she would be fired. She wasn't being paid a six-figure salary just to smile at guests as they arrived. She was being paid to handle situations just like this.

"I have just one favor to ask, Lieutenant."

"Ask away."

"I recall Mrs. Braxton's visit clearly. One of our best waiters, Raimondo, waited on her and Mr. Pierce. I would ask that you not ask Raimondo about his immigration status."

"Are you telling me that he is undocumented, Ms. Gardner?"

"No, I am not. I am simply making a straightforward request."

"Ms. Gardner, the objective of my visit is not to inquire about Raimondo's, or anyone else's, immigration status, and I have no reason to believe there is any cause for me to do so at this time. Please feel free to make sure Raimondo is aware of that fact."

She looked at him and nodded silently. He nodded back. She was good at her job, and she had handled the situation well, he thought. She was worth whatever they were paying her.

"Wait here," she said as she walked back toward the kitchen.

—⊶⊷—

Raimondo Flores looked nervous as he sat down with Lieutenant Hudson at a back table near the kitchen. He was a distinguished looking man in his thirties, and Walter guessed that he was probably married, with a couple of kids, trying to live out the American dream on the immigrant tightrope. If he fit the standard profile, he and his wife were probably both illegal, but their kids were probably native-born Americans. Life was tough enough in this city, thought Walter. No matter what he thought of the whole immigration issue, he had to admire the sheer fortitude of New York's Raimondos, who worked in the shadows and were an indispensable lubricant to the city's machinery.

"Thank you for agreeing to speak with me, Mr. Flores," said Walter, trying to sound as unthreatening as possible. "I have only a few questions and then I'll let you get back to your work."

Raimondo nodded silently.

"Have you served Mrs. Braxton before, Raimondo?"

"Oh yes, many times. She's a regular customer, and I am always her server."

"Has she come in here with Mr. Pierce before?"

"Maybe once or twice. I recognized him, but he's not a regular customer."

"Does she ever come in with this man?" said Walter, showing him a photo of Carlton Schuyler.

"Oh, yeah, lots," said Raimondo, his face breaking into a smile. "He's a funny guy. He always says to me, 'Raimondo, this is an Italian restaurant, right? So why don't you have spaghetti and meatballs on the menu?' One day the chef heard him say that, and he quick made some up and served it to him. Mr. Schuyler said it was the best spaghetti and meatballs he ever had. The chef, he says, 'It better be. My Mama taught me how to make that in the kitchen of our tenement on the Lower East Side. Mama is still the best cook I ever met.' Mr. Schuyler, he clapped his hands and said, 'Bravo.' Like I said, he's a funny guy." Walter was beginning to think that Carlton Schuyler was a lot more charming than his daughter had led him to believe.

"Mr. Flores, what do you recall about the demeanor of Mrs. Braxton and Mr. Pierce on that day? I mean, did they appear happy? Friendly? Relaxed?"

"No, sir," said Raimondo, hesitantly. "I don't think so. They seemed, you know, serious."

"Do you recall if they brought any documents with them to review while they ate?"

"No, not that I remember. They just leaned over the table across from each other and talked, you know, quiet like."

"Did you hear anything that they said?"

"No, I did not, Lieutenant," said Raimondo, sounding more than a little offended. "It was clearly a private conversation, and I left them alone. I wouldn't last long on this job if my customers thought I was eavesdropping on them."

"Do you remember what they ordered?"

"Mr. Pierce ordered the sea bass, but Mrs. Braxton only ordered a small antipasto."

"Is that what she always orders?"

"No, that's why I remember so clearly. Mrs. Braxton, she has a wonderful appetite. She always orders an appetizer, main course, and dessert, and she always eats every bite."

"And what about on that day, did she at least finish her salad?"

"No, she didn't. She ate maybe a couple of bites. And Mr. Pierce never touched his meal. What a waste of a fine piece of fish, you know?"

29

THE FOOD AT THE 9TH AVENUE DELI wasn't as good as what he'd eaten at Hell's Diner, but then again, not much he'd ever eaten was. But the 9th Avenue Deli made up in proximity for what it lacked in flavor, and he'd decided that, as much as he wanted to go back to Hell's Diner, the last thing Deacon Jones needed was for the place to develop a reputation as a cop hangout.

There had been a message waiting for him to call Levi Welles when he got back to his cubicle. It was almost past lunchtime, and he was starved after inhaling the delectable aromas at Pagliacci, so he'd called Levi and asked him to meet for lunch at the deli. They'd both ordered corned beef and Swiss on rye with a side of coleslaw, and Walter had also ordered fries. The food was good, and the view out the window onto the Garment District was always fascinating.

"So how goes your investigation?" said Levi, tucking into his sandwich.

"I'm collecting a lot of information, but I can't seem to make it come together," said Walter as he worked on his fries. He told Levi what he'd learned about Ted Junior and his wife from his last conversation with Virginia.

"I'm speechless," said Levi, putting down his sandwich.

"Join the club."

"Have you been able to eliminate anybody yet?"

"Not really. We've scrubbed everyone's alibis, and they all held up pretty well. The problem is, they all depend on the confirmation of a relative or an acquaintance, and they all tend to turn into pumpkins around midnight, when everyone except Carlton Schuyler and Virginia claim to have turned out the lights and gone to sleep. And of course, that's when the murder took place. So everyone has an alibi and no one has an alibi."

"But you remain convinced that the murderer was either a member of the family or a close acquaintance of the family?"

"Absolutely, Levi, especially after that conversation with Virginia. There are too many squirrely dynamics going on inside that family to think that it wasn't. It's turning out that The Perfect Family is anything but that, and anyway, statistically, murders like this are almost always committed by a family member or a friend. And if it is someone else, I'm cooked, because I'll never find him at this point."

"Might I suggest," said Levi, finishing off his last forkful of coleslaw, "that you focus more closely on Teddy's last day, from the beginning right up to the time of his murder?"

"Actually, I've had the same thought. Up to now, my theory of the crime is that the motivation goes much farther back and much deeper into the family history, but I've made an appointment with Caroline Schuyler to go over his schedule for that Friday to see if it might yield anything."

"I think that's a good move. At worst, no one will be able to accuse you of not covering all the bases."

"And there are plenty of people pretty eager to do just that. Frankly, I'm not pleased with the way I've handled this case. Normally, that would have been one of the first things that I would have done, but I've allowed myself to get distracted, and I've got a lot of catching up to do."

"By the way, speaking of distractions, how are things going with the Virginia Braxton situation? You don't have to talk about it if you don't want to."

"It's all right, Levi. In a way, it's pertinent to the case. I think we have things straightened out between us, and in a lot of ways it's because of Teddy's death. I don't mean to sound medieval, but it's like Teddy Braxton had cast a spell over that entire family, and now that he's dead they're all starting to wake up from it. Virginia is a brilliant, and essentially good, young woman, and I think she's beginning to realize that her feelings for me were to a great extent a result of her badly dysfunctional relationship with her father. And I have to understand that my feelings in return were a result of everything going on at home. It will all pass, and we're both happier for it."

"I'm glad to hear it, for both your sakes."

"So am I."

"And you haven't eliminated her as a suspect yet?"

"No, Levi, I haven't."

"Just so you know, I don't see her for it."

"Just so you know, neither do I."

They were just about to get up and pay the check when Levi's cell phone rang. He listened for a few seconds and said, "That's interesting," all the while looking at Walter. He hung up without saying goodbye.

"What was that all about?" said Walter.

"I think you might have a very interesting head start on learning about Teddy Braxton's last day."

"What do you mean?"

"I just got a call from a contact inside the administrative offices of the circuit court."

"And?"

"And at eight-fifteen on the morning before his death, Teddy Braxton sent in a letter formally announcing his resignation from the district court, effective immediately."

30

CAROLINE SCHUYLER SEEMED OBLIVIOUS TO THE STARES as Lieutenant Hudson escorted her to his cubicle in the detectives' squad room of Midtown South Precinct headquarters. She was dressed modestly in a navy blue pinstriped business suit, but she was a striking woman no matter what she wore, and too many of the detectives had seen the crime scene photos. He brought her a cup of coffee once she was seated. She didn't flinch when she took her first sip.

"I'm impressed," he said.

"By what?"

"By the fact that you didn't gag on the coffee. Most people think it's an interrogation tool when they taste it."

Caroline laughed that throaty laugh of hers and said, "That's only because they never tasted my father's coffee. He still makes it from the same old percolator that was in the tenement he grew up in. He says nothing else tastes like real coffee to him. Speaking of which, Daddy told me that you met him and that he showed you the old place and that he also treated you to a Reuben at Hell's Diner."

"He most certainly did. Don't tell me you've ever eaten there."

"Lieutenant, I'm an elite athlete. My body is a finely tuned machine. So you bet I have. When I train I need all the calories I can get, and Hell's Diner serves me the tastiest calories I've ever eaten. I'm my father's daughter, after all."

"Your father's quite a guy, so I guess that's a good thing."

"I guess it is, too," said Caroline. "I wish I hadn't disappointed him so."

"How are you doing, Caroline?"

"I'm doing much better. Thank you for asking, Lieutenant. A woman in my position doesn't necessarily warrant anyone's concern."

"Well, you still have a right to your grief, even if you have to keep it to yourself."

"You know what?" said Caroline, looking at him with those remarkable blue eyes, "I'm not sure I ever grieved. The only feeling I recall experiencing at the time was relief, and now I don't feel much of anything at all, except maybe....... puzzlement, for lack of a better word."

"Puzzlement?"

"Lieutenant, you seem like a pretty thorough investigator, so I'm going to assume that you've learned enough about me and my past to know that my affair with Teddy Braxton was the most uncharacteristic thing I've ever done in my life. I look back at that episode now, and it's like I'm watching someone else doing all those things. I'm a religious person, and I think I'm a fundamentally ethical person, so I must, and I do, take complete responsibility for my behavior. But it just wasn't me, Lieutenant. That is not who I am. It's like I dreamed the whole thing and now I'm awake, but I can't shake off the dream. I'm embarrassed, I'm ashamed and, most of all, I am utterly at a loss to explain myself. Barbara Braxton was like a second mother to me, and now I'm not sure I can ever look her in the eye again. I'd do anything to make it up to her."

"Just so you know, you're not the only person to feel that way, not by a long shot."

"I guess someday I might find that comforting, but not right now."

"Caroline, I don't want to take up too much more of your time, so would you mind if I asked you a few questions?"

"Not at all. That's why I'm here."

"I'm trying to put together Teddy Braxton's last day to see if it will offer any clues to what happened. Since you were his clerk, I was hoping that you would be able to help me with that."

"I'll help you where I can, but I'm afraid this isn't going to be easy."

"Let's see how we do, OK?"

"OK. We both got into the office around seven-forty-five and had a cup of coffee while I updated him briefly on the status of a couple of cases. Then he went to his chambers and was there, I presume by himself, from eight to eight-thirty. He came out and told me that he had a nine o'clock meeting with Brad Pierce at the offices of Braxton & Pierce that would last until about nine-thirty. He then asked me to meet him at his Park Avenue townhouse at ten. We were there together until about one o'clock. Please don't make me tell you what we did there. I then returned to work, but he didn't. I didn't see him again until seven that evening at the hotel for the dinner."

"Do you know what he did while he was in his chambers for that half hour between eight and eight-thirty?"

"Yes, I do. He was typing and sending his letter of resignation from the district court to the clerk of the administrative judge."

"And were you aware he was going to do this?"

"Yes, I was. We had discussed it thoroughly. I'm so sorry. I should have come forward with that information sooner."

"Let's not worry about that now. How did you feel about the resignation?"

"At the time, I felt just fine about it."

"And do you know why he was meeting with Brad Pierce?"

"Yes," said Caroline, for the first time averting his gaze and looking down. "He met with Brad Pierce to tell him that he had resigned from the bench, effective immediately, and that he would be returning to the firm of Braxton & Pierce, also effective immediately. In addition he informed him that I would be joining the firm as a senior partner."

"Did Teddy tell you how Brad reacted to that news?"

"How do you think he reacted, Lieutenant?"

"I don't know," said Walter. "From what I've heard, the firm was for all intents and purposes broke. Perhaps he was relieved to hear that Teddy was coming back to save it."

"Perhaps he would have been, except for the fact that Teddy also informed him that he would no longer be a partner, but that he was welcome to stay with the firm as an associate if he so desired. Brad was crushed."

"Was he also angry?"

"Teddy said it was the angriest he'd ever seen Brad. But can you blame him? He'd devoted his entire life to the firm, and to Teddy, and now there he was in his sixties, broke and on a salary an entry-level law school grad would probably have turned down. But poor Brad, Teddy eventually got him calmed down. He always said that he could talk Brad into or out of doing anything. It just wasn't in Brad to say 'no' to Teddy. Although it's not like anyone else was any better at it."

"But, Caroline, there's something I don't understand. Teddy was a very wealthy man, and at least many millions of that wealth came from the law firm. I thought he and Brad were equal partners in the firm. Why isn't Brad equally wealthy?"

"They were equal equity partners, Lieutenant, but not equal revenue partners. Teddy always kept the lion's share of the revenue because, he said, he was the rainmaker, and he and Brad would still be out doing real estate closings for fifty grand a year if it weren't for him."

"And Brad accepted that?" said Walter, incredulously.

"Poor Brad," said Caroline. "He's such a mild man. He was devoted to Teddy, and money didn't matter that much to him, so he just went along. Brad made a decent income over the years and he was a bachelor, but he always gave away anything he accumulated to the church and to his causes. The man was broke."

"And what about Ted Junior?"

"The same was going to happen to him. Teddy said that the worst mistake he ever made with Young Ted was carrying him along for too many years. He said he hoped Ted Junior would up and quit the firm and finally make something of himself."

"Did he tell him that?"

"No, he left it to Brad to explain it all to Young Ted."

"And did he?"

"I don't know, Lieutenant. Teddy didn't hang around to find out."

"Nice guy."

"That's Teddy."

"But I don't get it, Caroline. I've had everybody in New York, including Police Commissioner Donahue himself, telling me that Teddy Braxton was the most charming, charismatic man they had ever met, but it sure doesn't seem that way to me."

"Teddy could turn on the charm like it was a light switch, but I had begun to learn that it wasn't as much a genuine part of his nature as it was a tool in his toolbox. The Teddy I just described to you is the real Teddy, believe me. You know, charisma is a two-edged sword. In the right hands, it can inspire people to great things, but in the wrong hands it can be used to manipulate people terribly. And remember, Teddy was first and foremost a penniless orphan from the South Bronx. He was a survivor, and I think the older he got the more that essential part of his nature reemerged, no matter how wealthy and successful he'd become."

"I'm no Freud, but that makes sense to me."

"I know this all sounds like a lame excuse for my behavior, but it makes sense to me, too."

"Caroline," said Walter, pulling a manila envelope out of his desk drawer, "do you think you might take another look at these crime scene photos and tell me if you see anything that might be helpful to the investigation?"

Caroline was suddenly hesitant, and for the first time Walter felt the wall go back up, but she agreed. Walter laid out the photos in front of her and, unlike the last time, she stared at them for a solid few minutes. Then she looked up at Walter.

"I'm sorry," she said. "I'd love to help you but I can't."

"Are you sure, Caroline?"

"I'm sure."

Walter couldn't help noticing that she didn't say that she didn't see anything, only that she couldn't help him. He was positive that she was lying, but he couldn't prove it, and he knew that Caroline was a stubborn woman. He couldn't make her talk if she was unwilling. After he had escorted her out the door, he went back and stared at the photos for a long time. Caroline had seen something in those photos, something that would help him solve the crime. But what?

31

IT HAD BECOME SO EASY TO RECITE THE OLD LIES, thought Bradley Pierce as he looked across the small table at Walter Hudson. They were back at the Amsterdam Club and he was fairly sure that the young detective would not be as charmed by his tales today as he had been the last time they'd met.

But were they really lies, or just old fables told out of habit, fables told to protect the truths that sustained him? His religious discipline had taught him that habit and repetition were indispensable elements of one's faith journey, especially during those inevitable times when faith faltered. It was like reciting Morning Prayer at Trinity Church down on Wall Street, which he did every morning without fail. During the times in his life when his faith had been strong, it was merely a comforting daily ritual, but during those awful crises of doubt it had been essential. When he felt that faith had deserted him forever, he clung to the rituals, and his faith had always returned, stronger than ever.

So he wasn't lying, he convinced himself, he was simply clinging to ritual until the old truths reemerged. But what truths?

The truth was that when he first met Teddy Braxton his affection and respect for the man had been genuine. He had loved struggling side by side with him to establish the firm, and initially it had been a true partnership. It had been Brad's connections in the New York legal establishment and among the moneyed elite, and his unquestioned brilliance as a legal theorist that had given the fledgling firm the credibility and the initial client base that it had so desperately needed.

They made little money in those first few crucial years, but what they had made had been shared equally. As the years went by, and Teddy kept more and more of the firm's revenue for himself, Brad's faith in him had faltered. But Brad also had to admit that his own role had faded into relative insignificance as Teddy's star shone brightly in the New York legal firmament. And the money had never meant anything to Brad in the first place, so what had really changed? The firm was still named Braxton & Pierce, after all. His income was adequate for his needs, and he still enjoyed the role he played in the firm. He was a shy man, after all, and he was more than content to yield the spotlight to his dynamic partner.

The other unshakable truth in Brad's life was that he was still as deeply in love with Barbara deGroot Braxton today as he had been on the day he first laid eyes on her over forty years ago. It had been a bitter defeat for him when Teddy had won her over so effortlessly. But in the end he had remained to her, and she had remained to him, all that he had ever wanted: a devoted, faithful friend.

He was also no fool. He knew that Bunny had taken a lover many years ago when it had become apparent that her marriage to Teddy, no matter what else it was, was never going to be a faithful one. Had he secretly hoped that he would be that lover, that he would be the man who would give Bunny the unique affection and faithful devotion that she so deserved? Of course he had. But he had also known from a young age that he did not possess that capacity, that boundless craving for physical passion that all the other young men he had grown up with, gone to school with, and worked beside seemed to possess in such abundance. And Bunny Braxton was a passionate woman. She needed a man who would crave her above anyone or anything else, and he had finally accepted the truth that he could never be that man. So once again, he had stood back, silently offering his celibacy to her as his one priceless gift, the one true expression of his devotion. That celibacy had become one of the most precious elements of his faith, and he rejoiced in it.

Had it been enough in the end? He didn't know; perhaps he never would. All he knew was that what had been true from the beginning still was. Between him, Teddy Braxton, and Bunny deGroot, nothing had ever really changed. And now, what was done was done. Only a fool thought he could go back and alter the past. He faced his adversary calmly, knowing those truths would sustain him.

"I recall that you enjoyed the Glenlivet that last time you were here, Lieutenant," he said, smiling, as a waiter silently entered the private room and placed two glasses of the amber magic on the table. "I hope you don't think it was presumptuous of me to order some for you."

"Thank you very much," said Walter, "but I think just one will be fine for me today."

"Surely," said Brad, signing the chit that the waiter offered him. "But please feel free to change your mind."

"Mr. Pierce, I seem to remember that the last time we were here you paid with your personal credit card," said Walter, thinking now was as good a time as any to put the man on the defensive.

"Did I? I don't recall. Sometimes I just don't pay attention, I guess."

"No, the waiter didn't bring you a chit the last time; he just held out his tray and waited for your credit card."

"Lieutenant, you can hardly expect me to…"

"Was it because your firm was broke? Were you behind in your bills here? Had they suspended your account and put you on a pay-as-you-go basis?"

"My dear Lieutenant Hudson, what can it possibly matter at this point?"

"You're probably right. Things have turned out pretty well for you since Judge Braxton's death, haven't they?"

"I'm not sure that I appreciate the implications of that question, but to answer it directly, yes, they have. You must have read the announcement in yesterday's *Times* about the formation of the Braxton Family Foundation and my role in it."

"And that you will be winding down the affairs of Braxton & Pierce. How do you feel about that?"

"As you can imagine, I have mixed feelings. Of course, building and sustaining Braxton & Pierce was my life's work, and it meant a great deal to me. But this is New York. Law firms, even great law firms, come and go, and the work is, how shall I say it, ephemeral in nature."

"Unlike the Lord's work, which lasts forever."

"Lieutenant?"

"I remember you telling me how the ministry had always been your true calling, and how when you first met Mrs. Braxton, before she ever met her husband, and while you still had an 'understanding' with her, you and she had shared a dream of doing missionary work together. It seems like it's all come full circle."

For one awful moment Walter thought the man was going to burst into tears, but if he had been, he quickly regained his composure.

"It will give me the opportunity to do the work that I've always dreamed of doing, that is true. It is also true that I will enjoy doing that work with Bunny Braxton, a woman I have admired for many years. But if you are somehow implying that I would have killed my good friend and law partner to achieve that goal, I am afraid that you are way off the mark."

"But you must have been very angry with him that day."

"I'm not sure I'm following, Lieutenant."

"Mr. Pierce, I know that Teddy Braxton visited you at your law offices on the morning before his murder, and that he informed you of his intention to resign from the bench and rejoin Braxton & Pierce on terms that were, to say the least, damaging and profoundly humiliating to both you and Young Ted. I mean, it must have been bad enough that he was taking away your partnership status and reducing your income dramatically, but it must have been infuriating to know that you were being replaced by his latest lover."

"Teddy was just doing what he felt he had to do to save the firm," said

Brad, his voice flat, "and Caroline Schuyler is a fine young attorney, no matter what else she may have been at the time."

"So you admit that the firm was broke."

"That was Teddy's judgment, not mine, but it is true that the firm was struggling. After a long talk with Teddy I had to admit that it was all for the best."

"Oh, please, Mr. Pierce. You can't tell me that after perhaps a twenty-minute conversation with Judge Braxton you were just fine with everything and that there were no hard feelings."

"I'm a human being, Lieutenant. Of course I was initially angry and hurt. But even after a brief conversation with Teddy I had to admit that he was doing the right thing for the firm, and I told him that I was willing to stay on and do my bit to help him. It was hard to remain angry with the man."

"Is that what you and Mrs. Braxton were talking about over lunch at Pagliacci later that day?"

"Only briefly," said Brad, but he was starting to fidget. "We mostly talked about family matters and enjoyed a pleasant meal together."

"That's funny, she told me that you were discussing setting up a 501(c)(3) corporation for a non-profit organization that she and some of her friends were setting up to promote the arts in the local schools."

"Then maybe that's what we discussed. Perhaps I'm confused. We did, in fact, set up a 501(c)(3) together for that purpose."

"But that was six months ago, wasn't it? At least that's what your administrative assistant told me."

"Please, Lieutenant," said Pierce, raising his arms in a gesture of defeat, "I really don't remember."

"And the waiter at the restaurant remembers clearly that neither of you touched your meals."

"I go out to lunch almost every day. Perhaps the waiter is right, I don't know."

"But your admin tells me that you almost always eat a sandwich at your desk, and the waiter at the restaurant said that it was highly unusual for Mrs. Braxton not to eat her entire meal, including dessert. So what were the two of you discussing that had you both so upset?"

"Clearly my memory of that lunch is very cloudy, Lieutenant, so I don't know how you can expect me to answer that question." By now the man was perspiring freely, but Walter was relentless. Back to my old form, he thought.

"You're right, Mr. Pierce, let's change the subject. I was very remiss in our first conversation not to ask you of your whereabouts on the night of the Judge's murder. You were at the hotel for his speech, weren't you?"

"Yes, I was. I never denied that. I didn't stay long, though. I said hello to a few old friends and colleagues and left."

"And where did you go?"

"I went straight home. I still live in the small townhouse in Greenwich Village that I purchased over thirty years ago. I think I was home by ten."

"Did you speak to the Judge before you left?"

"I think I spoke to him briefly, but I really don't recall."

"You weren't still angry at him?"

"Oh, I don't think so," said Brad, but Walter could see that by now the man was seeing traps everywhere.

"Mr. Pierce," said Walter, withdrawing an envelope from his jacket pocket, "I was reviewing some photos last night that were taken at the event. They were taken by a newspaper reporter. I'm sorry, this is only a 5x7, but I think you can see it well enough." He took the photo out of the envelope and laid it on the table, facing Brad Pierce, who scanned it quickly and looked up.

"It's a photo of Caroline Schuyler," said Brad, looking up, a puzzled expression on his face. "She looked particularly lovely that evening, and I'm sure the gossip sheets took hundreds of photos."

"That's all I saw at first, too. It is kind of tough to take your eyes off her, isn't it?" said Walter, smiling. "But then, like I said, I took another look at it. Why don't you take another look. Check out the background, off to the right side."

Pierce looked at it for a few seconds and then suddenly paled. Walter knew that Pierce had seen what he had the night before as he pored over the hundreds of photos one more time, not knowing what else to do.

The images of the two men were small but distinct. The one looked angry, his hand raised, an index finger pointing at the other man, who had both hands raised, palms out, staring at the other man with an exasperated expression.

"Are you still going to tell me that you weren't angry at Teddy Braxton that night, Mr. Pierce?"

"Perhaps I was still a little overwrought, after all," said Pierce, glancing at his watch and hoping that he still had time to make it to Evensong at Trinity.

"Did you notice the time stamp on that photo, Mr. Pierce?" Pierce looked down at the photo once more. "Tell me what it says. I was tired, maybe I misread it."

"It says, '11:21PM, May 8, 2015.'"

"That's what I thought it said," said Detective Lieutenant Walter Hudson.

32

IT WAS four-thirty, and Walter couldn't decide whether to go back to work or just go straight home. He headed over to the subway station to pick up the 3 Train, thinking that he could make up his mind on the way to Penn Station, where he could get off and go back to work, or keep going another two stops to the Times Square station where he could hop on the 7 Train and go home. But his mind was made up for him when his cell phone rang.

"Hello, Eduardo."

"Lieutenant, where are you?" said Eduardo Sanchez, sounding anxious.

"I'm downtown, why?" said Walter, trying not to sound annoyed.

"I'm here at the Empire-Excelsior with Stan Kraszcinski. He's got something here that you're really gonna want to see."

It was the 3 Train in any event, thought Walter. "I'll be there in twenty minutes," he said.

Stanley Kraszcinski looked a damn sight better than the last time he'd seen him. The man's color was good and he was positively beaming. His windowless office still felt cramped, but the atmosphere had certainly brightened, the smell of failure no longer tainting the air.

"Good to see you, Stan," said Walter, shaking the man's hand. "You look great."

"It's all because of you, Walter."

"Well, it was mostly Commissioner Donahue's doing, but I'm glad everything worked out. So what have you found that got Officer Sanchez here so worked up?" Eduardo grimaced, but he was too excited to be embarrassed.

"I've been working around the clock on this murder for the past three weeks, and I think I finally hit pay dirt." He clicked some keys on his desktop computer and turned it so that they could all see the screen.

"What am I going to be looking at, Stan?"

"Like I told you last time, Walter, the security cameras that night were practically worthless. Half of them hadn't even been turned on, and the others hadn't been aimed properly, but at least they were running. So I decided to look at the images that the few operating cameras took. As I suspected, they were worthless, just hours and hours of video of the ceilings in the hallways, or hours of video of another camera taking pictures of the ceilings in the hallways."

"Except," said Eduardo, barely able to contain himself.

"Except one, that was hanging from the ceiling near the elevators on the north side of the building," said Kraszcinski. "I found one that, even though it wasn't pointed where it was supposed to be, was pointed at a hallway mirror."

"And the mirror was reflecting what?" said Walter, feeling his excitement starting to build.

"It was reflecting the doors for the bank of elevators that went to the top floors."

"Don't all the elevators go to the top floors?"

"No, they don't," said Stanley. "Some geniuses at Otis Elevator decided that it's more efficient to have some of the elevators skip the first fifteen floors on the way up and only stop at the top ten floors. There's another bank of elevators that only go up as far as the 15th floor."

"And on top of that," said Eduardo, "the top floors are where all the suites and expensive rooms are, so it's a perk for the high paying customers. Not that I'll ever learn that from personal experience..."

"Not that any of us ever will," said Walter, "but let's cut to the chase. What did you see?"

"Here, take a look for yourself," said Kraszcinski, as he pushed a button on his keyboard.

The lighting wasn't good, and the angle wasn't ideal, but Walter could see all the elevator doors fairly clearly. It took a second for his eyes to adjust, but once they did he was able to identify distinct images of people getting on and off the elevators, their facial characteristics clearly distinguishable. The images weren't continuous, which he found annoying, but it seemed that they were only about a second apart, so he doubted that anyone getting on or off the elevators would slip through the images.

"Can you slow this down, Stan? There are a lot of people and I'm having trouble keeping up with the images."

"Don't worry Walter, we're almost there," said Stan, his finger poised over the "Pause" key. "Three, two, one and...there!" He hit the key.

Walter stared at the frozen image for a full ten seconds before he finally saw the person he was afraid he would see.

It was Brad Pierce.

Officer Sanchez and Stanley Kraszckinski looked uneasily at Walter, who continued to stare at the frozen image, frowning.

"I don't get it," said Kraszcinski, "I thought you'd be ecstatic. We just solved the murder for chrissake."

"I'm sorry, Stan," said Walter, "this is great work and it's very helpful. Thank you."

"So what's the problem?"

"It's just that I have a lot of questions, that's all."

"My God, Walter, we've got the man on camera leaving the scene of the crime right about the time the murder was committed. What more could you want?"

"Some things just don't make sense to me, that's all. You know how it is, Stan. I have some knowledge that you don't have, and I'm trying to make the puzzle come together."

"Don't worry, I know the drill," said Stan, but he was suddenly starting to look nervous.

"Look, Stan," said Walter, "do me a favor and keep a tight lid on this. I don't want the press getting ahold of any of this until I've had a chance to do some follow up."

"Don't worry, I'd never talk to reporters, you know that," said Stan, but sweat was starting to pop out on his brow.

"Stan?" said Walter, a sense of dread starting to tickle his stomach.

"What, Walter?"

"Tell me you didn't."

"What are you guys talking about?" said Eduardo.

"Walter, look…."

"Aw, Stan, you called the commissioner, didn't you?"

"Walter, I just wanted him to know that he hadn't misplaced his trust in me, that's all."

"Aw, shit, Stan," said Walter as his cell phone began to ring. He picked it up, uttered a few "Yessirs," and hung up.

"What was that all about?" said Eduardo.

"It was all about how I have to go back downtown and get myself an ass full of splinters, that's what it was all about," said Walter, feeling as weary as he sounded.

"I'm really sorry," said Stan.

33

WALTER COULDN'T SEE HOW THINGS COULD GET ANY WORSE until Commissioner Donahue's admin, a cheerful young redhead named Patricia who was the only person who had a key to the commissioner's private hideaway except for the man himself, led him down the hallway and showed him in. He had assumed that he and Donahue would be meeting alone, but that had been wishful thinking on his part.

"Good evening, Madame Mayor," he said trying to keep the fear, if not the shock, out of his voice. He had met Mayor Deborah Kaplan once before, shortly after he had solved, with the help of Leviticus Welles, the "Points of Light" case, the case that had led to the murder of her predecessor and to Walter's own promotion to detective lieutenant. She was an unprepossessing woman, fifty-five or so, medium height, a trim build, and auburn hair with streaks of gray he hadn't noticed at her inauguration.

"Good evening, Lieutenant Hudson," said the mayor. "It's such a pleasure to see you again. How are Sarah and the children?" Deborah Kaplan had the politician's gift of remembering names and faces, and it slightly unnerved Walter.

"They're all doing fine, ma'am, thank you for asking."

Commissioner Donahue was, as usual, standing behind the bar looking for all the world like the Irish barkeep that somewhere deep in his heart, Walter was convinced, he truly longed to be.

"Let me pour you a Bushmills," said Donahue, "and you can tell us all about your good news."

The Bushmills was going to go down harder than usual, and Mayor Kaplan must have noticed the dour expression that he couldn't keep from his face.

"It *is* good news isn't it, Lieutenant?" she said.

"I think it is," said Walter, "but maybe not as good as you've been led to believe."

"What do you mean?" said Commissioner Donahue, sliding a generous two-finger glass of whiskey over to Walter, suddenly not sounding at all like the affable neighborhood publican.

"Sir, ma'am, I've reviewed the videos that Stanley Kraszcinski told you about, and I confirmed that the man coming off the elevator is Bradley Pierce, a man long associated not only with Teddy Braxton, but with the entire Braxton family. The time stamp on that recording coincides almost perfectly with the estimated time of the murder. And I can also tell you that in the course of my investigation, including extensive discussions with Mr. Pierce himself as recently as this afternoon, I have learned of events--events on the day of the murder--that give him a more than credible motive to kill Teddy Braxton."

"Such as?" said Donahue.

"Such as that on the morning of May 8th, the day of the murder, Teddy Braxton went to the law offices of Braxton & Pierce and told Mr. Pierce that he was leaving the district court to rejoin the firm and that Mr. Pierce, along with Ted Braxton, Jr., was losing his partnership and being demoted to essentially junior associate status. The buyout price for his partnership would be the one hundred dollars that he and Judge Braxton each contributed when the firm was founded."

"That just doesn't sound like the Teddy I know," said Mayor Kaplan.

"Ma'am, I'm sorry to say that the Teddy Braxton I've come to know in the course of my investigation bears little resemblance to the Teddy Braxton many people thought they knew and have described to me. And the family, the family that tries to present the image of billionaire Cleavers out of 'Leave it to Beaver,' is anything but."

"What do you mean by that?" said Donahue.

"Sir, I'll spare you both the most distressing details for the moment, but I've learned that Teddy Braxton had been a serial philanderer his entire life. In fact, he told Mr. Pierce that he intended to bring his current lover, Ms. Caroline Schuyler, into the firm as a senior partner."

"Caroline *Schuyler*?" said Mayor Kaplan. "I know both Caroline and her father, and I find that almost impossible to believe, Lieutenant."

"Ms. Schuyler herself confirmed it to me, as well as Mr. Schuyler, who effectively terminated both his friendship and his business relationship with the Judge over the affair. Mr. Schuyler is a man who is not ashamed of his violent past, and who, by the way, has also been engaged in an affair with Bunny Braxton for the past twenty years."

"Are you sure about that? I just had lunch with Bunny Braxton last month," said Mayor Kaplan. "I've known her for years. Such a lovely woman."

"Yes she is, ma'am, and I wouldn't hold anything against her. She is a truly admirable woman, a woman devoted to this city and to the welfare of her family above all else. There's more, but I'll spare you."

"I think that would be for the best," said the mayor.

"All I'm trying to say ma'am, sir, is that yes, Brad Pierce had a motive. And on top of everything else, the man has apparently been platonically in love with Bunny Braxton for over forty years. But a lot of other people, people close to the Judge, had motives, too."

"But none of the other people was caught on camera leaving the scene of the crime," said Donahue, "so I guess I don't understand why you seem so bound and determined not to arrest the man as your prime suspect. For heaven's sake, everything points to him."

"First of all, Commissioner, we have a logistical problem. Brad Pierce lives downtown, in Greenwich Village, and as I think you know, the murder weapon was found on the north bank of Spuyten Duivel, in the Bronx."

"Ah, you can explain that a lot of ways. If this Pierce is halfway intelligent, which I assume he is, he could have driven north, dumped the weapon and been back downtown in no time at that hour of the night. That's what I would have done if I'd wanted to throw the cops off."

"Bradley Pierce doesn't own a car, sir. He doesn't even have a driver's license. He never has. But you're right. I'm sure that any of us could come up with a credible explanation for the location of the murder weapon. We could quibble about how credible, but I won't argue about that right now."

"So why else don't you think he did it?" said Mayor Kaplan.

"Because I just can't make him feel like a murderer, ma'am," said Walter.

"He doesn't feel like a murderer to you?" said Donahue, staring at Walter, incredulous. "You are a trained investigator, Lieutenant, and in my experience a damn good one, which is why I put you on this case. And now you're sitting here telling me, despite all the evidence, that you're not going to arrest Bradley Pierce because he doesn't *feel* like a murderer to you? I have to tell you that I'm extremely disappointed, so disappointed that I'm tempted to take you off the case and order the man arrested myself."

"Give him a chance to explain himself, Mike," said Mayor Kaplan. "I'm sure you used your sense of smell on more than one occasion to solve a crime when the evidence was pointing in another direction."

"OK, Lieutenant," said Donahue, pouring them all a refill, "you've at least got the mayor on your side. What do you have to say for yourself?"

"Sir, we've both investigated enough murders to know that murderers come in all shapes and sizes: smart, stupid; big, small; strong, weak, whatever. But, at least in my experience, there's one quality that all murderers have in common."

"And that would be what, Lieutenant?" said Mayor Kaplan.

"They're all decisive, ma'am," said Walter. "At the critical moment, they are able to make a decision and carry through with it."

"And you're saying that Brad Pierce is not decisive?" said the mayor.

"Yes, that's what I'm saying. And I also know from all of my discussions with him and with others that Judge Braxton had always had the power to manipulate people, but Mr. Pierce more than anyone else. The man is incapable of defying the Judge."

"So why do we have the video of him leaving the elevator?" said Donahue. "You're not trying to tell us that just by some mad coincidence he was there to see someone else, are you?"

"What I'm saying, sir, ma'am, is that I think Brad Pierce was the person who brought the .45 to the hotel room. I think he went there with every intention of killing the Judge, but I also think that it took the Judge only a couple of seconds to dissuade him. I think he left the gun there and fled, either not knowing what else to do with it or because the Judge told him to."

"Mike," said Mayor Kaplan, turning to the commissioner, "that makes sense to me."

"Ah, it makes sense to me, too," said Commissioner Donahue. "I guess I owe you an apology."

"No need, sir. I could still be dead wrong, and I know that. I am in no way eliminating Brad Pierce as a suspect. I'm just not ready to put his picture on the front page of the *Daily News*, that's all. It would ruin him, quite possibly for no reason."

"And right or wrong, you still owe me, and the mayor, a solution to this crime. If Brad Pierce isn't the murderer, then who is?"

"Sir, I'm not prepared to say who it is yet, but I will tell you that I'm getting closer. I will solve this murder, and I will do it soon, I promise you that," said Walter, knowing that he was quite possibly getting out ahead of himself, and risking his career in the process. He rose to leave on unsteady legs. Would he ever leave this room sober?

Donahue was refilling his own and Mayor Kaplan's glasses. As usual, he seemed completely unaffected by what he had already drunk and, much to Walter's surprise, neither did Mayor Kaplan. He guessed a hollow leg was just another indispensable tool in a politician's toolbox.

"I'm glad to hear you say that," said Donahue, "and you can be sure I'll hold you to it."

"Yessir."

"Now, would you like to have one for the road with us before you leave?"

"Thank you very much, sir, but I really need to be getting home."

"You and Sarah must have your hands full, especially with your new addition," said the mayor.

"He is quite a handful," said Walter.

"Stay in close touch," said the commissioner.

"Yessir."

"And say, 'hi' to Sarah for me," said Mayor Kaplan.

"Yes, ma'am," said Lieutenant Walter Hudson thinking, what a world.

34

"YOU SMELL LIKE A DISTILLERY," said Sarah as Walter walked through the front door. It was 7:30 by the time he made it home, and he feared he might be in for another wrathful encounter with his exhausted wife. They had been civil to each other ever since that awful, angry night, but they had both shied away from talking about it, and the memory lingered between them like an unpaid bill.

"I'm sorry," he said, trying not to flinch, at least visibly. But as he looked around he noticed there was a different atmosphere in the house. The two girls had not yet retreated to the safety of their room, but were instead doing what they normally did: playing contentedly on the living room floor until they were ordered to bed by one or both parents. The aroma of a home-cooked dinner wafted in from the kitchen. Sarah herself looked freshly showered. Her hair was carefully combed, and she was wearing a pair of slacks and a blouse that she hadn't worn since Daniel had been born. If his eyes weren't tricking him, her face bore a hint of makeup and at least a trace of a smile. But the most remarkable change was what wasn't there, like Sherlock Holmes's dog that didn't bark in the night: the sound of a crying baby, a sound they'd been living with for so long that its mere absence was striking.

"I take it you've been spending more quality time with Commissioner Donahue?" said Sarah.

"Yes, and with Mayor Kaplan herself, who says 'hello' by the way."

"My God," said Sarah, her smile widening. "You mean she remembered me?"

"By name, with no prompting."

"I like her so much," said Sarah.

"You're not going to get any argument from me. I'm not sure I would have walked out of that meeting with the commissioner with my"…he almost said, "my balls intact," but he caught himself… "my badge still in my pocket if it hadn't been for her."

"It's hard to believe that when I was introduced to her I was still out-to-here pregnant."

"Speaking of out here pregnant, where's Daniel?"

"He's sleeping," said Sarah.

"He's been sleeping *all* afternoon, Daddy," said Beth, their oldest.

"All afternoon?"

"Since one o'clock, and I slept myself from one until about four. I feel like a new woman," said Sarah. "He's going to be famished when he wakes up."

"Is he OK?"

"He's fine."

"So, what's going on? Did all those prayers to the Virgin Mary finally work?"

"Perhaps," said Sarah, "but I think it had more to do with Hershey's chocolate syrup, if that doesn't sound too blasphemous."

"You're kidding me."

"No, I'm serious. He was awake and squalling as usual at lunchtime when I finally had to put him down and make lunch for Robin. You know she likes chocolate milk with her lunch and, as usual, I was in a hurry to get back to Daniel so at least poor Robin could eat her lunch in peace. I forgot to wipe my hands off after I'd mixed the Hershey's syrup into her milk, and a couple of my fingers were still sticky with the stuff. Well, he glommed on to one of my fingers that had the syrup on it and started sucking on it with everything he had. Then he did the same thing with my other finger. And then, instead of throwing up, he just burped. Then he took his bottle and fell sound asleep. I never thought I'd hear myself say this, but I think I'm going to have to wake him up soon."

"I don't think I've ever heard him burp in his entire life."

"It was really loud, Daddy," said Beth. "You should have heard it."

"So what do you make of all that?" said Walter.

"I don't know. I seem to remember reading a long time ago in one of my women's magazines that there is at least some informal evidence that there's something in chocolate that helps kids with colic, but I'd forgotten all about it. Now I'm thinking maybe there's something to it."

"Wouldn't that be a blessing,"

"It sure would. Look, before I wake Daniel up, why don't we go into the kitchen and I'll sit with you while you eat some supper."

"That," said Walter, "is the best suggestion I've heard all day."

Sarah had made a simple casserole, but to Walter it tasted better than anything he could have ordered at Pagliacci. They chatted about the day's events while Walter wolfed down two helpings.

He was getting up to clean his dishes when Sarah said, "I had an interesting visit today."

"Really?" said Walter, with a sense of foreboding. There was something in the tone of her voice that put him on his guard, like the almost inaudible whistle people hear just before a terrorist missile hits. "Who was it?"

"It was a woman named Virginia Braxton."

"What?" said Walter, feeling the casserole harden into a rock in his stomach. He had a tightening sensation in his groin, and his testicles felt like they were retracting.

"She said she met you because her father was Judge Braxton, the guy whose murder you're investigating. I never heard you mention her name."

"Sarah, we haven't had much of a chance to discuss anything lately. What did she want?"

"You don't sound too happy that she came over."

"It's just that I don't like it when my family gets mixed up in my police work, that's all. What was she doing out here?"

"She said she was delivering a lecture at St. John's this evening. I guess she's some kind of financial genius or something, even though she looked awfully young."

"Something like that."

"She seemed very nice, and she's very pretty."

"Sarah," said Walter, turning away from the sink feeling like he was turning to face the business end of an executioner's rifle, "I've never considered it a wise practice to discuss other women's looks with you, unless it was to talk about how ugly they were."

"Well, she certainly isn't ugly."

"So anyway, what did she want?" said Walter, hoping to change the subject, but fearing that no change could be for the better.

"She said that since she was in the neighborhood she just wanted to stop by and introduce herself. She said she wanted to meet the woman who was lucky enough to be married to you. And she told me an interesting story."

Walter Hudson was a simple man. He did not understand women. He did not pretend to, and he had no desire to. More than as the consequence of any residual guilt stemming from his interactions with Virginia Braxton, the fear that now coursed through him like hot lead injected into his veins with a horse needle was the result of the certain knowledge that any time two women chose him as the subject of their discussion, the result could not be good.

"Great," he said.

"Walter, you don't seem too comfortable with this conversation."

"Sarah, Virginia Braxton is a key figure in my investigation into the murder of her father. In fact, I have not yet formally cleared her as a suspect. I just think that it was improper for her to be making a social call on my wife, that's all."

"Well, do you want to hear what she said or don't you?"

"Of course I do. It may be important to my investigation," he said, thinking that he could probably slip that one by a lie detector.

"Anyway, she told me about how you protected her from that horrible sounding guy who'd been harassing her."

"There wasn't much I could do about that."

"She also said that you told her that you'd kill anyone who ever tried to take me away from you. She said it must be wonderful to have someone who cares about me that much."

"I'm sorry, Sarah, it was just an offhand comment that I shouldn't have made while I was questioning her about the, uh, infidelities of some of my other suspects."

"It's all right, Walter. I told her I knew that. I also told her that it's one of the things that made you so, you know, so attractive to me."

"Ah, Jesus, Sarah."

"It's okay," said Sarah, smiling at his discomfiture, "it was just girl talk, that's all." She hesitated for a few brief seconds and then said, "Walter, do you mind if I butt into your case for a minute?"

"No, go ahead," said Walter, eager for any change of subject.

"Virginia also talked a lot about how much better she's felt recently, and I couldn't help but feel that it had a lot to do with the death of her father. She never came right out and said that, of course, but just from the way she talked about him and about her past left me with that feeling. Anyway, it got me to thinking."

"Thinking about what?"

"Well, you know, it seems that a lot of times in a murder investigation you're looking for someone who hated the victim so much that he was driven to kill him. But sometimes I think that you should also be looking for someone who cared about another person so much that he would kill someone for their benefit, even if he didn't necessarily hate the killer."

"You know, Sarah, you're right. That's part of our training, and I try to keep it in mind. But it's easy to forget because the main focus of our training is to learn everything we can about the victim, since the victim was murdered, except in the cases of truly random killings, because of who he was and what he did in his life, good or bad. So we gather all this information into a big jumble and stare at it until we see a pattern emerge. It usually works, but the problem is that it tends to make us focus on what people thought about the victim, and why someone must have hated him. The virtuous killer is sometimes the last thing we think about. Thanks."

But Walter also knew that in this case, the more he learned about Teddy

Braxton, the more he realized how many people could have hated him enough to kill him. He also had to admit, though, that Sarah was right. He'd met many people: Brad Pierce; Carlton Schuyler; Albert the butler; Richard the driver; even Randall Brandt, who had spent much of their lives devoted to Bunny Braxton and to the deGroot family, people who just might kill to protect her and them, no matter what they felt, if anything, about the Judge. The problem was at least some of them, Brad Pierce and Carlton Schuyler in particular, had every reason to hate Teddy Braxton simply for who he was and what he had done. He could only hope that one thing would emerge from his investigation which would finally point him in the right direction.

Their thoughts were interrupted by the sound of Daniel fussing.

"I'll finish up the kitchen and get the girls to bed while you take care of the little guy, okay?" said Walter.

"Sounds good to me," said Sarah.

"And don't forget the Hershey's."

"Don't worry, I'm way ahead of you. And Walter?"

"Yes?"

"Let's try to get to bed as soon as possible tonight."

"Yes, ma'am."

"THAT SURE SCRATCHED AN ITCH," said Sarah as she lay contentedly in her husband's arms.

"I don't think I've ever called it 'scratching' before," said an exhausted but happy Walter, "but I'll call it anything you want if we can keep doing it."

"Perhaps we should send a thank you note to Hershey's," said Sarah.

"I'm sure they'd love it," said Walter, "but I'm not sure how they'd fit it into their ad campaigns."

Sarah had awakened little Daniel and repeated the process of letting him suck some chocolate syrup off her fingers, after which he'd guzzled down a full bottle, burped loudly and dropped an enormous, healthy load into his diapers. Sarah had joyously cleaned him up and, after a little playtime, put him back to bed, whereupon he had fallen again into a deep slumber. Sarah had joined Walter in their bed shortly thereafter.

"I don't know," said Sarah, "it certainly would expand their customer base."

"Well, they sure won me over," said Walter. He was about to roll over and go to sleep when he felt Sarah shift beside him and raise herself up on one elbow.

"Walter?"

"Yes?"

"You remember that I'm half Sicilian, right?"

"How could I forget? I thought your Uncle Paolo was going to carry out a vendetta at our wedding reception when he thought my cousin Donald was getting too familiar with his daughter. Why are you bringing that up?"

"Walter, I never expected you to live the rest of your life without finding another woman attractive."

"Sarah, I.…."

"You don't have to say anything, sweetheart. Just don't forget, whenever you feel like you might be losing your way," she whispered in his ear as she reached down between his legs and squeezed hard enough to make him gasp, "that I'm half Sicilian."

"I won't," said Walter, trying to get his breath back. "I promise."

"Good. We shall speak no more of this," said Sarah in her best Marlon Brando imitation. "Now, come over here and make some use of that stuff you've got while you've still got it."

"Yes ma'am," said Walter as he rolled toward his wife, knowing that he might never understand women, but would forever be blissful in his ignorance.

35

"YOU SEEM TO HAVE THAT CERTAIN SPRING BACK IN YOUR STEP," said Leviticus Welles as he placed a Styrofoam cup of steaming coffee purchased from a local bodega in front of Walter and kept one for himself. They were sitting in Walter's office at the precinct house. The office was cramped, but it had a window that looked out on to 9th Avenue, and it had come with his unexpected promotion to lieutenant, so he was proud of it.

"You can thank Hershey's chocolate syrup for that," said Walter, unable to conceal a grin at the puzzled look on Levi's face. "It's a long story. Thanks for the coffee."

"Believe me, it was more out of self-defense than generosity, but you're welcome," said Levi.

Walter sat back and regarded Leviticus Welles. Less than a year ago he had shown up in Walter's office a sad, lonely man desperately clinging to a job he didn't like and an employer he didn't trust, trying to recover from the long term unemployment and collapse of his marriage that had resulted from the devastating effects of the Great Recession. Levi had been an unexpected but critical source of assistance to Walter as he had solved the most important case of his life, and in the process he had displayed enormous latent talents that had helped him blossom both personally and professionally. His thinning hair was now carefully trimmed, his once pallid complexion was now ruddy and healthy, his once dowdy clothes now sharp and stylish.

He updated Levi on the developments with Bradley Pierce and his meeting with the Commissioner Donahue as they drank their coffee.

"That's all really interesting stuff," said Levi, "but I have to agree with you; I still don't buy Pierce as a murderer. I think it's really important that you've come up with a possible theory for how the .45 got into the room, but that's about it."

"I wish it had been that easy to convince the commissioner," said Walter.

"It sounds like you were lucky that the mayor was there."

"Yeah, but that's only going to get me so far. Commissioner Donahue deferred to the mayor, but I think if it had been up to him Brad Pierce would be behind bars right now, and I'm not sure he would have been wrong. And if I don't come up with the actual culprit soon he's going to demand that I arrest

Pierce, and I don't think a good prosecutor would have a whole lot of trouble convicting him. And as far as I'm concerned, the only thing worse than not solving this case would be to have the wrong man convicted."

"And that happens more than you and I would care to think about."

"Yes, it does," said Walter, "but it's never happened on one of my cases, and I don't intend to let it happen on this one. I'm hoping you're here to help me, Levi."

"I don't know whether it will help or not, Walter. It may just add to the confusion."

"Why don't you tell me what you've got."

Levi reached down and pulled a large manila envelope out of his briefcase. The briefcase looked new and it was made out of very expensive-looking leather.

"Nice briefcase you've got there, Levi. It doesn't look like the one that I remember you carrying."

"It was a birthday gift from Julie," said Levi, coloring slightly "as if just being married to her wasn't the only gift I needed."

"How did we ever get so lucky, Levi?"

Levi stared seriously at Walter with intelligent eyes magnified by his glasses. "I just don't know, Walter. I don't think I'll ever understand it. I'm beginning to think that there are some things that we're just not meant to understand."

"Me, too," said Walter. "That's why I'm a Catholic, but hopefully this case isn't one of them."

"I agree," said Levi, pushing his coffee cup aside and pulling a small stack of 8"x10" color photos out of the envelope. He chose half a dozen of them and spread them out on Walter's desk.

"What are we supposed to be looking at here," said Walter, "except for a lot of pictures of Teddy Braxton?"

"I was staring at the pictures of him that were taken at the hotel the night of his murder, and I thought I noticed something. So, anyway, I sat down at my computer at work and I downloaded as many pictures as I could find of Teddy Braxton down through the years. They were mostly on newspaper websites, but I also called the *Daily News*, the *Post* and the *Times,* and they gave me access to a lot of their photo archives that aren't available publicly."

"It's great to be a cop sometimes, isn't it?"

"Sure beats being a salesman," said Levi, referring to his past, unhappy career. "So, anyway, I found the pattern I was looking for, and I thought you might find it interesting. I've got over a hundred photos here, but I think the ones you're looking at are a good, representative sample. They were taken over the past twenty years."

"The only pattern I notice is that he's with a good-looking woman in every single one of them. Jeez, look at that one."

"Bunny Braxton was a stunner, wasn't she?"

"She still is," said Walter. "I guess I'll never understand that guy."

"Neither will I," said Levi. "Do you notice anything else?"

Walter stared for a long while, but finally said, "I'm sorry, Levi, but I don't think I'm seeing what you want me to see."

"Take a look at his ties, Walter."

Walter stared once again, but to no avail. "I don't get it, Levi. OK, they're all really nice ties, really expensive looking, but Teddy was a sharp dresser; we all knew that."

"But there's one thing they all have in common."

Walter stared once again. He was just about to give up when, suddenly, he said, "Oh, holy shit. It's the tie tack, isn't it?" It was large for a tie tack and looked to be made of some kind of stone set in gold. In the better photos the stone glinted a deep red. "Whatever made you notice that?"

"I noticed it first," said Levi, "because men just don't wear tie clips and tie tacks anymore. Teddy was such a fashion horse that it surprised me that he was wearing one. So I collected all the photos I could find of Teddy wearing a suit and tie, and in every single one of them he's wearing that tie tack, no matter how far back I go."

"So, what do you make of that?"

"To my recollection, that tie tack was never found at the murder scene."

"Hang on a second," said Walter, picking up his phone and punching a number. "Eduardo, you in the building? Good, come to my office." Then he turned back to Levi and said, "I think you're right, but Eduardo will know for sure."

Eduardo poked his head into Walter's office and said, "What's up?"

Walter picked out the photo that showed the largest and clearest image of the tie tack. "Did you recover anything like this at the crime scene, Eduardo?"

Eduardo stared for only a few brief seconds before saying, "No, sir."

"You're sure?"

"Positive."

"Could it have been stolen by someone in the room?" said Levi.

"It's always possible, but I doubt it," said Eduardo. "There were a lot of people, but they were all either cops or EMTs and I've worked with that EMT outfit before. They're good people. I'm no judge of this stuff, but that thing looks expensive. I know you don't want to hear this, but if the murder was just a random robbery, maybe the murderer took it."

"What, and not the Patek Philippe watch on his wrist?"

"Maybe he thought the tie tack would be easier to fence."

"I doubt it," said Walter. "That tie tack looks like a one of a kind. I don't think a fence would touch the thing. He'd take a Patek Philippe in a heartbeat. And besides, you'll never convince me that this was a random murder by some thief. Never."

"So what do you think happened to it, Lieutenant?" said Eduardo.

"I think that it was either lost in the confusion of the crime scene or someone took it for reasons we don't understand."

"Lieutenant," said Eduardo, "we did a damn thorough job of sweeping that room. With all due respect, we didn't lose a fucking thing. I'll bet my pension that it wasn't there when we arrived."

"Calm down, Eduardo. I agree with you, believe me," said Walter. "OK, thanks. Oh, by the way, have you made any progress on that other stuff?"

"Not yet. It's a pretty tedious process, but we'll know one way or another in a day or two at the most."

"Get in touch with me right away, either way, OK?"

"Yes, sir."

After Eduardo had left, Levi said, "What was that all about?"

"Oh, it's probably nothing," said Walter. "I'll give you a call and tell you all about it once Eduardo gets back to me. In the meantime, I've got to figure out what to make of this little tie tack."

"Sorry, I didn't mean to make the case more complicated for you."

"That's not it at all, Levi. My problem is that something is telling me that this is a key piece of evidence, that if I can figure out what happened to it it'll help me solve the case."

"Perhaps you should talk to Caroline Schuyler or Virginia Braxton."

"Caroline won't be of any help," said Walter.

"Why? Do you think she's still trying to protect Judge Braxton?"

"Not at all, but she's still clamming up on me, so she's trying to protect someone."

"Do you think she's trying to protect her father?"

"That's the most logical answer, but I just don't see him as the killer, Levi."

"Be careful not to dismiss him too soon," said Levi. "He's a very complex man, and he has all the motive in the world."

"Don't worry, I'm not dismissing anybody yet. That's my problem."

"Not even Virginia Braxton?"

"Not even Virginia Braxton."

"Good," said Leviticus Welles.

36

❦

"I'M REALLY, REALLY SORRY," said Virginia. "I hope I didn't cause you too much trouble."

She and Walter were sitting in a Starbucks on 78th Street and Park Avenue. They had agreed to meet there because Virginia had a meeting with a client nearby, and there was an easy subway connection for Walter. Walter had also insisted that there be no more meetings in her home, and she hadn't fought him. He'd purchased a "large coffee, black" for both of them. As a matter of stubborn policy, he wouldn't order anything but brewed coffee, and he refused to say, "venti," which he thought was ridiculous. He'd also ordered a pastry for himself, because riding the subway always made him hungry.

"It's all right, Virginia," said Walter, meaning it. "It cleared the air. Maybe it cleared the air for all of us. I'd like to know why you did it, though."

"I was already in the area, and I guess my curiosity got the best of me. I wanted to meet the woman who was lucky enough to be married to you."

"And?"

"What do you mean, 'and'?"

"I mean there's something you're not telling me."

"How do you know that?"

"Because asking people questions is what I do for a living, Virginia. And you're not answering my question."

Virginia stared out the window for a long time. It was mid-morning, the sun was shining, and Park Avenue was crowded with shoppers, tourists, and people in a hurry. A cab actually stopped to pick someone up. Must have been some out-of-towner's beginner's luck, she thought.

"OK, Mr. Smart-Ass," she said, turning back to him and taking a sip of her coffee, "I'll tell you, but I'll bet you another cup of coffee that you're making me tell you something you already know."

Walter just shrugged, so she continued.

"Walter, I know what our relationship can be, and I know what it can't be. I accept that, and you never have to worry about me. But it's hard for me, Walter, and I was afraid that as long as your wife was just some abstract notion it would be just that much harder. So I knocked on the door and I met her, face to face. Now she's not just that abstract notion. She's Sarah, a real live person I know now, a wonderful person. She's smart, she's funny, she's warm. She's a person who I would have wanted for a friend under different circumstances, and I know that I could never betray her in the way that I might have been willing to betray that abstract person. And Walter?"

"Yes, Virginia?"

"Don't mess with that woman."

Walter rested his eyes on her and said nothing. Some wild part of him wanted to say, "I could have loved you, too." But he knew that even those words would have been a betrayal, and he also knew from the look in her eyes that he didn't need to speak them. Something approaching a smile formed on her lips.

"Now," she said, breaking the spell, "why don't you get me that second cup of coffee that you owe me and ask me what you really came here to ask me."

"Two more large coffees, coming right up," said Walter, standing up.

When he returned, Virginia said, "Please promise me, Walter, that you'll invite me along the first time you order a 'venti macchiato.'"

"Don't hold your breath," he said. They sipped the hot coffee in companionable silence.

"So," said Virginia.

"So," said Walter, pulling a folded manila envelope out of his suit jacket, "I want to know if you can tell me about this." He extracted a photo of Teddy Braxton taken in the ballroom of the Empire-Excelsior Hotel on the night of his murder and laid it on the table. He saw Virginia blanch. "Christ, I'm sorry, Virginia."

"It's all right, Walter," she said, recovering quickly, "what do you want me to tell you about it?"

"Do you see this tie tack he's wearing?" he said, pointing.

"Yes?"

"Do you recognize it?"

"Of course I do."

"What can you tell me about it?" said Walter, his heart beginning to quicken.

"It was Mother's wedding gift to him. Before that it had belonged to her father. When Mother and Dad got married they were both completely broke, but Mother wanted to give him something nice, something lasting, so she got permission from Grandmother to give it to him."

"He wore it a lot?"

"I never saw him wear a tie without it. He absolutely loved it."

"Was it worth a lot?"

"That's not why he loved it, but yes. That stone is an extremely rare ruby. He never had it appraised because he never intended to part with it, but it is very valuable. On my recommendation, a lot of my clients keep a portion of their portfolios in collectables for diversification purposes, so I know quite a bit about these things. I would guess that just the stone is worth a quarter of a million dollars. A thief would love it."

"If he could fence it, and the stone would be worth only a fraction of that value if it was broken up to conceal its provenance."

"You're right about the valuation, but I don't think a clever thief would have that much trouble fencing it, although I could be wrong. You have more experience with that end of the rare gem market than I do, I imagine. But why are you asking?"

"Because we didn't find it at the scene of the murder, which puzzles me because I know from this photo that he was wearing it that night. And you're right, I don't think a thief would have left behind a perfectly generic but very expensive Patek Philippe that he could have fenced in five minutes within a block of the hotel, but taken a gem that would have been a problem at best."

"Well, even if you're right about all that, it doesn't surprise me that you couldn't find it," said Virginia with a dismissive wave of her hand. "Daddy was such a slob, there's no telling where it could have wound up. It drove Albert crazy the way he'd pay five thousand dollars for a Savile Row suit and five hundred dollars apiece for his shirts and ties, and then just throw them anywhere. Poor Albert was constantly picking up after him. I always told him that he was just enabling him, but he said he was just doing his job and, besides, he simply couldn't stand to see Daddy ruining his beautiful clothes like that. He also knew that it drove Mother around the bend, and by now you know how protective Albert is of Mother. I know the NYPD is very thorough in its searches, but I bet you missed it somehow. It's small, it's very light, and there are lots of little pockets in his suits. Check them again."

Before Walter could say anything his cell phone began to buzz. He glanced at the Caller ID and then looked at Virginia and said, "Sorry, I have to pick this up."

"Go ahead," said Virginia, turning back to the photo and staring at it.

"Yes, Eduardo, what's up?" He listened for a few minutes and then said, "OK, thanks," and disconnected.

Virginia looked up and said, "That was....," but then abruptly stopped in mid-sentence. "Walter, are you all right? You look like you've just seen a ghost. What was that all about?"

"Nothing, really," he said.

"Don't bullshit me, Walter. What's going on?"

"It's not anything I can talk about, Virginia," he said.

"Is your family OK?"

"Yes, they're fine. It's nothing like that. Look, I've got to go now. When is your appointment?"

"Actually, I'm a little late for it," said Virginia, glancing down at what Walter thought was a solid gold Rolex.

"Then we'd both better get going," said Walter.

Virginia gave him a light, chaste kiss on the cheek as they parted at the entrance to the subway. Walter stood at the entrance and watched her walk away.

37

MURDER IS A CRIME OF PASSION. The vast majority of murders are committed by someone related to or acquainted with the victim for deeply personal reasons. Even the most clinical mob executions are the result of hatreds and jealousies aroused by an intricate web of relationships sometimes stretching back generations.

Detective Lieutenant Walter Hudson knew, specifically because of those passions, that the duty of the criminal investigator was to remain detached, objective, and dispassionate. He also knew that, unlike all the other murders he had investigated in his career, he had failed fundamentally in that duty in the murder of Teddy Braxton.

Virginia Braxton stood out as his most egregious failure because he had failed not only professionally but personally as well. The personal failure had been a crime of passion, too, one for which he was not sure he could ever forgive himself. In the confessional booth, the priest had reminded him of the teaching of Saint Paul, that the simple fact of our faith, accompanied by outward acts of contrition, absolve us of our sins; but outside the safety of the sanctuary he found that to be cold comfort.

But Virginia had been only the first of his failures, the flickering but bright candle that illuminated all the others in stark relief. He thought of Carlton Schuyler, Brad Pierce, Albert Montcrief, Young Ted and Alicia Braxton, Caroline Schuyler, and even Randall Brandt. He had to face the fact that these people had not simply remained pieces on a chessboard that he would use to topple the perpetrator. Just like Teddy Braxton, they were all seductively charming in their own way, and he had allowed himself to fall victim to their charm offensive.

They had allowed him into their world but only, he now realized, on their own terms and for their own reasons. They were not interested in his kind of justice. Justice for them was a family affair, something with which the neighbors and Walter Hudson need not concern themselves. He had been merely a tool to get their way. And it had almost worked.

No more. Theodore Franklin Braxton, the fatally flawed man whom he had never met, but whom he had come to know so intimately through his investigation, was owed a killer. In Detective Lieutenant Walter Hudson's world, every murdered soul was owed that. And perhaps even more importantly, he thought, the world was owed the truth, that much-maligned commodity that seemed to be so disregarded by so many. Walter Hudson was not a sophisticated man, but he believed in the truth. He did not believe that truth was whatever conveniently fit one's narrative; it existed objectively apart from human desires and it needed to be preserved at all costs.

And now he would give Teddy Braxton his killer, and he would give the world, or at least New York City, the truth. It was his job.

He had bypassed taking a car out of the motor pool, instead, picking up the Metro North train to Placid Hollow after calling deGroot Farm to advise them of his visit. Albert had told him that he would send Richard to the train station to pick him up, so he was surprised when Virginia pulled into the front of the train station driving Albert's prized Mercedes. The top was down, and her hair had become tousled in the breeze, highlighting her youth and her beauty in a way that he was not at all sure was unintended. She was dressed modestly in a khaki, knee-length skirt and a simple lavender blouse, but she still managed to look stunning. He climbed in on the passenger side, and she planted a firm kiss on his cheek. She smelled vaguely of flowers.

"You look surprised," she said as she put the car in gear and pulled out of the station with barely a glance to check for oncoming traffic.

"It's just that Albert said Richard would come to get me, that's all."

"Oh, Richard would have driven you to the house in that boring old SUV," she said as she shifted the old car smoothly through the gears. "It's too beautiful a day for that. And besides, I thought it would be nice to spend a couple of minutes with you without my entire family looking on."

"Albert doesn't mind your driving his prized possession?" said Walter, determined not to let the conversation drift in a personal direction. He had hoped they were past that.

"Not at all," said Virginia, taking a sharp turn with a skill that would have surprised him if he still had been capable of being surprised by Virginia Braxton. "I'm the only one he lets drive this car. He won't even let Richard drive it, even though the poor guy does all the maintenance. I actually took my driver's test in it."

"Do you drive it much?"

"Hardly at all, but it's an awfully easy car to drive," she said, suddenly taking her hands off the steering wheel while turning to him and smiling.

"Jesus, Virginia!" said Walter, resisting the urge to reach over and grab the wheel.

"What a sissy!" she said, laughing as she put her hands back on the wheel.

In a few short minutes they were pulling into the long driveway of deGroot Farm. She turned once more to him and said, "Walter?"

"Yes?" he said, glad to know that he still had a voice.

"Um, you probably want to do something about that," she said, pointing at his cheek. "Mother might not approve."

At first he didn't understand what she was talking about, then his eyes widened.

"Shit!" he said, reaching into his pocket for a handkerchief. He wiped at his cheek and said, "Did I get it all?"

"Perfect," said Virginia, patting his cheek.

The pale stain on the handkerchief was unmistakably lipstick, and he briefly wondered how he would explain that to Sarah as he folded the cloth and put it back into his pocket. One thing at a time, he decided.

Albert was waiting on the front porch to greet him. He appeared grimmer than usual, but it was hard to tell with Albert, whose dignified demeanor clung to a fading era the way a lonely widow clung to her fading photos.

"Please come in, Lieutenant," said Albert, leading him to the rear of the house, "everyone is on the verandah waiting for you. I'm afraid you chose a busy day for your visit."

"What do you mean, Albert? I hope I'm not causing an inconvenience."

"I'm sure you're not," said Albert.

Walter cast a questioning glance at Virginia, who returned a mischievous smile and said, "I didn't want to ruin your fun." She grabbed his arm and escorted him in.

The "verandah" turned out to be a carpeted screened-in porch approximately the size of Walter's house, fully furnished with a dining alcove off to one side. Louvered windows and a sophisticated HVAC system made it usable year-round although it wasn't necessary today, and the warm, pleasant outside air circulated freely. The afternoon sun was now on the other side of the house, but the late spring light lent the room a pleasant softness. The sofas and chairs were upholstered in a pastel shaded summer motif. The side tables and the dining room set appeared to be handcrafted teak. A large flat screen TV dominated the sitting area, flanked by a stereo system.

As he had expected, the immediate Braxton family was there, but he was surprised to see not only Brad Pierce and Carlton Schuyler, but also Caroline, whom he wasn't sure was welcome in Barbara Braxton's home. Everyone was dressed casually, but more smartly than he would have expected for a relaxing summer Sunday, and their expressions were more strained than relaxed. An aroma of freshly baked pie-was it rhubarb?-wafted in from the kitchen.

"Good afternoon, Lieutenant," said Barbara. "Welcome once again to deGroot Farm."

"Thank you, Mrs. Braxton," said Walter. "I hope I haven't come at an inconvenient time."

"Not at all," said Barbara. "We were expecting you, after all. And you can call me Mrs. Schuyler from now on. Brad, or perhaps I should say Reverend Pierce, performed the ceremony for Carlton and me this morning. I'm afraid the children are all still digesting the news. We sprang the whole thing on them rather suddenly."

"Well, I, uh, congratulations," stammered Walter. "My congratulations to all of you. Mr. Schuyler, congratulations sir."

"Thank you," said Carlton Schuyler, beaming at his new wife. "Not bad for a street rat from Hell's Kitchen, huh?"

"I would have come at another time if I'd known."

"Not at all," said Barbara. "Have you come to us with news of your investigation?"

"Yes, ma'am, I have."

"Then your timing couldn't be better."

Or worse, thought Walter.

"Have you finally found the killer?" said Young Ted. "That would be tremendous news for all of us. I was afraid you'd spent so much time focusing on the family that you'd never find the actual perpetrator. Have you made an arrest?"

"Not yet, but an arrest is imminent," said Walter, thinking that Young Ted was the only truly innocent person there, including him. He desperately hoped to keep it that way.

"Then please, tell us," said Ted.

"My goodness, Lieutenant," said Barbara. "I'm afraid that we are once again being rude. Would you like something to eat or drink? We have coffee ready, and there are pastries fresh from the baker that I'm sure are still warm. Albert, perhaps you could ask Maria to bring the lieutenant something."

"That's very kind of you ma'am," said Walter, "but it won't be necessary. And I'd like Albert to stay, if that's all right with you."

"That would be fine, of course," said Barbara. "Anyone else?"

"Perhaps Richard, if he's available."

"Albert, can you please find Richard and invite him to join us?" said Barbara.

"Yes, ma'am," said Albert, turning to leave.

"Good gracious, Lieutenant Hudson, this is all getting rather mysterious," said Virginia. Walter was grateful that she chose to address him by his title in the presence of the family.

"I don't mean to be mysterious. In fact, I want to be as open as possible because, I'm sorry to say, Ted, that someone in this room murdered your father."

"Oh, for God's sake!" said Young Ted. "If that is what you still insist on thinking then you have utterly failed to find the killer, and it's time we got someone else on this case. Mother, perhaps it's time you called the commissioner."

"Ted," said Barbara, "I think we should let the lieutenant finish before we render any judgment on his findings."

"But, Mother.....,"

"Ted, please."

Ted sat back with his arms folded. Alicia put an arm around his shoulders and whispered to him, "Please, honey, try not to get too excited." She turned anxious eyes on Walter, her face unnaturally pallid and rigid with fear. He also saw something else in her face and suddenly thought to himself, "She's pregnant." He didn't know whether she had told the family, or whether she knew herself yet; but he'd seen that look three times in his life on his own wife's face, and there was no mistaking it.

"Thank you, Mrs. Schuyler," he said. "Mr. Braxton, I know how sensitive this is, so I will try to be as thorough as possible in my explanation, and I hope that by the time I'm done there will be little doubt about my conclusion." Young Ted opened his mouth to speak, but bit his tongue.

"Let's start with you, then," said Walter, looking at Ted, "because, frankly, you were the first person I eliminated."

"Well, I should hope so," said Young Ted.

"Be quiet, Ted," said Alicia. "Please continue, Lieutenant."

"First of all, you had a good alibi, but everybody had a good alibi. What you lacked was a motive. I knew that you were in trouble with the house you bought, and you stood to lose a bundle if your father ruled the wrong way on the property case. But I also think that you're a good enough lawyer to realize that his ruling wouldn't have made much of a difference in the long run. I had a long talk with Randall Brandt about that, as I know you did, given that he was a family acquaintance. You also didn't know, as Brad Pierce did, that your father planned to displace you at Braxton & Pierce, a personal betrayal that would have hurt you badly, personally, professionally, and financially."

Young Ted Braxton turned uncomprehending eyes on Bradley Pierce, looking like a puppy who had received an undeserved beating from his master. "Brad?" was all he managed to say. His weak chin began to quiver.

"Ted, I never had a chance to tell you. I only found out the morning of the murder, and I just didn't have the heart to say anything. And then, of course, the whole issue became moot. I hoped you might never find out. I wanted you to be able to keep a high opinion of your father in your heart."

"I'm very sorry you had to hear that from me, Mr. Braxton," said Walter, "but it is a fact you all needed to know. I hope that will become clear to you shortly."

"Brad's right," said Alicia. "None of this matters anymore. We both know that now." Young Ted managed a nod and, after a second, a brief smile. Alicia held him closer.

"I have unfortunately investigated patricides in my career," said Walter. "They are very rare, and they are only committed when the child is under extreme emotional duress. Concern about your house simply didn't rise to that level, and I found no other motivation for you to commit such an act." Alicia Braxton audibly sighed, while Virginia and Bunny both stared at him, stunned. He stared back. He was lying, and they knew it, but that was his prerogative as a cop. Young Ted's ignorance of the affair between his wife and his father was beyond doubt. The man was innocent, and Walter wasn't about to destroy his life for no reason. He saw that comprehension dawn on their faces, and they both nodded imperceptibly. The dead must often be buried more than once.

"And finally," said Walter, glancing at Caroline Schuyler, "I have it on expert opinion that you are a rotten shot. The worst one in the family. You never could have fired three rapid shots in such a tight grouping. So, as a cop, I'd say that you lacked both motive and capacity."

"But, damn it, I practiced harder than anybody!" said Young Ted. His wife beside him gave him a nudge, while Virginia laughed out loud.

"Oh, Ted, you are precious," she said, smiling at him. It was the first affectionate moment Walter had ever observed between the two.

"Me next," said Virginia, smiling at him impishly.

It'll be your turn soon, don't worry," said Walter. "But first, let's clear the air about Caroline Schuyler, since you are, after all, Ms. Schuyler, still technically out on bail as a suspect."

"I was hoping we wouldn't have to rehash all that," said Caroline.

"We don't," said Walter.

"We don't? Why not?" said Caroline.

"Because you were in the right room at the right time but with the wrong gun, and by the time the police entered the room and found you, the right gun, the murder weapon, had already been deposited on the Bronx side of Spuyten Duivel. It's as simple as that."

"While you're on the subject of the Schuyler family," said Carlton Schuyler, "what about me?"

"Well, Mr. Schuyler, your four poker playing friends are either the best liars I ever met or you have an airtight alibi."

"Perhaps both," said Schuyler, smiling.

"Perhaps," said Walter, remembering why he liked the guy. "I interviewed all four of them separately, and I couldn't find a single inconsistency between them. But I also know that you don't surround yourself with fools, and those guys were damn smart, despite the humble impressions they all tried to leave me with. I have no doubt that they all could have been covering up for you."

"But?" said Schuyler, with an almost amused expression on his face that let Walter know that, once again, this man was way ahead of him.

"But I tended to believe you when you told me that if you'd decided that Teddy had to go, you would have found a much quieter way to do it."

"But you didn't just take me at my word, did you, Lieutenant. I know you better than that."

"Of course I didn't. I asked my colleague in the intelligence division, Levi Welles, to do some research. It seems that the two men suspected of murdering your brother all those years ago both disappeared without a trace about a year later. The cops talked to you, but you were only thirteen, you didn't seem to know anything, and they had better things to do than waste time investigating the murders of a couple of pimps, so they just let it go."

"Yeah, I always wondered what happened to those guys," said Schuyler, his eyes boring into Walter's.

"I'm sure," said Walter. "In any event, even though I couldn't completely eliminate you as a suspect, I marked you down as a pretty low possibility. And besides, by that time I'd collected enough evidence to identify the killer."

"Please, Lieutenant," said Young Ted, "let's get on with it."

"You're right, Ted," said Walter. "It's time to get on with it. Don't you agree, Mr. Pierce?"

"Well, of course, I guess," said Pierce, reddening.

"Oh, really," said Barbara. "You can't possibly believe that Brad Pierce would harm a fly."

"I believe he would for you, Mrs. Schuyler. And he had all the motive he needed, didn't he?"

"Lieutenant," said Young Ted, "I'm afraid you're making absolutely no sense at all."

"On the day of the murder," said Walter, "your mother went to visit Brad at his office just after your father had left, where he undoubtedly told her the news he'd just received. Right, Mr. Pierce?"

"Yes, but I already told you that I'd gotten over that."

"Perhaps you had, but Mrs. Schuyler, a woman you cared for deeply, must have been devastated to hear it, and that must have angered you all over again, perhaps leading you to that altercation with Judge Braxton just before he was murdered."

"You can't seriously believe that Brad Pierce murdered my father," said Young Ted.

"I wouldn't, except that we have video of him exiting the elevator that led to the upper floors of the hotel just before midnight. Don't we, Mr. Pierce."

There was a stunned silence as all eyes in the room fell on Bradley Pierce.

"Mr. Pierce?"

"All right, all right, Lieutenant. Yes, I went up to the room."

"How did you know which room he was in?"

"I had to walk across the lobby from the ballroom to get to the elevators. I just walked up to the desk and asked. It was so chaotic that the young woman I asked just looked at her computer and gave me the number. She never even looked up at me."

"And how did you get in?"

"How do you think I got in? I knocked. Teddy let me in. And you are right; I had every intention of killing the man. For the sake of Bunny and for the sake of the entire family, the family that I felt was my own, he had to be stopped before he destroyed everyone."

"And you were carrying a gun with you."

"Yes, I carried it up in my briefcase. The hotel security had completely broken down by that time, and no one ever checked. I could have walked around with it in my hand and I don't think anyone would have noticed."

"And did you take it out of your briefcase once you were in the room?"

"Yes, I did, Lieutenant. And I pointed it right at Teddy."

"And what did Teddy do?"

"He just laughed," said Pierce, a look somewhere between wonder and shame passing across his face.

"Did he say anything to you?"

"Of course he did. Teddy always had something to say, especially when it was time to get the last word in." Someone—was it Alicia?--choked out a derisive chuckle.

"What did he say?"

"I hardly remember. I was very overwrought. All I remember clearly is hearing him say that I'd only be harming Bunny if I killed him, and that I should just drop the gun and leave, that the whole incident would be forgotten."

"And what did you do then?"

"I'm ashamed to say I panicked, Lieutenant," said Brad, but then his face fell and his eyes moistened. "No. Let me correct that. To my everlasting shame I did what I'd been doing ever since the first day I met Teddy Braxton. I did what he told me to do. I dropped the gun and I left. I'm so sorry, Bunny," he said, turning to Barbara Braxton. "I meant to do the right thing for you, and once again I failed."

"You are a rare man, Bradley Pierce," said Barbara. "You are true to yourself, just as you have been since the day I met you. And you have been true to me. You are my Polestar, Brad, and I don't know what I ever would have done without you in my life. You did not fail me; you have never failed me. Thank you, dear Brad." Tears filled Bradley Pierce's eyes, but a smile lit his face.

"But I don't get it," said Young Ted. "Someone shot my father to death. If it wasn't Brad, then who was it?"

"Mr. Pierce, what kind of gun did you bring to the hotel room that night?" said Walter, ignoring Young Ted.

"I, I don't know. You mean, what brand name was it?"

"No, Mr. Pierce, I mean what type of gun was it? A .22? A 9-millimeter?"

"I don't think I can tell you. You see, I bought that gun thirty-five years ago when my Greenwich Village neighborhood wasn't as safe as it is today. I bought it from a not-too-reputable local gun dealer, brought it home, put some bullets in it, and set the safety; and then I put it in my nightstand drawer. I hadn't touched it since."

"Did it have a silencer attached?" said Walter.

"I really couldn't tell you. I honestly don't know what a silencer looks like. I just put the gun in the drawer the way it came."

"Was it heavy, Mr. Pierce?"

"Compared to what? I guess it felt hefty, but I've never picked up another handgun, so in a relative sense I don't know if it was heavy or light."

"I'm sorry, Lieutenant, but that all seems awfully difficult to swallow," said Young Ted.

"It would," said Walter, "except that we know that two people came to your father's hotel room that night to murder him. One of them left an unfired gun on the floor of the room, and one of them came and left with the murder weapon."

"Why haven't we heard any of this before?" said Young Ted.

"Because we had to withhold some facts that only the killer would know. I think you'll find out why in just a few minutes."

"Okay," said Young Ted, "but please, let's get on with it."

"In addition to the video from the elevator, we got lucky one more time with some videotape, but not from the hotel. It's video from one of the traffic cameras on the West Side Highway. At first we didn't even bother to look because we thought we were looking for a black SUV, and there are so many of them in this city it would have been impossible to find the one we might be looking for. But then, after my last visit here, I realized that we might be looking for another car, one that would be much easier to spot. Isn't that right, Albert?"

"Lieutenant?" said Albert, as all eyes turned to him.

"What we saw, driving north at approximately 1AM, was a light colored, 1975 Mercedes Benz 450SL convertible, with the top up. The images aren't good enough to identify the driver or if there were any occupants, but that's quite a coincidence, wouldn't you say, Albert?"

"Yes, I guess that would be quite a coincidence," said Albert.

"Oh, no," said Virginia. "This is impossible. There must be plenty of other 450SLs on the road besides Albert's."

"There are exactly twelve in the Greater New York area fitting that description," said Walter. "But we were also able to make out two letters on the license plate, an 'A' and a 'P.' There is exactly one of them. Right, Albert?"

"If you say so, Lieutenant."

"Would you care to tell us about what you did that night? Or would you prefer to have an attorney present?"

"Albert," said Caroline, "speaking as an attorney, I strongly suggest that you say nothing without an attorney present."

"You are not under arrest," said Walter, "and I have not read you your Miranda rights. I don't intend to. If any time is the right time to talk, it's now."

Something in Albert Montcrief's expression sagged, but if anything his posture became even more erect.

"You are correct," he said. "That was my car and I was in it."

"And did you drive to the Empire-Excelsior Hotel?"

"Yes, I did."

"Why?"

"In order to kill Teddy Braxton, Lieutenant."

"But Albert, why?" said Young Ted.

"Ted, Virginia," said Albert, turning his eyes to Bunny Braxton's two children, "I have spent my entire life devoted to the care of the deGroot family. Your last name may be Braxton, but that is simply an accident of marriage. You are deGroots. Your father was not; he was a Braxton, a poor family of no account. You children grew up to be the fine, successful people you are because of your deGroot lineage, passed on to you by your magnificent mother. Your mother and I grew up together. We have been close all our lives, and she has always felt free to confide in me. She told me of her conversation with Mr. Pierce on the morning of the murder and everything she learned that day. Your father, despite his lineage, was once a fine young man, but over the years he, for lack of any better description, reverted to his base Braxton form. He was destroying all of you, and I simply could not stand by and let that happen."

"So what did you do, Albert?" said Walter.

"I parked the car on the street and went up to Mr. Braxton's suite, and I shot him to death."

"Let's back up a little bit, Albert," said Walter. "Where did you park your car?"

"On 34th Street."

"OK, and how did you get up to the Judge's suite?"

"I took the elevator, of course."

"Which elevator?" There's a bank of elevators on the north side of the hotel and one on the south side. Which one did you take?"

"I guess the north side, because that's the side of the hotel where I parked."

"So you walked into the hotel and went directly to the elevators?"

"Yes."

"That's funny, because that's the same bank of elevators that Brad Pierce used, the only one where the cameras were working. We looked and looked and looked, but we never saw you."

"Perhaps you just missed me, Lieutenant," said Albert. "I don't exactly stand out in a crowd."

"Perhaps," said Walter. "OK, then what did you do?"

"I went to his room."

"And how did you know his room number?"

"I, well, I went to the front desk, just as Mr. Pierce said he did."

"But Mr. Pierce had to walk through the lobby to get from the ballroom to the elevators. You weren't in the ballroom, so you didn't have to do that. And you just told me that you went directly to the elevators."

"Now that I think about it, you're right. I did go over to the front desk. I'm sorry for the confusion, I just forgot momentarily," said Albert.

"Okay, let's say you did. And I assume you simply knocked on the door, just like Mr. Pierce did."

"Yes, of course."

"And then what?"

"I shot him."

"And then?"

"And then I left, of course."

"Did you ever say anything to the Judge before you shot him?"

"No, no I didn't. I just shot him."

"Did you ever approach the Judge's body, to make sure that he was dead?"

"No, Lieutenant," said the now freely perspiring Albert. "I just left."

"What kind of gun did you use, Albert?"

"I'm not really sure. Just one of the guns from the house."

"Albert, you were a sharpshooter in the Army. Are you going to tell me that you didn't even verify the type of firearm that you were firing?"

"Lieutenant......"

"Oh, please, Lieutenant, stop tormenting the man. It's time to end this charade and you know it," came a clear voice from the other side of the room. "It was a Smith & Wesson .38 with a twelve round magazine in the handle. I'm sure the nine remaining rounds were intact when you found the gun."

All eyes turned in the direction of the voice.

38

❦

"**N**O!" cried Young Ted.

"Yes," said Barbara deGroot Braxton Schuyler. "Yes, Ted, it's true, and I'd rather you hear it from me in the end than to have our intrepid young Lieutenant Hudson point the finger at me." Carlton Schuyler sat stolidly beside her, expressionless. Clearly, Bunny had revealed everything to him, assuming he even needed to be told, before she had married him. Walter would have expected nothing less from either of them. "I had Albert drive me to the city in his Mercedes on Friday evening, about eleven o'clock. He dropped me off at the hotel, where I went to your father's room and murdered him. Albert then drove me back here sometime around one. Along the way I threw the gun into the Harlem River, or at least I thought I had. Albert had no idea what I had done, Lieutenant. I made sure that I threw the gun out the window when he wasn't looking. He was not an accomplice; I want to be clear about that. He only learned of what happened after the fact."

"But, why, Mother, why?" said Young Ted, tears beginning to stream down his face.

"Oh, Ted, I should think it would be obvious by now, but perhaps it's a blessing that sons rarely see their fathers for who they really are. Perhaps that's one of the essential fictions that hold our world together. But, Ted, there were some truths that I had to recognize, and I had to act on, before it was too late.

"There are some men, men like my dear, dear, Carlton," she said, looking at the man and lightly touching his shoulder, "who grow up hard, but who are ultimately able to escape their beginnings and permanently outgrow them. But those men are rare, Ted, and your father was not one of them. I had to watch, year after year, as your father's behavior became increasingly outrageous, until one morning I woke up and had to admit to myself that he was no longer the man I'd married. But even then I might have stuck with him, if I hadn't had to face the damage that he was inflicting on you, your sister, and my dear friend Brad. If you know me at all, you know that the only real priority in my life is my family, and I just couldn't stand by and watch your father destroy all that."

"Before we go any further," said Carlton Schuyler, still not betraying any emotion, "I'd like to hear Lieutenant Hudson tell us how he figured all this out. I mean, Albert and Brad cared deeply for this family, too. I know that there are some gaps in their stories, but even you admitted that you weren't able to eliminate them completely. Even now, as far as you know, Bunny might simply be covering for them."

"You're right, Mr. Schuyler, except for a couple of small details," said Walter. "Once I had my three suspects in place, I re-examined all my evidence. Who would have brought a thirty-five-year-old .45 to the hotel room, a weapon that, it turned out after we inspected it, hadn't been cleaned or fired, perhaps ever? Not Albert, who was a trained sniper in the Army. He would have brought a much more serviceable weapon that would be appropriate to the task. And he would have been more than capable of firing the tight, accurate grouping of shots that killed the Judge. The same goes for Mrs...... Schuyler, who hosted many of your parties and doubtless participated in the shooting practices. So there's no doubt in my mind that Brad came with the .45 and left it there."

"But you can't actually prove it," said Schuyler.

"I take your point," said Walter.

"And you just said that it could have been Albert, too!" said Young Ted. "So why are you blaming Mother?"

"You're right, Ted. One of my most important clues came from a conversation with your sister, when she off-handedly told me what a slob your father was, and how Albert was constantly picking up his expensive clothes off the floor and caring for them. When I took another look at the crime scene photos after that conversation, I couldn't help noticing that his suit jacket and tie were carefully folded over the back of a chair. Your father wouldn't have done that."

"But you just said it yourself, Lieutenant, Albert would have done that!" said Young Ted.

"You're right, Ted, but there are a few things wrong. First of all, while Albert was trying as hard as he could to confess to the crime a few minutes ago, he failed to mention that. He simply said he shot your father and left. And I also finally realized that that was what you were seeing every time I tried to show you the crime scene photos, Caroline. The second you looked at those photos you knew who had murdered Judge Braxton, and you told me, didn't you, how you would do anything to make up to Mrs. Schuyler for your betrayal of her. If you thought that pointed to someone else you would have told me right away."

Caroline stared back at Walter defiantly, but she said nothing.

"But then who drove Caroline off the road that afternoon?" said Virginia. "Don't tell me that Mother did that. And doesn't that implicate someone else, perhaps someone you haven't even thought of?"

"Caroline?" said Walter. "Do you want to explain that or do you want me to?"

"There was no black SUV that tried to kill me," said Caroline. "You're right, Lieutenant. It was just some asshole who changed lanes without looking. I thought if you believed some goon tried to drive me off the highway, it would divert your attention away from the family, that's all."

"Just like you sent me off on that wild goose chase to talk to Randall Brandt, right?" said Walter. "I have to give you credit, Caroline; you did more to impede my investigation than everyone else combined."

"Yes, you're right. I'm very sorry."

"But that still doesn't clear Albert!" said Young Ted.

"But Caroline also noticed one other thing in the photo, didn't you, Caroline?"

"Of course I did. I noticed that his tie tack was missing. His ruby tie tack. You're starting to annoy me, by the way."

"Don't worry, I'm going to annoy you more before I'm done."

"But Albert could have taken that, too!" said Young Ted.

"But he didn't," said Bunny Schuyler, looking at Walter. "I presume, since you are so thorough, that you have a search warrant with you, but I won't make you use it. The tie tack was a family heirloom, a memento of my father. I didn't want it taken as evidence or lost. You will find it in my personal jewelry box in my bedroom."

"Thank you, Mrs. Schuyler. I'll take your word for it. And then there is the last thing. It didn't show up in the photos of course, but Officer Sanchez, who I'm sure you remember from the crime scene, Caroline, noticed it right away, something a man wouldn't have left behind."

"I presume you are talking about the lipstick on his left cheek," said Bunny. She seemed to become lost in her own thoughts for a minute, and then she continued. "I don't know if anyone in this room except Carlton has lived long enough to understand this. I had not loved Teddy Braxton for many years, but there was still a certain poignancy in the memory of our past together. After all, we had raised two wonderful children, and that bond would never disappear. So after it was all over, I knelt down over him, smoothed his hair as best I could, straightened him out a bit and gave him a little kiss on the cheek. Then I heard movement coming out of one of the bedrooms, so I got up and left quickly."

"So in the end, you ruined your own life for the sake of the rest of us," said Young Ted.

"Well," said Bunny, smiling at her son, "before you get all misty about my selflessness, please remember that I didn't exactly go running to the police to confess. To be frank, if there had been an investigator just a little less competent than our Lieutenant Hudson on the case I just may have gotten away with it, and I would have done so gladly. And I also had a selfish reason for doing what I did, a reason that also lent a certain urgency to the undertaking, didn't I, Lieutenant?"

"Mrs. Schuyler, I…"

"My dear Lieutenant, I think that you have spent enough time living inside my head to warrant a less formal address, don't you? So why don't you just call me Bunny."

"As you wish….Bunny. I was prepared to hold back the detail that I believe you are referring to for a later time. I wasn't sure if you'd had the chance to talk to your family."

"Thank you. You are correct that I haven't told my family yet about my situation, but it's about time, especially since I just this morning received some encouraging news."

"Mother? What are you talking about?" said Young Ted, paling.

"On the morning of your father's murder, I had a brief doctor's appointment during which I was informed that I had a fairly advanced case of pancreatic cancer. I was given between six months and a year to live. It was then that I realized that I didn't have a moment to lose, that I could not die and leave you all exposed to your father's depredations, which only would have become far worse once he was free of me and my influence over his estate. But I also realized that I did not want to die without having at least some time to live out in the open as Carlton Schuyler's wife."

"But, Mother," said Ted, "why didn't you just divorce Dad, then?"

"Because a divorce would have broken up the estate, and I probably would have been dead before the whole process was finalized. I simply couldn't wait that long."

"But you said you've received some encouraging news," said Alicia, finally breaking her long silence.

"Yes, I have," said Bunny, "and it's all thanks to my dear Carlton. He happens to own a pharmaceutical company."

"Orion Pharmaceuticals," said Virginia, her eyes widening in recognition as she turned toward her new stepfather. "You bought it and took it private two years ago. They're a relatively small company, but I remember reading that they were doing some state of the art research on pancreatic and liver cancers. A lot of people thought it was pie in the sky and believed you were making a big mistake."

"Which didn't bother me," said Carlton, "since I was able to buy it for a song. And it turns out that their research was solid, and now it's worth five times what I paid for it."

"That was a prescient move on your part, Mr. Schuyler," said Young Ted.

"Not really," said Schuyler. "I bought it because my mother died of pancreatic cancer, and I promised myself on her deathbed that if there was ever anything I could do to cure it, I would. It kind of put me on the path I've been on ever since. Did you manage to stumble on that little tidbit, Lieutenant?"

"No, no I didn't, sir," said Walter. "As usual, you're one step ahead of me."

"Well, he's the only one in the room who is, then," said Virginia, smiling at Walter.

"I think there's one other," said Walter, smiling back at her.

"But, Mother, what is the encouraging news you spoke of?" said Alicia.

"I just received the preliminary results from the first round of my treatment, and they are very positive. I just may be with you all much longer than I thought, although I may be spending much of that time in jail."

"We'll see about that," said Carlton.

"Carlton, dear, whatever do you mean?" said Bunny, a flash of concern on her face.

"I mean," said Carlton, turning to look at Walter, the humor in his eyes turning to a hard glitter, "that as the lieutenant here knows, everything that we have discussed here this afternoon was off the record. Isn't that so?"

"Yes, sir, it was."

"And by the time anything goes on the record, I'll have everyone here surrounded by the best defense attorneys in the country. This case won't even come to trial for at least a year, during which time my wife will be free on bail. And I confidently predict that it'll snow in July before she's ever convicted of anything. And I'm never wrong when I make a confident prediction."

"You may very well be right, sir," said Walter. "In fact, I know you're right."

"You what?" said Carlton, looking puzzled for the first time since Walter had met him.

"How can you possibly know that, Lieutenant?" said Bunny.

"Because, as you know, Mrs. Schuyler, despite that wonderful story you just told, you didn't murder Teddy Braxton. For all I know, you may have been planning to do away with the Judge for all the reasons you just gave, but somebody just barely beat you to it, right?"

"Lieutenant Hudson," said Young Ted, "I'm not following you at all. If Mother didn't murder my father, then who did?"

Walter Hudson turned his head slowly, scanning all of the faces in the room until his eyes came to rest on Teddy Braxton's killer.

"Walter, you can't really believe......."

"I'm sorry, Virginia."

39

"MOMMY, HELP ME," said Virginia, her eyes still locked on Walter. He wondered how he had never seen the insanity lurking behind those lovely eyes, that beautiful face, before. Damn me, he thought. He almost shuddered to think how close he'd come to being completely taken in, both personally and professionally. It all now seemed so obvious in retrospect.

"My dear Lieutenant," said Bunny, a note of desperation in her face, "I just gave you my full confession. Please read me my Miranda rights and I will repeat it so that it can be used at my trial. You are wrong. I killed my husband, not my daughter."

"I admire your devotion to your daughter, Mrs. Schuyler. I admire your devotion to your entire family, but I cannot allow you to confess to a crime you didn't commit."

"I don't understand you, Lieutenant," said Bunny.

"The truth matters, Mrs. Schuyler."

"The truth," said Bunny. "And who left you in charge of the truth?"

"In this case, ma'am, the City of New York did."

"So tell me, Lieutenant Hudson," said Carlton Schuyler. "What suddenly makes you believe you know the truth now?"

"First of all, Mr. Schuyler, your wife described driving down to Manhattan Friday night in Albert's Mercedes around eleven and returning around one. We did, in fact, see the car heading north on the West Side Highway around one-fifteen, but we never spotted it coming south earlier in the evening. At first we thought that we were just missing it in the traffic, but then I learned something interesting during my last visit here."

"I'm glad you've found your visits to deGroot Farm instructive, Lieutenant," said Bunny, "but what possibly could you have learned?"

"When I was leaving, I saw Albert's Mercedes for the first time. I saw it because Richard had it out on the driveway to make a minor repair. Do you remember, Richard?"

"Yes, I was changing out a rear brake light. So what? What's so interesting about a brake light?"

"The brake light wasn't interesting, but the fact that Albert didn't know that the bulb was out was, because it made me think that someone other than Albert had been driving the car. I also know that a rear brake light is one of those things that's hard to notice when you're the driver. It's one of those things that someone has to point out to you, usually someone who was driving behind you when you put on the brakes. Sometimes, that's a cop."

"Aren't you stretching things a bit here?" said Carlton Schuyler.

"I thought I might be," said Walter, nodding to Schuyler. "I knew it was a real long shot, but I asked Officer Sanchez to make a couple of calls to the local police, and guess what? He got lucky. He found a nice, young Placid Hollow cop named Sherman Busby who remembered pulling over a yellow Mercedes on Friday afternoon. He knew the car, and he knew that it belonged to you, Albert. He didn't want to give out a ticket or anything, just give you a heads up. But you weren't driving it; Virginia was. Officer Sanchez asked if it was unusual to see someone other than Albert driving the car, and he said that the only person he's ever seen drive that car other than Albert was Virginia. Do you remember that, Virginia?"

"I probably do," she said, glaring at him.

"Oh, for God's sake," said Young Ted. "She was probably just running a few errands in preparation for the weekend, that's all."

"Perhaps, except I had another colleague of mine, Leviticus Welles, pay a follow-up visit to 'Chez-Vous,' the restaurant you took your clients to the night of the murder, Virginia. He found a valet parking guy who clearly remembers parking the car. He said the car was hard to forget, and so was the driver. It seems you have a lot of admirers."

"I guess you'd know, wouldn't you?" she said.

"But Lieutenant," said Young Ted, "that just proves that Virginia was where she said she was on Friday night."

"Yes, that's true, but Mr. Welles also paid a follow-up visit to the bartender from that night. He remembered you clearly, Virginia; even in Manhattan five hundred dollar tips are pretty unusual. But he also recalled that you left your guests alone for a rather long period of time."

"You would have left them alone, too, Lieutenant," said Virginia. "They were drunk, they were all chain smokers, and they were all trying to look up my skirt."

"I have no doubt that all that's true," said Walter. "But it's also true that 'Chez-Vous' is only two blocks from the Empire-Excelsior Hotel."

"Lieutenant, you can come up with all the interesting theories about my daughter that you want, although they all sound awfully improbable to me," said Bunny. "But you're forgetting one very important thing."

"What would that be, ma'am?" said Walter.

"I confessed. I did it. You don't need any far-fetched hypotheses to solve the crime. *I* did it. *I* told you that. No jury in its right mind will ever conclude beyond a reasonable doubt that Virginia murdered her father when someone else, someone with all the motive in the world, has confessed to it."

"Right up until yesterday I might have agreed with you, Mrs. Schuyler. I have to admit you gave quite a convincing confession. It must have taken hours of rehearsal with your daughter and Albert to get all the details straight. But it was Virginia who did all the things you confessed to. She shot the Judge. She was the one who lovingly folded his jacket and his tie, smoothed his hair, and who took the tie tack for safekeeping. And it was your daughter who, after finally having her father all to herself, even if it was for just a few precious minutes of her life, gave him a final kiss on the cheek and bade him farewell."

"I think you're the one who's concocted an outrageous story," said Bunny.

"I have to admit, I could hardly believe it myself, until the lipstick finally started making sense to me."

"Somehow, I doubt lipstick ever has or ever will make sense to you, Lieutenant."

"Most of the time you'd be right, ma'am, but in this one particular instance I think I understand at least a little."

"For example?"

"The lipstick found on Judge Braxton's cheek was a brand called 'Eros.' It's a pale, pinkish kind of color."

"Yes, Lieutenant, I know that," said Bunny, "I have a tube of it in my makeup bag."

"Perhaps you do," said Walter, "but you never wear it, at least I've never seen you wear it. You always wear a very bright red that complements your hair color and your complexion. Your daughter, on the other hand, is dark haired and has a complexion that is perfectly suited to a paler shade, which she has worn every time I've seen her."

"I hardly think you qualify as a makeup consultant."

"I completely agree with you ma'am, but luckily, I don't have to be one."

"And why would that be?"

"Because yesterday I got a call from the NYPD forensics lab informing me that they had finally been able to get a complete DNA sample from the lipstick that was found on your husband's cheek. It was touch and go for a while, but they finally succeeded."

For the first time, Bunny Braxton Schuyler's composure started to crack. Her skin went pale and her eyes widened, her left hand unconsciously reached for her husband's. On the other side of her, Virginia started to tremble visibly.

"Oh, no," said Virginia, as her eyes widened in sudden realization. "Your handkerchief."

"Whatever are you talking about, Virginia?" said Bunny.

"What she's talking about, ma'am," said Walter, "is that today when she arrived at the train station to pick me up, she leaned over and kissed me on the cheek when I got into the car. She then reminded me to wipe the lipstick off before we came into the house. The handkerchief, and the lipstick, are in my pocket. I'm guessing that the DNA extracted from that lipstick will match the DNA from the Judge's cheek. What do you think, Virginia?"

"That's illegally obtained evidence!" shouted Carlton Schuyler. "It will never be allowed into evidence. And without that, Lieutenant Hudson, you don't have much of a case. Ladies, gentleman, I think we're through talking."

"I'm no lawyer, heaven knows," said Walter, "but I've seen my fair share of murder trials, and I think the DNA evidence will be admitted. We'll let a judge decide that. And even if it's not, I believe the circumstantial evidence is overwhelming." He turned to Virginia. "I am so sorry, Virginia. You are a very troubled woman, and I blame myself for not seeing that sooner. Perhaps that will mitigate in your favor, at least when it comes to the sentencing. But now, I have to arrest you for the murder of Judge T. Franklin Braxton. A patrol car will be arriving any minute to bring you in." He walked over to Virginia and removed the cuffs from his belt.

Virginia suddenly rose from her chair and bolted to her mother's side, clinging to her.

"Mommy, do something! Please! You said you could take care of this! Please!"

"I tried dear, Lord knows I've tried," said Bunny, staring at Walter. "But now it has been taken out of our hands, I'm afraid. I hope you're proud of yourself, Lieutenant."

"Pride has nothing to do with it," said Walter. But it did, and he knew it did.

40

WALTER, LEVI, AND EDUARDO sat in a booth at the Broadway Deli a week after Virginia's arrest. They were all eating one of the deli's enormous sandwiches: Walter roast beef, Levi brisket, and Eduardo pastrami. Levi had barely made a dent in his, but Walter was making decent progress, and Eduardo had finished his sandwich and was working on his sides of fries and coleslaw. His eyes were beginning to drift over to the cheesecake on the pastry tray.

"How are you going to explain your lack of appetite at dinnertime to Angelina, Eduardo?" said Levi. "You know she hates it when you eat deli food at lunchtime, especially after you've eaten a loaded fried egg sandwich for breakfast."

"Who says I won't be hungry?" said Eduardo, "And how do you know what I ate for breakfast, anyway?"

"Because I don't think Angelina would have let you out of the house this morning with dried egg yolk on the front of your uniform, that's why."

"What?" said Eduardo, looking down at his shirt, then, "Shit!" as he spotted the offending stain and started to dab at it with a napkin he'd dunked in his ice water.

"Walter," said Levi after he and Walter had finally stopped laughing, "I guess there's something I still don't understand."

"What's that, Levi?"

"Why? Why did she kill him, and why did she choose that day? I mean, she'd been suffering emotional damage because of her father's behavior almost her entire life. What finally tipped her over?"

"It's going to be a long time before we know for sure, if ever," said Walter. "Virginia is out on bail, but she's heavily sedated and on suicide watch at Bunny's Park Avenue townhouse; and of course no one in the family is talking to me."

"Do you think she'll ever go to jail?" said Levi.

"I guess the lawyers and the judges are going to have to work that out, but with Carlton Schuyler's money and Bunny Schuyler's influence behind her defense, I guess I'd be surprised if she did."

"It's a shame either way. She's such a brilliant young woman, and now her life is ruined. Do you have any guesses about what set her off?"

"I've heard some rumors, but that's about it. It's funny how people start talking once the news is out. Apparently there had been some kind of chatter among Judge Braxton's staff that Caroline had let slip that there might be wedding bells in her future, and somehow Virginia had gotten wind of that."

"Holy crap," said Eduardo.

"Holy crap is right," said Walter. "Virginia considered Caroline a sister more than a friend. Knowing that her father had already had an affair with her sister-in-law, I think Caroline's affair with her father had brought Virginia right to the breaking point. Any talk of marriage could have made her snap. But I'm not sure we'll ever know." They all got up to leave.

"I guess there's a lot of stuff we'll never know," said Eduardo.

"You're right, Eduardo," said Walter. "One of the things I've learned on this job is that we never really know what makes people do the things they do. But there are a couple of things I do know. I know that when we get back to the precinct house Captain Amato is going to be waiting there to pin a brand new, shiny detective's shield on your uniform."

"Congratulations, Eduardo!" said Levi, shaking the man's hand.

"Thanks, Levi," said Eduardo, beaming.

"I also know," said Walter, "that I never would have solved this case without your help, Levi. Only you and I will ever know how much you helped. I don't know what to say."

"You don't need to say anything, Walter."

"And I also know," said Walter as they walked out into the warm air and the bright sunshine, "that it's a great day to be a cop."

"Damn right," said Eduardo and Levi.

"Damn right," said Detective Lieutenant Walter Hudson.

THE END

CPSIA information can be obtained at www.ICGtesting.com
Printed in the USA
BVOW02s1323090316

439706BV00001B/1/P